WRITERS CRUSHING COVID-19

AN ANTHOLOGY FOR
CORONAVIRUS RELIEF

PIEDMONT AUTHORS NETWORK

LIGHTSPEED
BOOKS

RCG
PUBLISHING

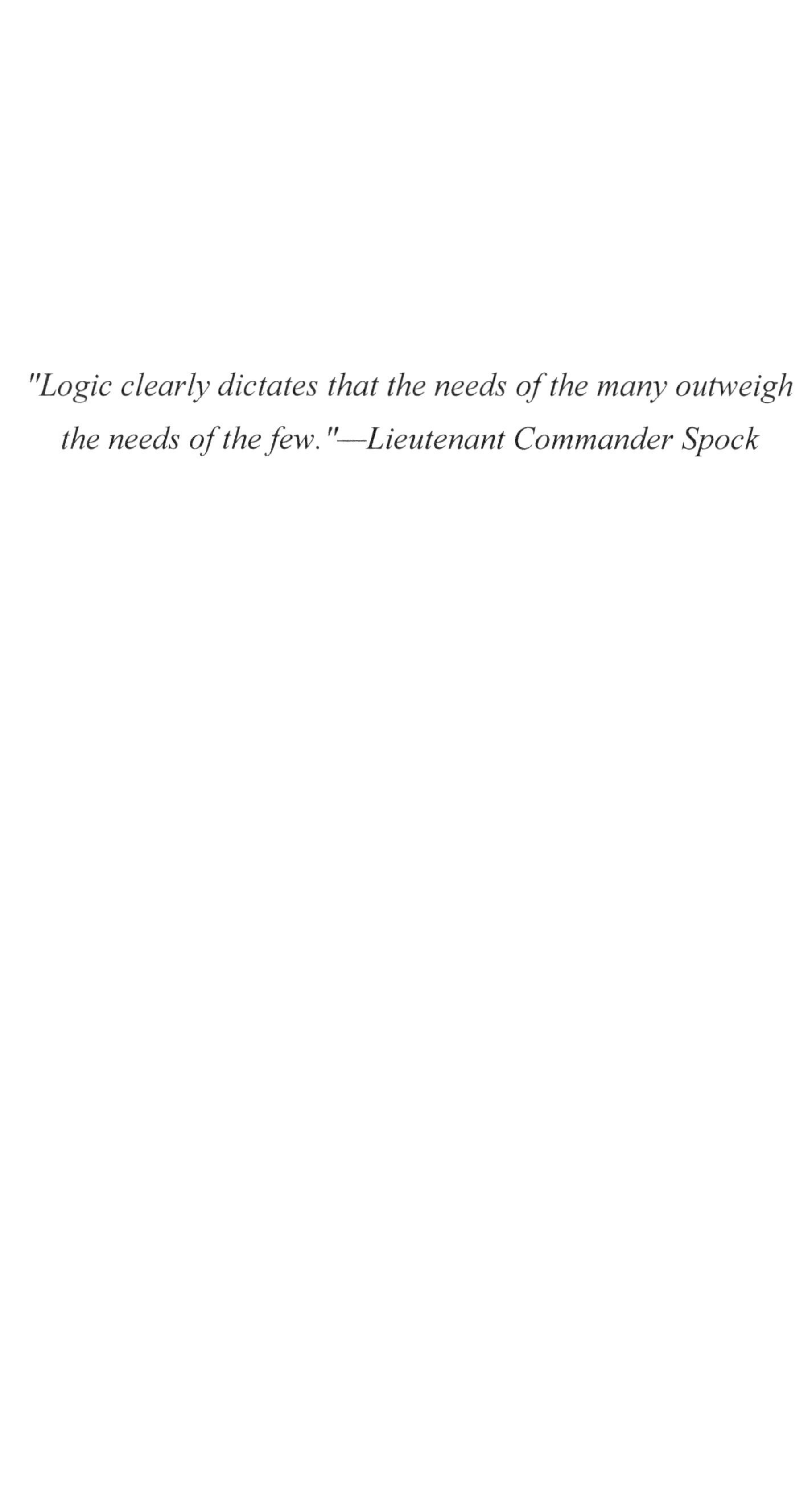

"Logic clearly dictates that the needs of the many outweigh the needs of the few."—Lieutenant Commander Spock

WRITERS CRUSHING COVID-19: An Anthology For
Coronavirus Relief

Copyright © 2020 by Piedmont Authors Network
All rights reserved.

Some of the contributions to this anthology are works of fiction. Where applicable, names, places, characters, and incidents are the product of the author's imagination or are used fictitiously. Any resemblance to events, locales, or persons living or dead, is coincidental.

For The Many

Introduction

A lot of us are in or around the same age demographic. Which means we remember things like the Viet Nam war, Woodstock, the moon landing, and a president's resignation. Many may even remember a president's assassination. It's safe to say, though, not many of us, if any, can remember the Spanish flu of 1918. We may have heard about the polio outbreak of 1952 and some of us may have had family members or friends affected.

This novel plague, COVID-19, not only will *we* remember but our kids and grandkids will remember it as a major event in *their* lives.

So, this is for them. *Writers Crushing Covid-19* is a collection of short stories, essays, and personal letters from some of the best authors in the business. Several authors, like Karen McCullough and J.L. Delozier, have dealt with the virus on a personal level, as one suffering from the illness and a doctor on the front lines. E.A. Aymar's touching thoughts to his young son will bring you to tears. There's humor, who-dun-its, paranormal, and suspense. And there's even a western.

The authors who donated their time and words are just as varied as the stories themselves. Multiple award winners, NYT Bestsellers, multi-published, and debut authors. Every single author in the anthology jumped at the chance to give back. Proceeds are going to the Book Industry Charitable Foundation.

This Anthology would not have been possible without the selfless dedication of the following individuals: our skillful editors Micki Bare and Karen McCullough, tech genius Tim Caviness, and last but not least Larry Kelter for proposing and editing this work.

We thank you for *your* support so that *we* can support others.

Stay safe,

Lynn Chandler Willis
President
Piedmont Authors Network

TABLE OF CONTENTS

A Letter To America's Medical Students

J.L. Delozier

Dr. J.L. Delozier worked for the federal government for fifteen years caring for America's veterans and deploying to disasters through the Disaster Emergency Personnel System. She left federal service to see patients and teach as an Associate Clinical Professor of Medicine for Penn State College of Medicine.

In early January, she received a fax from the CDC about an abnormal cluster of pneumonia cases in Wuhan, China. Although the details were sparse, her specialized training in mass casualty, pandemic, and bioterrorism scenarios allowed her to see the future. A plague was coming.

Six weeks later, medical schools across the country pulled their students out of clinical rotations, deeming it too dangerous for them to shadow physicians during the COVID-19 outbreak. This letter was written shortly thereafter.

Sarah and Daniella,

I see your distress. You're worried not just about our shared concerns of illness, family, and finances, but also about your schooling, your futures. You've worked so hard and sacrificed so much to get to this stage, and in a span of six weeks, it's been whisked away indefinitely. You're in limbo, a viral-induced no man's land, as is our entire country.

I also see you're eager to help, chafing at being sidelined when you entered this career specifically because you are the helpers, the ones the inimitable Mr. Fred Rogers said we should seek out when trouble calls.

But America needs you to be patient. When the second wave of illness hits—and if history and my training have taught me anything, it's that there will be another wave—you're our second line of defense. Already dozens of physicians have fallen to COVID-19. In a year or two, when many, too many, of us front-liners are gone, you'll have your chance. By then, your readiness will match your desire.

In the meantime, mindfully, medically, ignoring the hyperbole and fear, watch what's happening around you. I've always taught you to listen to the patient, for they will tell you their diagnosis. America is now our patient. COVID-19 has laid bare our country's underlying disease. Inequalities in health care and the ability to earn a living wage, racism, classism, political partisanship—they're all out there, hidden in the numbers and language of public health. Over the past three months, you've received a crash-course in epidemiology in a living lab, more vivid and visceral than any textbook could be. Review the websites of the Centers for Disease Control, World Health Organization, and your state health department daily. Think about how they approached the data and what that data means for the real world. Crunch the numbers down to the patient level, to an "n" of one. That's what it means to be a physician.

The next time we meet, no matter how many months have passed since you sat in a classroom, you'll be ready. I believe in you. Truthfully, I believe in you more than I believe in the generation above mine, the generation which holds the bulk of our country's political, financial, and institutional power. Why? Because you'll have watched and learned from this delicate dance, this interplay of disease, politics, money, religion, individuality, and dogma. What didn't work? What needs to work better? America is telling you its diagnosis. Listen. You are the cure.

Sincerely,

Jennifer Delozier, MD

As a physician, J.L. Delozier draws inspiration from science that exists on the edge of reality—bizarre medical anomalies, new genetic discoveries, and anything that seems too weird to be true. The first of her four thrillers was nominated for a "Best First Novel" award by the International Thriller Writers organization. Her short fiction has appeared in the British crime anthology, *Noirville: Tales from the Dark Side,* NoirCon's e-journal, *Retreats from Oblivion*, and *Thriller Magazine.* Her first sci-fi short story won a Roswell Award and appeared in *Artemis Journal.* She lives in Pennsylvania with her husband and three cats.

FOR PHILLY

Micki Bare

The rock was upturned ever so slightly, as if someone kicked it out of place. When she noticed it, panic rose from Jeanine's gut, spreading like disease to her extremities.

Was she here?

Unable to move forward or turn back, Jeanine contemplated her options. If she continued into the cabin and her mother was there, one of them was going to die. If she left, she was leaving behind the one thing that could save her brother's life.

Her eyes darted between gaps in curtains, straining to see a shadow or flicker—movement of any kind. Seeing nothing, she closed her eyes and listened.

When school was still held in buildings, before the pandemic, her science teacher took her class outside once a week just to listen. "Eyes and mouths shut," Mrs. Brennan used to say. When Jeanine looked back at her science journal, she was always amazed at the lists of different things she was able to hear when she took the time to listen.

Today, she waited to hear something that could help her decide whether to move forward with her plan or run. The creaking of an old plank, worn furniture being dragged across loose flooring, the gravelly breath of a chain-smoking, addicted, bi-polar, self-absorbed monster.

The cabin was where her mother stayed when she wasn't living with her latest boyfriend or on the couch of an acquaintance who'd believed one of her elaborate pity stories. It's where Philly, her eight-year-old brother, was found after he ran away when he was placed with the third foster family in the span of a year. It was the family that wouldn't take Jeanine, the family that was happy to take one child—preferably the younger one, because teens are much more difficult—but not two.

In the quiet, Jeanine realized that even if she did see or hear something, she still had to go inside. She could live with having to kill her mother in self-defense. The worst that could happen was prison. How much different could prison be from a group home for teens in the system? She'd still be able to write her brother. And he'd be able to visit.

She was not afraid of dying, either. Not if it happened trying to save her brother's life. What she couldn't face was a future without the dimpled smile of her kid brother.

She was shocked when he texted that he'd forgotten his bag. No one checked for the bag when the authorities "rescued" Philly from the cabin. Insulin was not easy to get in the post-pandemic world. "It's going to get better," the caseworker said. "We just have to be patient. Anti-virals and vaccines are still backing up production."

She looked at the jagged rock again and picked it up. It was heavy. Jeanine paused and let all the rage that built up over the past few years flood her heart. Losing their dad to the virus. Watching from a distance as their mother signed away her parental rights. Losing everything but a trash bag of clothes and a few personal items.

Jeanine hadn't seen any of her friends since the day they closed the schools. She fell two grades behind in the 18 months it took for home schooling—and the infrastructure to make it feasible—to become mandatory.

With gentle, slow steps, Jeanine approached the door. She pushed it open, slamming it against a chair. The chair tumbled into a lamp, which also fell, causing the light bulb to explode into a thousand pieces.

When the clatter quieted, Jeanine looked around the dim cabin. She checked the bedroom, under the rusty cots, in the closets. She checked the bathroom, jerking the shower curtain off its rings.

When she was certain no one was inside the cabin, she dropped the rock and began looking for Philly's bag. She opened draws, tossed aside pillows and cushions, opened the freezer and refrigerator—

"You're not going to find it," a raspy voice shouted at her.

Every ounce of blood in Jeanine's veins went cold. She turned to find her mother in the doorway. Her gray, wiry hair had grown past her shoulders and was matted. Red lipstick bled through the wrinkles around her taut mouth. She had an open pack of cigarettes shoved in the side pocket of a stained, oversized, blue and pink housedress.

"What are you talking about?" Jeanine finally answered. Her mouth had gone completely dry.

"You know. Don't act like you don't know. Now clean up this mess you made," she demanded, pointing to the toppled lamp and strewn pillows.

Jeanine swallowed hard. "What won't I find?"

Her mother laughed. "You wanted to sell it, too. Admit it. And now you're angry that I beat you to it!"

"Sell what?"

"Clean this up! Now!" her mother barked back.

"I'll clean it when you tell me what you took. What you sold."

Her mother squinted her eyes and lit a cigarette. "I'll tell you what I sold when you get this crap cleaned up."

Jeanine closed the refrigerator door and took a step toward her mother. "You don't tell me what to do. You signed a paper saying you didn't want to be my mother."

Jeanine's face burned hot. She took another step. "What did you take, Charlotte? What was it? Tell me!"

"Don't call me that! I'm your mother. Signing a piece of paper didn't change that! I'm still the one that gave birth to you." Charlotte's voice cracked. She began to cry. "I love you. I always have."

"Then tell me."

"You know already. It was in his bag. He left it," Charlotte answered. Her hands flailed as she babbled on. "It was probably expired anyway. Do you know how much that sells for? I needed that money. You abandoned me. Just like your father. You all abandoned me."

The fire that was building in her heart sank to her stomach as her mother confirmed her worst fear. The insulin was gone. It'd been sold on the black market.

"You don't love us. You never did! You know you probably killed your son. He needed that medicine. And you stole it." Jeanine was screaming now.

So was Charlotte. "You liar. He's not dead. And that social service lady will get him what he needs. What about my needs? Ever think of that? Get out of here!"

Charlotte picked up the chair and threw it. Jeanine ducked and grabbed a knife.

Charlotte laughed and threw down her cigarette. "What are you going to do, stab me? You ungrateful witch!"

Charlotte pulled a gun from underneath her housedress and shot. The bullet hit the freezer door.

Jeanine ducked behind the kitchen island and threw the knife. It bounced off her mother's arm—the one without the gun. She pulled out her phone and dialed 9-1-1, dropping it as she hit send.

Another blast rang out. This time the bullet hit the light over the island, shattering it above Jeanine's head.

"Stop! Please!" Jeanine yelled.

"Not so tough now, are you?" Charlotte answered. "Get up. Let me see you. Or are you afraid to die?"

Sirens blared in the distance.

"Those are for you. I called. They're coming for—"

BLAM! BLAM!

Jeanine screamed in pain. A bullet ricocheted off the sink and hit her shoulder.

"Are you dead? Are you hit? You dying?"

Jeanine held her shoulder and stayed quiet. If Charlotte thought she was dead, maybe she'd leave.

BLAM! THUD!

For the next few minutes, all Jeanine heard were sirens. Tears streamed down her face. The pain was sharp. She watched as a red stain grew bigger on her shirt. A small pool of blood formed on the floor next to her hip.

Lights strobed across the walls. Car doors slammed.

"This one's gone," a voice said. Then, "Is anyone here?"

Jeanine opened her mouth, but nothing came out.

"Get the truck! It looks like she took a bullet," a voice yelled.

Jeanine woke up to the sound of a monitor blip, blip, blipping next to her head. Her arm, shoulder, and neck were immobilized. She was in pain, but all she could think about was her brother.

"Nurse, my brother. Can you help me find Philly? He was sick. Foster care. Insulin. She sold it."

"Shhh, relax. It's good to see you, young lady," the nurse responded. Let me get your social worker. She's just down the hall."

A few minutes later, the social worker pushed Philly into the room. He was in a wheelchair, but otherwise, looked well.

"Philly!" Jeanine called out. Then she looked at the social worker. "Did he get his insulin?"

"He had a bit of spell. When he started to go into shock, his foster mother brought him directly here. He was stabilized in the ER. He gets to go home today. And he has enough insulin to get him through until his prescription can be filled."

Jeanine closed her eyes. He was safe—for now. And that was enough. It had to be.

THE END

Micki Bare is the author of Thurston T. Turtle Moves to Hubbleville, Thurston T. Turtle and the Legend of the Lemonade, and Thurston T. Turtle and the Precarious Puppy (Jan-Carol Publishing, 2010, 2012, 2015). A graduate of N.C. State University, her career in early childhood career spans more than two decades, with service as a teacher, administrator, and marketing director. She loves to write, garden, cook, and hike. She's currently working on middle grades novels. She is a member of SCBWI, PAN, and Asheboro/Randolph Chamber of Commerce. Micki is also a Talkabook certified author (Talkabook.com). She and her husband reside in Asheboro, NC. Visit mickibareauthor.com.

THE LONG LOOK BACK

Brendan DuBois

When the door to his room swung open, Eric Randall smiled at seeing his sixteen-year-old grandson Micah lope in, holding a work pad in one hand. Micah was a good kid, the son of his daughter Grace, and unlike a lot of his teen friends who were into gaming, gaming, gaming all the time, Micah seemed to enjoy spending time with his Grampie Eric.

Even if today was just a school project.

Eric had CNN up on the main screen on the other side of his room, and he toggled it off when Micah sat down across from him. Once again, the sound didn't seem synced with the picture, and Eric made a mental note to call the facilities manager and get it fixed. Lord knows he paid enough each month here for the meals, medical care, and upkeep, and making sure the video matched the sound shouldn't be an issue.

"How goes it, Grampie?" Micah asked, settling in to one of the two comfortable chairs in the living area, near an empty settee.

"Eh, I can't really complain," he said, which was true. He was pretty damn old, older than he ever dreamed he'd reach, and the medical staff here—while pricey—managed to keep his aching and leaking body parts together.

Micah was a good looking kid, slim, dark-skinned with black hair that was trimmed pretty short, almost like a crewcut, and he had on brown shoes, khaki slacks, and a light blue polo shirt with his school's name—ST. MARY'S ACADEMY—embroidered in white over the left-side pocket.

Eric said, "Your mom said you wanted to interview me for a history project."

"Unh-hunh," his grandson said, slim fingers flying over the keyboard of his tablet. "We're each supposed to do a report on the COVID-19 pandemic. You were around then, right?"

Eric nodded. "Yep. Fresh out of college. Copy editor at *The Boston Globe*. Sure, I remember it well."

"What can you tell me about it, Grampie?"

He smiled. "Ah, c'mon Micah, you can do better than that. Thirty minutes on Google will tell you everything you need to know."

Micah looked up, smiling. "Yeah. I guess you're right. Okay, what do you remember specifically? I mean, it happened in the spring of 2021, right?"

"Twenty-twenty," Eric said. "At least get the year right."

"Ah, no big deal. A fact check scan would flag it."

"You hope," Eric said. "You kids and depending on your tablets and all to correct all of your mistakes. God help you all if the computers decided to go on strike."

His grandson smiled and did a little roll of the eyes, and Eric smiled right back. "Okay, enough of goofing around. Well… What I remember most is that we weren't really prepared for it. I mean, we thought we were prepared for it, we thought the hospitals and the governments would know what to do, but they didn't."

"Wow, really?"

Eric raised a hand. "Ah, it shouldn't have been a surprise. Big governments, big bureaucracies, they're never ready for a sudden change. They always deny, cover up, over-react or under-react. Go back to your Google and look up Pearl Harbor. Lots of warnings that the Japanese were going to attack, and they were ignored. And look up Clark Field in Manila, nine hours after Pearl Harbor was bombed. Even with that much warning, most of the American air fleet was destroyed on the ground. And Hurricane Katrina in 2005. Even with all the warnings that a big hurricane would someday hit New Orleans right in the nose, nobody was ready."

He took a moment to catch his breath. Lots of talking, and truth be told, he didn't have much opportunity to talk at length around the facility.

"Yeah, so people shouldn't have been surprised when it seemed like nothing was done right to address it. That's how it goes most times, unfortunately."

Micah kept on typing away. "When did you notice?"

Eric said, "Most of the world knew in December 2019, when the word first came out of… Wuhan. Yeah, that was it. Wuhan. It seemed like something that China could handle, or at least Asia. Word was that it came from a market that sold bats. Lots of jokes were being made about bat soup and stuff. Then people started dying in Asia, and then it spread… to Italy, France, Spain, the United States. Within four months, more than three million people around the world were infected, with more than two hundred thousand dead. And that was just the start…"

Eric paused again, not because he couldn't catch his breath, but because all of the old memories, stories, photos, and videotapes came rushing back to him, even if he thought they had been carefully stored away.

"And what did you do, Grampie?"

"Me? Just tried to live, tried to adapt. At first we didn't take it that seriously. Then the cases popped up in the United States. At first it was, okay, we can control this by closing the restaurants, or movie theaters, and other places of gathering. People were told not to wear masks, and then told to wear masks… It was a confusing time. Different states had different rules and reactions. Some countries nearly collapsed. Places that sheltered senior citizens—most as old as me!—were nearly wiped out by the virus. In some cities, they ran out of spaces to hold bodies. It was a terrifying time. Back then, nobody really trusted anyone in the media or in politics. People got paranoid about their neighbors from other states."

"But Grampie…what did you do?"

Good question.

"Micah, all this talking is making me thirsty. Get me a cup of water, will you?"

"Sure."

His young and intelligent grandson went to the right of the room, where there was a little kitchenette installation—his meals were taken in the common dining room—and he drew a glass tumbler of water and brought it back.

Eric took a good sip and said, "Me? I just took it, day by day. We were told to wash our hands a lot. Which I did. Then we spaced apart our work areas at the newspaper. And I started wearing masks while going out. Then we started working from home. Then the governments shut everything down, and we were told not to leave our house. Some grocery items, including toilet paper, if you can believe, ran short. Yeah, a scary time."

"But… It got better, didn't it?" Micah asked, still tapping away on his pad. "Eventually?"

"Oh yes, it did, but it was a hard time. Very hard time… It seemed every week the death rate climbed up, and every week, officials in the government spent more time fighting with each other than cooperating."

Eric's words drifted off.

He shifted in his chair.

His grandson looked up.

Eric said, "But there was good out there, as well. People looked out for each other. Phone calls, Zoom video meetings, stuff like that. There was a shortage of hospital ventilators, and lots of companies retooled themselves to make 'em. There was also a shortage of facemasks, and volunteers made them at home and donated them to whoever needed it."

"That sounds great," Micah said.

"And there were other things as well," Eric recalled. "In my apartment building, an elderly woman lived alone, and she was scared to death about going out, because she was vulnerable and could have died. But I contacted her, started getting her groceries, started to talk to her, and found out during World War II, that she had been an Army nurse in France. And if it hadn't been for the COVID, I would have never known her. Other people did the same, all across the country, all across the world. In most cases, most places, the good outweighed the bad."

Micah typed some more, looked up and said, "When it finally ended…what happened next?"

"We picked up the pieces, and moved on," Eric said. "Like people do after all disasters.   Like the Black Death.   Great wars. Depressions.   Humans… We have the funny ability to look around and decide to forge ahead."

Micah typed some more, and Eric said, "Got enough?"

"I think so, Grampie," Micah said.   "If I need anything else, I'll buzz you."

"Okay, then.   Hey, your mother gave me some great news yesterday.   You were accepted for early admission to MIT.   Are you going to accept?"

As his grandson was preparing to answer, Eric reached out for the glass tumbler of water, misjudged, and knocked it over.   The water spilled out in large globules, and the tumbler started its slow fall to the floor, the one-sixth Lunar gravity easing its way.

Micah quickly got off the chair and caught it before it hit the floor.

"Sorry, Grampie, guess I wasn't quick enough," he said.   "Want me to wipe up the water that spilled?"

"No, no, it'll dry itself," Eric said.   "But answer the question.   Will you go to MIT next year?"

Micah smiled.   "It's a long way to Earth."

Eric smiled back.   "Not as long as the trip to get us here."

THE END

Award winning and New York Times bestselling mystery/suspense author Brendan DuBois is a former newspaper reporter and a lifelong resident of New Hampshire, where he lives with his wife Mona, their hell-raising cat Bailey, and one happy pup named Cooper. He is also a one-time "Jeopardy!" game show champion, and is also a winner of the game show "The Chase." He is currently at work on a number of projects with New York Times bestselling author James Patterson. Their first two collaborations, THE FIRST LADY and THE CORNWALLS ARE GONE, were released this past March 2019. He is currently working on another novel with Patterson, as well as a new Lewis Cole mystery novel and a number of short stories. Since 1986, DuBois has published more than 170 short stories in markets such as in Playboy, Analog, Asimov's Science Fiction Magazine, Ellery Queen's Mystery Magazine, and Alfred Hitchcock's Mystery Magazine.

He can be reached by email at brendan@brendandubois.com

Nothing Could Be Finer

Diane Kelly

I donned the homemade red-and-white gingham mask that matched my ruffled apron, picked up the watering can, and stepped out of the diner. Standing on tiptoe, I lifted the can to water a hanging basket of purple pansies. The afternoon was cloudless and bright, the sunshine warming my auburn hair and freckled skin. But it would take more than sunshine for Mother Nature to distract me from the fact that the world was in the throes of the COVID-19 pandemic.

As if reading my mind, the Universe sent a car my way. Under normal circumstances, the sound of an approaching vehicle wouldn't catch my attention. Carolinas' Finer Diner sat on a relatively busy roadside just before the turn that led into town. But with so little traffic on the roads now, the rumble of the engine drew my eyes to the highway to see who had dared to venture out.

A Watauga County Sheriff's Office patrol car rolled slowly by. Our mountaintop town was too small to support a police department, and was instead overseen by the sheriff. An unfamiliar yet formidably broad-shouldered man sat behind the wheel of the cruiser. Though a white mask concealed the bottom half of his face, he was exposed from the bridge of his nose upward. The timber wolf tones of his short hair told me he was no spring chicken, but the music drifting from his open window—AC/DC's "You Shook Me All Night Long"—told me he wasn't ready to be put out to pasture.

The deputy glanced toward the diner, and our gazes met over our masks. He raised his left hand from the steering wheel in a casual wave and his gray-blue eyes crinkled with an unseen smile that set every nerve in my body sizzling. *Now I know how the hash browns feel.* As he rolled on, he turned his attention back to the road, curled his fingers over the steering wheel once again, and rounded the corner, disappearing from view.

Did I just experience a surge of unadulterated lust, or had it been merely a hot flash? These days, it was more likely the latter. At 52, I was no spring chicken myself. But I'd been divorced over a year now. Maybe it was time to get back on the horse. I only hoped the next horse I rode didn't turn out to be another jackass in disguise.

I carried the watering can inside, tucked it behind the counter, and picked up a menu to fan myself. I called back to my partner in the kitchen. "Hey, Lina! The new deputy just drove by. Heard anything about him?"

"Not much," she called back. "When the town shut down, the gossip mill did, too. All I know is he's from the Memphis area."

Hmm. Small-town mountain life might seem slow and routine to a man from a big, bustling city like Memphis. Then again, maybe that's precisely why he'd taken a job here, to escape to more serene surroundings. Heck, I'd come up here last year from Atlanta for a much-needed post-divorce detox, fell in love with the place, and immediately made plans to relocate. It only seemed right to move to the Carolinas, with my name being Carolina, and it had been kismet when I'd met another fiftyish divorced woman with the same name who worked in the hotel's restaurant. She'd sat down for a drink with me after her shift. With well-honed cooking skills but no capital, her dream of owning her own eatery had faded over time, seemingly destined to remain a wistful wish. I, on the other hand, had spent the last twenty years as a stay-at-home mom, only recently sending my youngest off to college. But what I lacked in work experience, I made up for in determination and my divorce settlement.

On a whiskey-fueled whim, we two Carolinas decided to launch Carolinas' Finer Diner. Bet you'd thought that apostrophe had been misplaced, huh? We bought a defunct beauty shop and remodeled the interior to fit our needs, but left the pink exterior intact. To avoid confusion, my partner went by the nickname Lina and I went by Carrie. Our diner catered to the breakfast and lunch crowd, opening our doors at 6:00 each morning and closing them at 2:00 every afternoon. In light of the fact that we'd rushed into this joint venture only knowing each other a matter of days and with our business plan hastily scribbled on a napkin, you might think our diner would be doomed. But we'd beaten the odds, as well as numerous bowls of blueberry muffin batter, and were in the black by our third month in business. Now, we weren't just business partners, but also good friends.

I returned the menu to the stack and pressed the button on the cash register. The drawer opened with a *ding*. After counting out the day's earnings and leaving tomorrow's start-up cash in the till, I made out a deposit slip and stuffed both the slip and the $368 cash into a zippered bag to take to the bank. It was only half our usual daily take, but others were earning nothing. We'd count our blessings.

I ventured back to the kitchen to help Lina finish cleaning up, but found she was nearly done already. Our income might have been cut in half by the pandemic, but so had our dishwashing duties. With us serving only take-out orders, we had no plates, silverware, glasses, or mugs to wash. See? Another blessing.

Lina untied the bandana holding her dark curls back, and shook them loose. "Another day, another dime."

Given that Lina sourced our eggs from her backyard chicken coop, we had a steady supply. The same could not be said of our other usual staples. It had been hit or miss the past few weeks, deliveries being unpredictable and some ingredients impossible to find, but so far we'd managed to make do. I gestured to the refrigerator and pantry. "How're supplies holding up?"

"We're out of bacon and sausage," she said, "but that's probably a good thing. The cholesterol levels in this town are as high as the altitude. The blueberries are running low, too."

"Technically, we can still call them blueberry muffins if there's at least one blueberry in them, right?"

"And lose our five-star Yelp rating? Not on your life. I've got some blackberries and raspberries left. I'll make mixed-berry muffins and pancakes tomorrow."

"Sounds like we've got the morning's breakfast special." I cocked my head. "What would you think about offering free meals to first responders in uniform?"

Though our diner earned a profit, we weren't rolling in dough. In normal times, we made just enough to cover expenses and pay ourselves a modest salary. Still, first responders were putting themselves on the front lines during this pandemic rather than sitting at home watching Netflix all day. We should show some gratitude.

"I think it's a wonderful idea." Lina slid a muffin pan into the dishwasher before turning to me, a brow raised in accusation. "I also think your motives aren't entirely pure. You were so flushed when you came inside I thought I'd have to put you in the freezer to cool you down."

There was no point in denying it, so I didn't bother. "I can't help it if I got a little flustered by his broad shoulders and sexy eyes."

"Got a good look at him, then?"

"Not really," I said. "The lower half of his face was covered by a mask."

"Don't get ahead of yourself," Lina warned. "For all you know, he's only got one tooth. Or untrimmed nose hairs. Or worse yet, maybe he's sporting one of those porn-star mustaches behind that mask."

I snapped a dish towel at her. "Or maybe that mask is hiding a nice smile."

"You even sure he's available?"

"He waved at me with his left hand. He wasn't wearing a ring."

"He might be single on account of the nose hairs." She put a hand on her hip and cocked her head. "You were married for twenty-five years and you haven't had a date since your divorce. Do you even remember how to flirt?"

"Maybe it will come back to me. Like riding a bicycle."

She put out her hands and performed a hula. "Can't hurt to shake your backside a little."

I rolled my eyes. "I'm a middle-aged woman. My backside shakes whether I want it to or not."

We locked up and headed out. I circled by the bank on my way home and made the diner's deposit at the drive-through. Tomorrow, I'd do it all again, the routine as soothing as the diner's comfort food.

****

At the crack of dawn the next morning, Lina and I were back at it, slinging hash, baking biscuits, and frying eggs. The air in the kitchen was heavy and humid, but scented with the delicious aromas of fried potatoes, vanilla, and pepper gravy. While some of the customers who called in orders grumbled upon learning there'd be no bacon or sausage, most took the news in stride, adapting to our revised and improvised menu.

During a lull, I stepped to the front windows and looked out across the mountains, which were green up close but morphed into grayscale in the distance. Being able to see for miles helped a person keep things in perspective. While the virus was disrupting everything now, like earlier calamities this pandemic would be a tragic but temporary trauma, a time in our lives we would someday look back on and say *remember when?* We'd lose some loved ones, but humans were a stubborn and resilient species. By and large, we'd survive, maybe even come out stronger and smarter.

A few minutes later, I was lining up to-go orders along the front counter when the deputy rolled up in his cruiser again. He still wore a mask, but this time, rather than heading on, he slowed and pulled to the curb to read the sandwich board sign out front. Along with the diner's phone number to call for takeout, I'd noted the morning's breakfast specials, including our apple fritters. I'd also noted our new "First Responder Free Meal" benefit. He retrieved his cell phone from the breast pocket of his uniform. The next thing I knew, the ancient landline mounted on the wall next to the register rang.

As I lifted the receiver, a fresh buzz sparked through my circuits and my throat tightened. "Carolinas' Finer Diner," I said, cringing to hear the squeakiness in my voice. "What can I get you?"

A voice with a deep timbre and sexy southern drawl responded. "How about a couple of those fritters? I'm in the cruiser out front."

"I'll get them right out to you, Deputy. On the house. Would you like a coffee to go with them?"

"You're singing my song."

"Cream? Sugar?"

"Give me some sugar."

"You got it." I hung up the phone.

Lina propped her elbows on the ledge again and wagged her brows. "I see the deputy's back."

"Mm-hm. He asked me to give him some sugar. Too bad he was talking about his coffee."

Lina and I shared a girlish giggle as I rounded up one of our signature pink paper bags. Using a pair of tongs, I dropped two fresh-from-the-fryer fritters into it. I filled one of the diner's souvenir travel mugs with coffee, stirred in a dash of sugar, and attached the lid. After grabbing a napkin, I headed outside. I set the bag, napkin, and coffee down on a picnic table near his patrol car so we could maintain a safe distance. As I backed away, he climbed out of his cruiser.

His eyes sparkled, the friendly crinkles back again. "Thanks, Carrie."

My hand reflexively went to my chest, a finger pointing to myself. "You know my name?"

"The guys at the sheriff's department told me."

So he'd asked about me, huh? The thought turned my insides as warm and gooey as the diner's apple compote. "I hope they didn't tell you all my secrets." *Maybe I haven't forgotten how to flirt, after all.*

"Nope. I'll have to find those out on my own."

He's flirting back, isn't he?

He picked up the bag and coffee, raising them in salute. "Thanks for breakfast. I'm Victor Vance, by the way."

"Nice to meet you, Deputy Vance. Enjoy the coffee and fritters."

"I will." He stepped to the cruiser, but cut me a sideways glance before climbing in. "By the way, you didn't quite get the phone back on the hook."

What? It took a moment before the import of his words sunk in. He heard me joke with Lina about giving him some sugar! My face flamed like a grease fire on the grill and I darted back inside.

***

Deputy Vance drove up again late the next morning. Too embarrassed to face him, I ducked behind the counter and spied from behind the cash register as he pulled his cruiser into the parking lot. My heart pulsed like a blender on high speed.

When the phone rang, I called to Lina in the kitchen. "It's him!" I hissed. "You have to take the call!"

"Can't!" she called back. "I'm up to my elbows in dishwater. Buck up, buttercup!"

Taking a deep breath to steel myself, I answered the phone.

Deputy Vance's voice came over the line. "How about a short stack of pancakes and another coffee with sugar?"

"Yes, sir." I hung up the receiver, double-checking this time to make sure it was fully seated.

When his order was ready, I rushed out the door, set it down on the picnic table, and called "Enjoy!" as I dashed back inside.

He wasn't letting me off the hook that easy. He phoned the diner again. "Why don't you grab some coffee and keep me company while I eat?"

Looked like I hadn't scared the guy off. *Might as well take a chance, right? After all, I'd taken a big chance with the diner, and that had turned out well.* "Okay."

I poured myself a cup of coffee and went outside, taking a seat at one end of the long picnic table. He sat down at the far end on the opposite side. As I watched, he reached up and lowered his mask. He had plenty of teeth, no errant nose hairs, and no porn-star mustache. In fact, he had a warm, friendly smile. A smile claimed my mouth, too, and I lowered my mask to show it to him.

"When this is all over," he said, "I'd like to take you on a proper date."

"I'd like that, too."

He raised his coffee in toast to what might come, and I did the same. "To better days ahead."

The End

Diane Kelly is a former assistant state attorney general and tax advisor who spent much of her career fighting, or unknowingly working for, white-collar criminals. Lest she end up behind bars herself, she decided self-employment would be a good idea. Realizing her experiences made great fodder for novels, she put her fingers to her keyboard. Diane writes funny mysteries that feature feisty female lead characters and their furry, four-footed friends. Diane is the author of over 30 novels and novellas, including the *Death & Taxes*, *Paw Enforcement*, and *House Flipper* mystery series. Find Diane online at DianeKelly.com, on Twitter and Instagram @DianeKellyBooks, and her author page on Facebook.

Suburbia Apologia

Chris Knopf

I wrote this essay about three years ago when I was contributing to various blogs. It never ran anywhere, but now with COVID-19, long-time city dwellers are flocking to the 'burbs in big numbers, and undoubtedly, many are feeling sheepish about it. I'd like to help with that.

When the lockdowns came, my wife and I were already ensconced in our ranch house in a neighborhood of one-acre lots twenty minutes outside Hartford, Connecticut. As the following essay demonstrates, I've always loved suburbia, in particular the close-in variety with well-established character and easy access to the city. But now I'm so grateful for the mammoth supermarkets, wide-open spaces, and friendly neighbors who are all out gardening, walking their dogs (ours also get to hang out in a big fenced-in yard, a privilege few city dogs enjoy), exercising, and airing out the kids. The mood is all kindness and cordiality, an unspoken but palpable understanding that we're a community eager to support one another, if only by a refreshing conversation at a distance that never gets closer than about a dozen feet.

I once spoke with a woman who moved from Manhattan, where she'd lived her entire life, to a small, suburban town in Virginia. She was smitten with her new home and all that surrounded it, describing the experience lovingly as, "Living in a bowl of lettuce."

The modifier "leafy" is often placed in front of the word "suburb" and that's likely the only occasion when the arbiters of what's good and bad about contemporary living express anything favorable, however obliquely, about the way most Americans live.

Let me repeat that. For all the obsession with rural small towns and dazzling urban cores, most Americans live in suburbia. Let's start from there and build out. (I have a literary point to make, just hang in there.)

I'm sixty-seven-years old and have lived and worked in suburbia nearly my entire life. The only time I lived in an apartment building was about four months right after college. I had a year in London (in a flat carved out of a single-family house), and our home just over the western border of Hartford, Connecticut, where we lived for twelve years was pretty urban, but we had our own house with a lawn, a garage and an above-ground swimming pool. So I am as fully a creature of the suburban world as you can get, and I'm stepping up to defend it.

In 1957 my father, who was born and raised in Philadelphia, and spent his childhood playing football on city streets and moving around almost entirely on trolleys and smelly subways, moved his family out to the uncharted territories of Gulph Mills and King of Prussia (not made up names), a whopping ten miles from Philly via the new, yet already traffic-clogged Schuylkill Expressway.

These early suburban developments had the pick of the best property, most of which was formerly farmland or old, colossal family estates. My father bought into one of these situations, picking up two acres of nearly virgin forest of towering oaks, may apples, ferns, tulip poplars, dogwoods, thick moss, and about a trillion tree frogs.

This was a place within a forested paradise of hundreds of acres comprising streams, cliffs, abandoned houses, trails, Tarzan-grade vines, poison oak/ivy/sumac, and hopeful love notes carved into the bark of long-suffering silver beech.

All just a quick hop from downtown Philadelphia, even with the traffic.

In those days, parents generally let children and pets fend for themselves, even in city neighborhoods. My parents brought this habit to the suburbs, where even the faintest protective impulse faded away. There was now all this land for us to play in, so why bother with supervision? It seemed redundant. When we got home from school, we changed out of our school clothes and into our play clothes, and then ran out of the house. From there we'd risk death in a thousand ways for a few hours, before coming home for dinner, at which time the only requirements were to have washed our hands and not fight over the serving bowls.

This arrangement was even more liberating on Saturdays, when we had the time to either ride our bikes to the farthest reaches of Southeastern Pennsylvania, or grab the commuter train and travel back into the congested, crime-ridden city tumult our parents thought they'd delivered us from.

In essence, this was the type of idyllic childhood the likes of which we'll probably never see again, because never will geography, social evolution, and parental naiveté so neatly conspire to the good of formative youth.

But even today, there's much about suburban living that goes unappreciated. For example, what is the difference between a small town and a suburban town? Often nothing, except the suburban town has ready access to the cultural and financial advantages of a nearby metropolis. You can have main streets or village clusters with storefronts, surrounded by tightly knit neighborhoods, and social magnets, like high schools, churches, and synagogues that allow for a strong sense of place. And yet within a few miles, you can have things like The Franklin Institute, Academy of Music, and the Philadelphia Museum of Art, complete with a statue of Rocky Balboa.

I've read my share of Cheever and Updike and other literary works that invariably portray the suburbs as a culturally arid, psychological wasteland, a realm of alienated, alcoholic housewives and office dweebs slowly succumbing to lives of quiet desperation. While there's much to learn from these stories, the underlying sociology is built more on a kind of intellectual and artistic snobbery than awareness of facts on the ground. Why would a taste for roomy living quarters, trees and shrubbery, and neighborhood bar-b-cues automatically correlate with mental, emotional, and moral depravity?

Do you really think the average married couple with two kids and a mutt living in a split-level is more screwed up than a pair of Yuppies in Brooklyn with a closet full of Goth clothing and an artisanal cat?

One of the reason writers so readily denigrate the suburbs is they can get away with it. Suburbanites have been pariahs for so long, we're resigned to it. I think the proverbial visitor from another planet would find that ironic, since what you clearly get with a nice suburban town is the best of all worlds: access to cultural amenities, small town intimacy and convenience, and abundant natural and man-made beauty.

I think it's important to distinguish my preferred habitats from the outer rings. I can understand the attractions of exurbia, which can easily feel like full-fledged country living. For one thing, you can grow and raise your own food out there. That written, I once lived in an apartment (as usual, one of three in a former single-family building) which had a backyard where all the tenants grew corn, peas, zucchini, tomatoes, and asparagus. Today, my wife tends luxuriant flower gardens, but if the mood ever comes over us, we could become nearly self-sustaining on less than a quarter acre of our big yard.

However, there's something about the cultural vitality of the city infiltrating close-in suburbs that weakens as you move further away. To me, it's a gravitational pull, and once I've driven beyond its reach, I feel unmoored and adrift.

Speaking of driving, the only modern phenomenon more reviled than the suburbs is the automobile, the thing that made it all possible. I enjoy trains, hate buses, fear airplanes, and totally love cars. To me, they often rise to the status of sentient beings. Steeds, that can transport you to the corner drugstore or all the way to Los Angeles. Loyal, embracing, and uncomplaining, aside from the occasional warning light on the dashboard.

If you live where I do, the car means convenient access to the wonders of the city (aside from the agonies of traffic), or leisurely flights to the countryside. All completely safe from infectious human interaction, provided you stay in your lane when approached by a million-ton tractor trailer. And that vegetable garden of my dreams would easily balance out the subsequent carbon footprint.

I don't deny there are flaws and fallacies in the suburban life, but these are well-aired by those who resentfully ignore the sublime reality of what is good.

So, buck up, fellow suburbanites. Hold your commuter heads high, tend the lawns, clear the snow, fight the municipal status quo, and know you are the unheralded heroes of our time, the silent and uncounted denizens the 21st century.

THE END

Chris Knopf has published 17 mystery/thrillers, receiving multiple awards and starred reviews. His short stories have appeared in Alfred Hitchcock, Ellery Queen and the Akashic noir series. He spent 45+ years in advertising and also contributes to non-fiction publications.

Moonlight Goes Viral (A Dick Moonlight PI Short Thriller)

Vincent Zandri

"Los Angeles County Sheriff's Department spokeswoman Shirley Miller told CNN deputies responded to a Saugus home around 3 a.m. Monday for a family disturbance. The sheriff's department said a man allegedly punched his mother.

"'This is the first arrest I've heard of that started out over an argument over toilet paper,' Miller said."

--The Mercury News

Chapter 1

The front entrance to Lanie's Bar was still locked. There should be a law against such behavior. But then, I guess that was the law since the Chinese Wuhan Corona Covid-19 virus began ravaging the land like the return of the plague. Not that I'd seen any evidence of it. Oh sure, I'd heard horrific stories coming out of New York City and other big, congested metropolises where folks of all ages and ethnicities live on top of one another. Stories of mass graves, of bodies piling up like cord wood, of people crying out for ventilators, of zombies walking up and down Broadway devouring the flesh of the innocent.

But way up here in Albany, not a damn thing has happened. Okay, that's not entirely true. We've had a few deaths related to the virus. Or so the news tells us. But everybody knows the fake news lies like hell to get ratings, so who knows what to believe. I do know this: old folks who are said to be the most vulnerable to an infection that invades the lungs suffered the deaths. The lungs fill up with fluid, eventually collapse, and you kick the bucket. You just can't fight it if you're really old and fragile.

But only thirteen confirmed Corona Virus deaths in Albany and because of them, you gotta shut down my favorite bar? *Every* freaking bar? More than twenty Albany County residents died last weekend alone from car accidents. Another dozen from drug overdoses, and three from falling down the stairs in their home sweet homes. And yet, a gumshoe like me…a man who's got a piece of bullet in his brain and who can die at any time should it shift…can't get a stinking beer at a bar.

There ought to be a law.

CHAPTER 2

I tried the door once more. It was a stupid, if not futile, maneuver. Naturally it was bolted closed and no way was it opening any time soon. I stared at my reflection in the glass. I'd let my salt and pepper beard go in the month since this whole pandemic thing started. My scalp was still pretty bald. A passerby with decent eyesight could easily make out the dime sized scar on my right temple where the .22 caliber round entered it back when I tried to commit suicide. Naturally, I fucked it up and lived. Call it the story of my life *and* death.

I was wearing my old black leather coat over the same clothes I'd been wearing for about a week now. A black t-shirt that had *The Ramones* printed on it in big bold letters, and a pair of worn Levis jeans over black combat boots. You could not see the Colt .45 I was carrying these days thanks to the coat.

Technically speaking, I was no longer licensed to carry. But these were dangerous times when basic supplies were limited, when a man couldn't go out for a quick beer, and when tempers were not only running high, they were running at a hair trigger, DEFCON 4 level.

One last try. The door was still locked.

How did Einstein put it? Performing the same action again and again only to get the same result is the definition of insanity. I just wanted a fucking beer and a conversation with a pretty woman.

Is that too much to ask at a time like this?

CHAPTER 3

Choices. Go home dry or at least head to the local mega mart to buy some beer with my credit card. That is if I had any credit left on my credit card. Work had been tough to come by lately now that the economy had crashed to Great Depression-era levels. No one had the extra cash lying around to spend money on a private eye. Not even to take pictures of their cheating wives or husbands. Everybody was out of a job, or so it seemed, and it was the government's fault. The Governor was telling people to stay home, to not go to work, to cover their faces, to stay away from one another, to not go to church, to not get married, to not have parties, to not exercise outdoors, to not have fun of any kind. Or else!

When the government started lobbing orders at me, I was the type to defy them. No one tells me what to do. Not me, Dick Moonlight. Captain Head Case. You see, I could die at any moment. It was important I live every minute to its fullest. No bureaucrat governor wearing an expensive Italian suit and who wouldn't make middle management at Walmart if his daddy wasn't governor before him was going to tell me what to do. At least, that's what I liked to tell myself.

I got back in my third-hand Jeep Wrangler, and drove up the hill to the supermarket. The place was crowded, judging by the number of cars and trucks parked in the lot. I parked in the first available space, got out, and entered the busy store.

I tried to think. What essentials did I need to survive the next few days of quarantine? I jotted down a list in my brain. Beer, coffee, hamburger, beer, vegetables, fruit, beer, and oh yeah, toilet paper. I was out of toilet paper. I needed beer *and* toilet paper.

First things first. I made my way through the throngs of people wearing medical grade masks. Many of them looked at me with horror since I chose not to wear one (just try to arrest me). I maneuvered my way into the beer aisle. In New York State, you could no longer get a haircut, but you could buy all the over-the-counter booze you liver desired. Made sense too with all the sin taxes the state brought in from the sales. I guess Expensive Suit Governor also thought it might be prudent to allow his lemmings to be sedated as much as possible during this viral madness.

Two men were standing in the way of the cooler door, blocking it entirely. They were big men with beer bellies that made them look like they swallowed a basketball apiece. They were both wearing matching navy blue nylon track suits over white t-shirts. For footwear they wore white basketball sneakers, laces untied. Their round faces were baby smooth and their blonde hair was slicked back on their heads with…what did my on again/off again girlfriend, Lola, call it? Product. Twins. Identical twins.

"You mind?" I said.

The one closest to me turned quickly.

"Mind what, da?"

Da...Russian. Go figure.

"I'd like to grab some beer, you don't mind?"

The second one smiled.

"When we are finished, you may get beer, da?" He smiled when he said it in his heavy Russian accent. He gazed at his twin brother. "My, my, so much beer, I just can't seem to make up mind, Boris."

"Da, Vlad. Look at all that beer. It is ass blowing."

"No, you dumb cocksucker, Boris. It is *mind* blowing. Mind...blowing. Ass blowing is something else."

"Whatever," Boris said shrugging his shoulders. "Mind, ass, mind. What is difference?"

"In your case, there is no difference," Vlad said.

I couldn't take it anymore. Time was wasting and I needed beer. I shoved my way in between them, grabbed an eighteen pack of Bud and bulled my way out of there.

"What the fuck?" Boris said. "You are rude American, da?"

"He thinks he owns supermarket," Vlad said.

I glanced into their matching blue eyes. When, on cue, they both opened their tracksuit jackets to reveal the black grips on their matching semiautomatics, I couldn't help but open my leather coat, exposing my piece.

"Mine's bigger than yours, assholes," I said.

I felt their stares as I exited the aisle for the paper goods aisle.

CHAPTER 4

I'll be damned, but the place hadn't been emptied of all the toilet paper and paper towels. It had been fucking *ravaged*. I stood at the far end of the aisle and did my best to locate anything that might pass for toilet paper. That's when I saw it. One lonely package of no name brand, single ply TP, shoved way in the back on the top-most shelf. Must be the paper goods-starved public had missed it entirely.

A wave of urgency washing up and down my body, I double-timed it down the aisle, and with my free hand extended upwards, grabbed the package of TP. But that's when another, far bigger hand also reached out for it. I looked to see who the hand belonged to.

Boris. Or was it Vlad? It was impossible to tell who was who.

"You are too late, rude American, da?" he said. "This toilet paper belongs to Russian bears, da?"

Rage filled my veins. My little cold war was about to get hot.

"I was here first," I said, yanking the package out of his hand.

The two brothers eyed one another again.

"What do you think, Boris?" Vlad said. "Maybe we should shoot him on spot."

Vlad went for his gun. But that's when I dropped the beer and drew my .45. I was enraged. Crazy enraged. These Russian thugs had no idea the crazy man they were dealing with.

Outdrawn, they both slowly raised their hands in surrender.

"Looks like the toilet paper is yours, cowboy," Vlad said with a grin.

"Da," Boris said. "Go wipe your ass with it, Billy the Boy."

"It is Billy the Kid, numb nuts," Vlad said. "Billy the fucking kid. Get it right."

"Whatever," Vlad said, his hands high. "Kid, boy, kid."

I didn't want to stand around listening to their stupid banter. Grabbing the beer, I hightailed it out of the aisle, paid for my shit, and exited the store.

Pronto.

CHAPTER 5

My credit card worked. Thank God for small miracles. I tossed the beer and toilet paper in the back of the Jeep and drove out of the lot. I hadn't managed to grab any food, so I made my way through the McDonald's drive-thru, which was still open. I purchased a super-sized Big Mac meal with the credit that was left on my card, and scarfed it on the way home.

It was all I could do to make it to The Port of Albany and my flat inside the old red brick tanker dispatch building. I raced to the bathroom with my new package of toilet paper and relieved myself of my McDonalds. You'd think that by now I'd have learned about the ill effects of fast food on a man well past forty years of age. Seated on the throne, I gazed at the toilet paper dispenser.

Empty. Only the brown cardboard roll left over. Thank God I was able to score the last package of TP. Thank God I was quicker on the draw than the Russian Twins.

Tearing into the package I pulled out a roll and went to place it on the dispenser. But an abrupt noise coming from the front of the first floor flat gave me pause. Pulse picked up, mouth went dry. Was somebody intruding? In my overheated brain, I couldn't help but see the Russian Twins. Had they followed me all the way out here?

Quickly taking care of business, I then washed my hands and took all the toilet paper with me into my bedroom. Pushing the bed aside, I pulled up a four-by-four section of floor boards and tossed the TP into a concrete lined hole that also housed my less than legal assemblage of ordnance, including six grenades, two M16s, and twenty thirty-round magazines. Plus one AK47 and three banana clips. Assorted pistols and knives.

Replacing the floorboards, I pushed the bed back in place. That's when I drew my .45 and slowly, quietly made my way towards the front of the flat. The sun had gone down and the place was dark. But darkness was a good thing. It concealed me.

Then came a bump. It wasn't something that goes bump in the night. Far as I could surmise, it was someone coming in through one of the front double-hung windows.

"Be quiet stupid fucking moron, Boris," a voice said. "You alert rude American crazy man."

The accent was Russian. It had to be the twins.

"I am quiet, dry old babushka," Vlad said. "It is fucking darker than witch's titties."

"It's *colder* than witches titties, idiot," Boris said. "If you are going to live in America, learn to speak like America."

"How do you know witch's titties are not black?"

"Just shut up and get inside," Boris said. "My stomach is rumbling. We need that toilet paper."

I tiptoed to the front vestibule only a foot or so away from the front door, concentrated my aim on the window. When one of them stepped inside, I'd pop them on the spot. It was legal to shoot an intruder, especially if he was threatening your life.

More noise. Me, taking careful aim.

The front door was thrown open. I turned quick and…

CHAPTER 6

When I came to, I heard voices. Russian voices.

"Keep looking, Boris. It has got to be here somewhere."

"We have been looking for long time and still nothing," Boris said. "Maybe it is in Jeep, da?"

"I checked Jeep," Vlad said. "Nothing. *Nyet*."

"But I really, really have to go."

A loud belly laugh followed.

"You have to shit at time like this?" Vlad went on. "Must be Mother Natural is calling."

"I can't help it," Boris said. "I already told you stomach is rumbling. And it is Mother Nature, not Mother Natural."

"Whatever," Vlad said. "Point is, you need toilet paper now. Because rude American has nothing in shit house."

As my world came back into focus, I found myself duct taped to one of my kitchen chairs. The kitchen was a wreck, all the cabinets opened, the dishes pulled out, some of them shattered on the floor. I could hear the twins opening drawers and closets. Made me wonder the train wreck they were creating with the rest of the flat.

Over my right shoulder, I could see out past the wood deck to the Hudson River. Some riverbank spotlights located on the Troy side cast a white glow on the slow-moving river.

"Enough is enough, Boris," Vlad said. "Maybe if we get rude American crazy man to talk, he will reveal location of toilet paper, da?"

"You mean go all Putin KGB on him?"

"Da, da."

"Why not, Vlad," Boris said. "We have checked everywhere and I am about to explode like Trident missile."

Oh shit, they're gonna torture me…

For a brief second I thought about screaming. But then, my flat was located in the abandoned Port of Albany. My only neighbor was another PI bud of mine who went by the unlikely name of Steve Jobz. That's Jobz with a Z. He lived on a houseboat that was moored way too far to the north for him to hear me. Plus, he was probably passed out drunk by now, or banging some dame half his age or both.

The Russian Twins entered into the kitchen.

"Where is toilet paper?" Vlad said. "My brother has to take dump."

"Tell him to use his hand," I said.

Vlad made a fist and balled it in my face. The lights went on and off in my head. I knew that if he hit me too hard, he could dislodge the piece of bullet in my brain. If that happened I'd probably stroke out and die. Oh well, goodbye cruel virus-infected world.

Boris grabbed one of the steak knives from off the counter, stepped forward. His face was tight as a tick and if I had to guess, he was turtling his ass cheeks with all his strength.

"Tell me where toilet paper is now," he said. "Or you lose finger."

Vlad reached out for my hand, slapped it onto the kitchen table. His grip was as strong as a Russian bull, and that was saying something considering I could bench press three hundred pounds.

"I don't know where it is," I said. "It blew out of the Jeep on the way here."

"Liar," Boris said.

He stepped forward with the knife, pressed the blade against my pinky. He hadn't even cut me yet and the pain was already electric.

"Is hiding toilet paper really worth losing finger?" Boris went on.

His face was growing paler by the second, his entire body tense. I could tell he was about to experience a colon blow of epic proportions. Hey, we've all been there at some point in our lives. But out the corner of my eye, I couldn't help but see a boat slowly moving upriver. It was outfitted not only with the standard port and starboard side lighting, but also red, white, and blue LED flashers. It was an APD police boat.

The Russian Twins caught sight of the boat at the very second both their foreheads reflected the bright red laser beams that came from the electronic sights on the SWAT team's sniper rifles.

"Duck!" Vlad screamed.

The twins dropped to the floor as the window exploded and the rounds ravaged the wall mounted cabinets. I had no choice but to sit there and pray the shooter's aim was true. The front door slammed open then, and the sound of jack boots filled the flat. Three SWAT cops entered into the kitchen, automatic rifles aimed point blank at the Russian Twins. The SWAT cops were dressed in black tactical gear. Their helmets had clear visors. Two of them planted their combat-booted feet onto the backs of both Russians while the third cuffed them with thick flex ties. When the cop stood back up, I could see that he was making a sour face.

"Who crapped himself?" he said.

"I could not help it," Boris said. "It was impossible to hold any longer."

"Shut up already," Vlad said. "You embarrass yourself in front of rude American police."

CHAPTER 7

SWAT didn't waste any time pulling the Russian Twins up off the floor and carting them back outside to what I assumed was an awaiting SWAT van or an APD cruiser. Meanwhile, a uniformed APD cop entered into the kitchen along with a plain clothes cop. It was homicide detective Nick Miller.

"You okay, Moonlight?" the tall, white, jar-headed cop said while shoving his hands into the pockets on his Burberry trench coat. "Who'd you piss off this time?"

"It wasn't my fault," I said.

"Never is," Miller said.

"How'd you know I was in trouble anyhow?"

"There was that little bit about you drawing your hand cannon on the twins in the paper products aisle. Supermarket CCTV picked it up and they immediately notified us. You weren't answering your phone and the bars are closed. So I sent out the troops by land and by sea. Or by river anyway."

"You make me feel special."

"It wasn't about you," he said. "The twins have a rap sheet two miles long. They've been on our radar for a while."

"Glad I could be of service, Miller."

Uniformed Cop pulled a fighting knife from his utility belt and began to cut the tape that bound me to the chair. As he was working I gave Miller my initial statement regarding the evening's festivities. From the moment I entered into the supermarket and ran into the two Russian Twins hogging the beer aisle, to having to pull my gun on them in the paper products aisle (I know, grossly illegal. But desperate times call for desperate measures). I also told him how they followed me home, busted me upside the head and duct-taped me to the chair while they ransacked my house in search of paper gold.

"Paper gold?" Miller asked.

I looked up at him from the chair.

"You know," I said, "Loo roll, butt wipes, bum wads…"

"Toilet tissue," he said. Then glancing at his watch. "Speaking of which. I need to head to the supermarket. I'm clean out of paper gold myself."

"This damned virus," I said, standing. "You're never gonna get any tonight. The hoarders will make sure of that."

The old detective pursed his lips, straightened his already perfectly tied necktie.

"You wouldn't by chance have an extra…"

"Follow me, Miller."

Together we made our way out of the kitchen and into my thoroughly tossed bedroom. Pushing the bed aside, I pulled up the floorboards, grabbed a couple rolls and handed them to him.

"No wonder those two numbskulls couldn't find your stash," the old detective said, cradling the TP in his arm. "But was it really worth taking a chance on losing your finger?"

"It's the principle that counts. They invaded my house. I don't care what they were after. I don't cooperate with dirty rotten assholes."

He tossed one of the TP rolls in the air, smirked, and caught it.

"Touché," he said.

He started for the bedroom door. I followed him out of the house. SWAT was gone and the Russian Twins were now seated in the back of an APD blue and white. The uniformed cop who freed me from the chair had a black bandana wrapped around his face.

"He afraid of catching the virus, Miller?" I asked.

"I think he can't stand the stench of Russian gangsters," Miller said.

Then, turning to me, he went to shake my hand.

"No more hand shaking," I said. "Remember?"

He frowned and, staring off into the lonely distance, slowly shook his head.

"Sometimes I feel like it's the apocalypse," he said after a long beat. "This Wuhan virus just might get us all in the end."

"Look at it this way," I said. "As a species, we had a hell of a run."

He thought about that for a while, then slowly walked away, disappearing into the darkness. About facing, I made my way back inside the flat. I had once hell of a mess to clean up.

THE END

Vincent Zandri is the New York Times bestselling ITW Thriller Award winning author of more than 45 novels and novellas, including The Remains, The Embalmer, and The Girl Who Wasn't There. He lives in Upstate New York. Visit his website for a FREE Dick Moonlight PI Thriller at *www.vincentzandri.com*

FRAGMENTS FOR MY SON

E.A Aymar

I imagine it would take a week.

I'd wake feverish, after feeling unsteady the night before. That unsteadiness would have been worrisome, the way any cough or cold or fever nowadays brings concern. But I likely would have taken Tylenol and gone to bed.

I'd wake sweating, my shirt soaked through. Your mother would take my temperature (she'd be healthy, she's always the healthy one) and I'd sleep fitfully through the day, beset by nightmares, grinding my teeth until my jaws ached.

The next day coughing would wake me, and the fever would persist. I'd make my way out of bed and to the closet, so I could change out of my damp clothes, and discover that your mother has taken everything she needs (her clothes, books, bathroom supplies, iPad) out of the room.

I'd talk to both of you through the door, your mother worried but trying to stay calm, you telling me about something you saw on television, because you're only six and too young to understand this type of stuff.

I'd call a doctor, and the doctor would tell me that I was showing symptoms of COVID-19. The doctor would tell me I should remain isolated, self-quarantined.

The next few days would be a mix of fevers and coughing, and then body aches would start. There'd also be moments of respite where I'd watch television or maybe try to read a book. I'd be too tired for the effort of writing; that act, stolen.

As the week came to a close, the fever would encompass me like a net. I'd start to wake on the floor, next to the bedroom door, or in the bathroom.

On the stretcher, being carried out of the house, I'd see you and your mother watching me from the door. I think I'd see tears covering your face. I don't think I'd see anything more.

****

There is a common, somewhat clichéd sentiment among crime fiction writers: write what scares you the most. That approach has never worked for me, even if the concept is both powerful and provocative. My greatest fear, after all, isn't the common ground crime fiction generally treads. I'm not fond of serial killers, for example, but I don't live in fear of them.

My greatest fear is leaving you.

And that's a possibility, given that I've reached an age where friends are starting to discover cancer in their bodies or suffering heart attacks, when death ceases to be unusual. And this is also a troubling age for men, in particular. We've considered ourselves invincible up through our thirties and then, seemingly suddenly, death is possible. We've also considered ourselves the center of the world – both our own world, and the world of everyone else we know (that's such a guy thing). And for that to be taken away is unimaginable.

Again, this is really more of a thing that happens to men. We rarely understand the moment. Women are much better at that, and generally more realistic than we are. Men constantly try to re-shape reality, which makes us naïve. And dangerous.

And vulnerable.

***

So many of my friends talk about being quarantined with their families in the bleakest terms. And, let's face it, kid, the start of this essay was pretty bleak.

The thing about worry – as consuming and helpless as it can feel – is that, when you worry, it's almost always about something that hasn't happened. It *could* happen, but it hasn't. You're not helping yourself when you do that. You're not fixing anything.

Move in a different direction.

Take a look at reality, grasp it like a ledge, and pull yourself up.

***

I was going through a pretty stark unhappiness before this pandemic hit.

I'd see you in the morning, in the rush to get ready for work and school. The drive to your school took less than ten minutes, and then I'd head to work. I'd come home around seven at night and it'd be time for your nightly routine of dinner, bath, and bed. Weekdays never deviated.

I bitterly hated that I barely saw you during the week. Whether it meant finding a job closer to home, or home schooling, or making enough as a writer to do that full time, I wanted something that would give me a few more precious hours with you every day.

These past months, I've sat next to you while you do your schoolwork. We've taken breaks in the day to ride bikes, or make cookies for your mother, or laugh together at *Spongebob Squarepants*. My patience hasn't always been great, but I can honestly say it's improved, and I'm a better person and father because of that. Sometimes you want to do things I'd normally refuse, like a playful water fight with the hose that leaves us drenched, or watch too much television on the couch. I've relaxed and allowed those things and it's been wonderful.

You've laughed more.

I was never one of those men reticent with their words, a father who rarely says "I love you," but I think I've been even more loving than I was, and that fills my heart.

You fill my heart.

****

Funny thing is, I wasn't exactly psyched to be a dad. I was sort of dragged into the whole thing. I liked my life before this. It was nice and selfish and I slept a lot.

Having a kid seemed like *a lot* of work and responsibility, and I imagined that those were things I could shirk once you were born. And that first year was rough. But something happened near the end of that year, one of those interminable days when you were crying and I was exhausted. You laughed. And I'd never heard you laugh, and there is no better sound than a baby's laugh.

And then, another time, you were on the play mat trying to lift your head, and you grunted, and a baby's grunt aches inside of people. I realized then that I would do anything to help you, anything at all.

Fine. You won.

***

One thing I've realized, in my six years as a parent, is how little parents truly control. When I was your age, there was no world beyond my mom and dad. School and friends were subject to their control. My parents were the ultimate rule, the foundation of my life.

But how helpless they must have felt. I was born when the Vietnam War was ending, the first moment in the latter half of the twentieth century when America realized it wasn't invulnerable. Presidents had recently been assassinated or exposed as corrupt, and we were heading into a Cold War that we weren't confident of winning – or confident of what winning would cost. I was aware of none of this.

You're not aware of what it means for 100,000 Americans to die, and for the national and state governments to have contradictory, unsatisfactory approaches to dealing with a crisis. There is no foolproof plan, aside from remaining at home, and our country doesn't welcome that approach.

But children give parents a strength they never thought possible. Yes, any concepts of a valiant struggle or a stance against darkness are often illusory. But the willingness to fight isn't. The desire to be better than what I was, to be stronger than what I was, was given to me in ways I never imagined, from you.

Your mother and I will do everything we can to protect you.

And so nothing is truly hopeless.

***

I imagine it will take time.

Some things never truly return. Many of our favorite restaurants and stores remain closed. Online and virtual communication are enhanced. Work is conducted remotely as often as possible; not because it's safer, but because companies realize that employees can be trusted to work from home, and they see the unnecessary expense of retaining a large office. Schools offer more robust distance-learning features. The environment improves.

The majority of people live through this, in the way that the majority of people always survive catastrophe. We persist, and the world is more recognizable than we now expect.

I can see into forever with you, and that's where I want to walk. Sometimes the path is dark, sometimes it's treacherous, sometimes there are crevasses which seem impossible to pass.

It takes time, but we'll get there.

Don't be scared.

I'm your father, and I'll hold your hand, and I'll walk with you.

I promise.

THE END

E.A. Aymar's most recent thriller, THE UNREPENTANT, was published in 2019. His next thriller, THEY'RE GONE, will be published in November under his pseudonym E.A. Barres.

His past thrillers include the novels-in-stories The Swamp Killers and The Night of the Flood (in which he served as co-editor and contributor). He has a monthly column in the Washington Independent Review of Books, runs D.C.'s Noir at the Bar series, and is a former Board member of the International Thriller Writers. He was born in Panama and now lives and writes in the D.C./MD/VA triangle.

Flowers for a Dead Man

Jeffrey S. Hargett

Sara told me she loved me with all her heart. What a load of crap that turned out to be. Cousin Kevin said love was the brain's creation, nothing more than hormones, pheromones, and trigger-happy neurons. Turns out he didn't have a clue either. Hearts and brains have nothing to do with love. They have nothing to do with hurts and hate either. That kind of stuff lives in the soul.

Need proof? Check my grave. Nothing left of Franklin David Jones but ash and bones. My baby blues turned to dust years ago, right along with my adorable dimples and dashing smile. That's how 23-year-olds like me end up when the Fairlane's got a new set of whitewalls and the girls need impressing. And I did my impressing with all eight cylinders.

That's how I met my Sara.

I'm not really sure what it was about me that caught her eye. She did have a lot to choose from though. Momma raised me to be a modest boy, but still, it wasn't me the ugly stick took to beating. Leastways, I never thought so. But I suppose it could have been the Fairlane's apple-candy red. It did have a dozen or so pounds of the shiniest chrome you ever saw. Most girls like shiny. Sara did too, but I think what got her motor running was the 200 horses under the hood. I ain't met a woman yet that didn't like a little muscle. She had all 642 of mine flexing from the get-go.

Now, Momma raised me to be honest, so I'll admit that Sara

caught my eye first. Sara caught just about everyone's eye first. Men tend to notice things like a woman more beautiful than dawn with hair the color of a sunrise.

She'd just got done waiting tables at Charlie's Grill down on Worth Street next to the old Firestone. Charlie dressed his girls in yellow with frilly, white aprons cut to accent hips and hind ends. Charlie's customers were good tippers. I liked to watch from the Fairlane. Watching was free and it didn't require tipping. Besides, the burgers over on Main cost less and came with fatter fries.

When Sara stepped outside Charlie's, I lost every bit of sense I'd collected in twenty-three years. Maybe it had something to do with those hormones and trigger-happy neurons Cousin Kevin always went on about, but I thanked God for my Fairlane. If I'd not been in the driver's seat, I'd have been a red-faced fool. Those swaying hips of hers had my engine revving. Love may live in the soul, but it stirs things you can touch.

I spent the whole night wondering what her name was and where she lived. I'd have followed her, but the sheriff gets involved when guys do that. So I did what any other guy my age would do in that situation. I called Stephen, my best friend since second grade. Now Stephen always gave advice you'd only take on a dare, but she'd left me in a daring frame of mind. And for once, that low-life best friend of mine didn't lead me astray.

I put a ring on Sara's finger less than four months later. I said my "I dos" and meant them all, but just because a man's got a wife at home don't mean he can't still impress the ladies in town. I might have been a married man, but I still looked good sitting on 200 horses. When a girl lets her eye linger on you, she expects you to be a gentleman and return the favor. Momma did raise me to be a gentleman.

Nobody ever mistook Franklin David Jones for Ward Cleaver. Some guys got the makings for TV dads. Some don't. I was who I was. Folks can say about me just whatever they please. It don't mean I didn't love Sara. Maybe if I'd had a daddy helping Momma raise me I'd have been a better husband. Then again, maybe not. It don't much matter now. I'm dead and can't change a damned thing.

I've got Stephen to thank for that.

Along about September, Stephen calls. He'd found him some cute brunette from the other side of town and his Mercury was in the shop again. Far be it from me to deny my best man a lift in his hour of need. Besides, I was more than a little curious about what kind of girl dates a low-life like Stephen. I loaded Sara into the Fairlane and we set out to salvage what little dignity he had left.

Now I'm willing to overlook a few faults when a girl has a pretty face, but that Angie girl he found didn't know how to shut up. The girl yammered straight through dinner, the whole way to the drive-in and right through the pre-show cartoons.

I kindly yanked Stephen's butt out of the car and dragged his "gonna get me some" grin all the way to the concession stand. The boy thought he was Rock Hudson out with Doris Day. Even asked me if I found Angie attractive. Was he kidding? Anything wearing a skirt's attractive when you're 23. Didn't mean he was getting lucky though.

I'd have spent my whole check on popcorn, Goobers and Raisinets too, just on the chance it'd keep that girl quiet. The funny thing is, every time she got quiet I found myself looking over my shoulder.

Stephen was my best friend, but ain't nobody allowed to mess around in my Fairlane except me and Sara. My Fairlane, my rules.

Angie's battery finally ran low just about the time the second feature ended. I enjoyed a good three minutes of quiet on the drive back until Stephen somehow set Angie to squealing. A sudden commotion like that startles a man. I jerked the wheel and the next thing I know I'm Park Lawn Acres' newest resident.

I always did hate cemetery names. I do have to admit though that I'm decomposing under the greenest damned grass in the county. Of course, it'd be a whole lot nicer if all the neighbors weren't dead. Some of these poor souls have been here since Moses saw God. The living might not be able to see us, but we can see each other. We're like faded Polaroids and shimmer when the moon's right.

Some take to moping about and peering at tombstones, sometimes theirs, sometimes not. I thought at first they were searching for someone. They're not. They're just doing what I'm doing. Remembering. The dead don't got much else to do but remember. And we got forever to do it. Dying's a serious thing. I don't recommend it. It takes a spell adjusting to being dead. Some never do. Some go mad. Maybe they were mad before, but now they've got angry and crazy in a gift-wrapped box. Mine comes with a pretty bow.

I never saw Angie here in Park Lawn Acres. Maybe she's staring at tombstones over in Poplar Grove or one of the church cemeteries. Maybe she's still jabbering at drive-ins and squealing in back seats. One thing's for certain. She ain't with Stephen. Stephen's with Sara. My Sara. They've been here. Together. He puts his hand on her shoulder while she plucks stray weeds and places flowers next to the headstone. Flowers! What damn good are flowers to a dead man?

I'd almost come to terms with it, being dead, being a ghost. Never did figure out why I didn't pass on to someplace else. I never really expected it to be Heaven. God knows Momma tried. I always figured I'd be dodging red devils and pitchforks, but this is where I am. The smile-flashing Franklin David Jones everybody loved stays put six feet under. The Franklin David Jones that still feels the loves and hurts and hates stays put too. Ghosts don't leave their corpses behind. Ain't a matter of won't, it's a matter of can't.

Maybe that's what stokes our anger. That, and seeing a new gold band on your wife's finger that matches the one your former best friend's wearing. I can't help but wonder which came first, them patting down the dirt on my grave or Stephen moving in on my wife. At least he don't come here much anymore. Sara does though. She brings a little girl with her. She's got baby blue eyes. Just like me. And she cries every time Sara brings her here. Just like me.

Smiles fade and dimples disappear. You're left to linger on, cling to hates and hurts and loves because you can't lay a hand to anything. The worst part about dying? It's the living that comes after. Especially on the days they bring you flowers.

THE END

Jeff Hargett is a grandfather from North Carolina with an imagination full of magic and dragons. He stays young and fit by dining on epic fantasy whenever possible. He is currently writing an epic fantasy series that he hopes to publish while he can still wield a pen. He's a firm believer that when this world doesn't suit you, you should write a world that does. He enjoys interacting with readers and other writers and spends far too much time loitering around his blog: strandsofpattern.blogspot.com

THE JOURNEY THROUGH COVID-19

Karen McCullough

There are so many ironies and quirks to the story. Irony one: if my trip to visit family had been scheduled for just a week later, I wouldn't have gone. And I wouldn't have gotten the disease that has dominated my life for the past six weeks. Irony two: Until I can get a test for antibodies, I won't get a formal diagnosis. My one goal and hope throughout has been to stay out of the hospital. I succeeded, and because of that I haven't been tested, so it may never be official. But I know that I've had COVID-19.

I don't know exactly where or how I got it. I flew to visit family on March 5, returning on March 13. Given the timing of symptoms, I likely picked up the germ on the trip out or shortly after I arrived. Did I get it from the very large man in the next seat on one flight who wheezed throughout? Or in the crowded, bustling Atlanta airport? Or maybe on the also crowded playground where we took the children a couple of days after my arrival? Someone else or somewhere else entirely? That's one answer I'll never have.

Almost a week into the visit I started to have symptoms that I realize in retrospect pointed to what was about to happen. For a couple of days I had mild headaches. I attributed those to the change in routine which meant I didn't always have as much caffeine as I was used to.

I thought I felt fine on the trip home. That night, though, the anvil dropped—on my lungs. At least that's what it felt like. My chest got very constricted, like someone had tied a band around it and was pulling it tighter and tighter. I couldn't draw in a deep breath. I started hacking a deep, dry cough that raked my throat raw.

The weeks since then have been an up and down time. Like most people with the disease, fatigue has been a huge issue. As far as I know, I haven't had a fever, but I don't generally run fevers no matter how sick I am. We don't even own a thermometer.

I've had better and worse days and the contrast can be dramatic. Several times I actually thought I was getting better, and then the next day I'd wake up the with weight on my chest again and the fatigue pinning me down to the recliner. On bad days my chest hurt, I coughed so hard my throat was raw, and it was all I could do to walk from one end of the house to the other.

I'm in the vulnerable age group and have a few continuing health issues. I couldn't help worrying that I might take a turn for the worse and end up in the hospital, possibly dying. I've done quite a bit of meditating on that, but it's a different essay. I did consult with my doctor's office and also with a good friend who is a nurse. Both believed I had COVID-19, but my symptoms weren't severe enough to require further medical intervention. At some of the worst times, I teetered on the brink of calling for help. But then I'd improve just enough. At the urging of a nurse, I borrowed a pulse oximeter, which let me check my blood oxygen levels. It was reassuring to see those readings stay in the normal range when my chest felt so tight it was painful to draw a deep breath.

After three weeks of illness, I had a solid week and a half of feeling I was getting better. Then things went downhill again. Badly and fast. One evening I started having pain in my chest. As I got ready for bed that night, I noted a headache that got steadily worse. I wondered if I had suddenly developed a massive sinus infection. My face hurt, my teeth hurt, even my eyeballs hurt. I couldn't sleep. Tylenol had no effect on it. Finally, in desperation, I took some ibuprofen at three in the morning and it helped enough that I fell asleep for an hour or two. Over the next day, the pain in my head faded. But pain in my chest, the oppressive fatigue, and the racking cough returned for several more days. Then they slowly faded again.

I'm now ten days past that last episode. Two days ago I woke for the first time feeling almost normal again. I like to think that after a five-week battle, I'm finally over it. My energy hasn't fully returned yet, and my lungs don't feel completely right. Eventually, I'll need to be evaluated for possible permanent lung damage. But for the moment I'm counting myself very fortunate.

Don't believe anyone who says, "It's no worse than a cold or flu." Yes, some people get light or even symptomless cases. My version was only moderate, and it was a nightmare, the worst illness I've had in many years, including several bouts of flu.

A few people have asked me privately why I'm so sure I've had COVID-19 and not a more standard cold, flu, or allergy issue. There are two reasons, one fairly simple and one more complex.

The simple reason can be summed up in three words: no head congestion. Throughout, while my chest hurt and my throat grew raw with coughing, my sinuses stayed clear and nothing has dripped from my nose or down my throat. Even though I had some bad headaches, there was no mucus.

I do suffer from seasonal allergies, though they're worse in fall than in spring, but those make my head stuffy and my eyes itchy. I sneeze a lot and my nose runs. The same with colds and flu. They generally start with congestion in my head that may spread to my lungs, but I can't remember ever having a flu (and I've had it several times) that started with a direct and ferocious attack on my lungs.

The more complicated reason is that this disease has simply felt different. Aside from the lack of head congestion, every other symptom has been subtly different from anything I've experienced before. I can't remember ever feeling that same sort of chest constriction, like something was wrapped around my lungs, keeping them from expanding the way they should. And the cough was different. I've had bronchitis with a nasty cough, but that always seems to involve lots of goo. There was none with this. As people have mentioned about COVID-19, the cough was dry. And it seemed to come from somewhere down deep.

The progression of the illness is different. In my experience, flu comes on, gets worse, lays you low for a week or two, and then starts to go away. It can take a week or more for a complete recovery, but generally that's it. Not like COVID-19. This disease comes in waves, attacking hard, receding, attacking hard again. At least twice I thought I was over it, only to have it come back.

I've talked to my own doctor's office and to friends in the medical profession who all agree my symptoms indicate COVID-19. Because I got it early in the outbreak, when testing was limited, I would've had to go to the hospital to get it confirmed. Fortunately my condition never got dire enough to make that a necessity. I can live with not having that formal confirmation. I'm glad to be living. Period.

THE END

Karen McCullough is the author of almost two dozen published novels and novellas in the mystery, fantasy, paranormal, romance, and romantic suspense genres. Her publishers include Avalon Books, Worldwide Mystery Library, Kensington, ImaJinn Books, and Five Star/Cengage. She's won several awards, including an Eppie Award for best fantasy novel and been a four-time Eppie Award finalist, a Daphne finalist, Prism finalist, Rising Star Award finalist and several others. Her short fiction has appeared in a number of anthologies and small press publications in the mystery, science fiction, and fantasy genres. While pursuing her writing, she also spent fifteen years as a computer programmer, then ten years as editor, managing editor, and senior editor, with two different multi-national trade publishing companies. After leaving the corporate world, she started her own web design/development business. She's now retired and writes full-time. Karen has three grown children, a bunch of grandchildren, and lives in Greensboro, NC with her husband of many years.

Website: http://www.kmccullough.com.
Facebook: https://www.facebook.com/KarenMcCulloughAuthor
Twitter: @kgmccullough
Pinterest: https://www.pinterest.com/kgmccullough
Bookbub: https://www.bookbub.com/profile/karen-mccullough
Amazon: https://www.amazon.com/Karen-McCullough

THE COUGH

Lynn Chandler Willis

Marty Ludlum scrutinized the bank manager stringing up the yellow tape. The fat sumbitch draped it through the front door handles like he owned the damn place. He'd already posted "Lobby Closed. Please use drive thru" signs on the glass doors; now he strung the barrier to make sure people got the message.

"We ain't using the damn drive-thru," Marty mumbled.

Dwayne Shelby stirred in the passenger seat of the Buick. "Say what?"

"The drive-thru. How we supposed to rob a bank using the drive-thru?"

Dwayne laughed 'til he coughed. He scratched at his spotty beard. "Well, we'd already be in the get-away car so there wouldn't be no need for Benji."

He had a point. Marty had a strong dislike for Benji, even if he was Dwayne's first cousin. He was a snot-nosed kid as far as Marty was concerned.

"So, what are we gonna do?" Dwayne said. "I mean if they've got the drive thru open, someone's gotta be in there, right?"

Marty didn't answer. Instead, he sat there in the driver's seat and stewed. Why couldn't just one thing in his life go as planned? Just one thing. That's all he asked.

Marty waved his hand at the red brick building with the yellow tape strung across the front. "You do see the tape, right? You think they're just gonna open the door for us?"

Dwayne stared at the doors like he fancied himself a genie and they would open by mental telepathy or some shit. Marty turned the engine of the LeSabre and slowly pulled away from the parking lot across the street from the bank.

"So what are we gonna do?" Dwayne said.

Marty didn't answer right off. He had to think.

Dwayne lit one of those cheap cigarettes made from leftover tobacco, and the stench nearly gagged Marty. "Roll the damn window down," he grumbled.

He didn't want to go home reeking of cheap cigarettes. Sharon would gnaw his head off and his only goal in life was to keep her happy. That and stuffing his pockets with some extra money.

Dwayne cranked the window halfway and blew a stream of smoke through the opening. "So what are we gonna do?" he said again.

Marty gave the Buick a little gas to make the light. "We're gonna go home and think, Dwayne. That's what we're gonna do."

Dwayne coughed again. He took one last pull from the smoke before flinging it out the open window. "Say, before we go home, you mind stopping at the Walmart? I told Ramona I'd check and see if they had any toilet paper yet."

Marty gave Dwayne a side-eye stare. He sure was coughing a lot more than normal. The guy wasn't real healthy to begin with. "You ain't got the virus, do you?"

Dwayne took a swig from his travel coffee mug. "I hope not. Wouldn't want to expose you to it. Your diabetes and all." He hocked a loogie then spit out the window. "Just smoker's cough, probably."

Marty had no doubt about that. More likely lung cancer. He drove into the Walmart parking lot, carefully navigating around the multitude of cars. The town only had so many people in it and Marty'd bet half of them were right here at the Super Center. He dropped Dwayne at the front doors then circled around and parked near the end of a row.

From there he could see shoppers moving through the parking lot. Everyone wore a mask of some sort. A bandana or something hand sewn. One woman even wore a winter scarf wrapped tight around her face. And here it was springtime.

Marty studied the cart guy who rounded up the buggies. He, too, wore a mask. *Interesting.* Thoughts began circulating through Marty's head and he figured the day may not be a total loss.

He jumped when Dwyane opened the passenger door. Empty-handed. "What happened?"

"They won't let you in unless you got a mask. Never heard of such a thing." Dwayne buckled his seat belt and settled his skinny ass in the seat. "Mind swinging by the Save-A-Lot?"

Marty pointed the Buick east and headed to the other side of the small town. Population two thousand. He'd bet money that right then, at that very minute, a thousand of the town residents were at the Walmart. Spending money.

Quite the opposite, the Save-A-Lot's parking lot was near empty. Four lonely cars and two trucks were the only vehicles occupying spaces. Marty pulled into the fire lane and Dwayne hopped out.

While Marty waited, he ran numbers in his head. How many customers pay with cash versus plastic? He figured at least half. It was a one-bank old mill town. People always carried cash.

Dwayne slid back in the car, a four-pack of top-quality toilet paper clutched in his hands like a prize. "Jackpot," he said and laughed. He coughed again.

Marty tapped his fingers on the steering wheel, happy like, as he drove down Main Street. He didn't even get angry at the old mill where he used to work. Prick bastards sent his and two-hundred others' jobs over to China and closed up shop five years ago. Where the hell was he supposed to get another job? He was fifty-eight years old with high blood pressure and diabetes. And he had bad knees. "I got an idea."

Dwayne turned to him. "Yeah?"

"We're gonna rob the Walmart."

Dwayne scratched at his beard, head tilted, left cheek raised high.

This pissed Marty off. "What? You got a better idea?"

Dwayne started to say something, stopped. Began again. "There's a bunch of people there, Marty. Some of 'em probably know us, too."

"Masks, Dwayne. Everyone has to wear a mask." Marty shook his head, pissed that he had to explain the obvious.

Dwayne's leathery face remained scrunched up. "You can wear one of those bandanas all day long and I'm still gonna know who you are, Marty."

"I ain't talking about a bandana, Dwayne. We use the hunting masks we got for the bank job." Every male in the state owned a hunting mask, Marty figured.

Dwayne stared at Marty while his face slowly returned to the normal wrinkles. Finally, he said, "That might work."

Not that Marty needed Dwayne's blessing on the heist because Dwayne usually did what Marty asked, but he liked knowing he was on board.

"Maybe you can come over tonight and we'll plan it," Marty said.

Dwayne nodded. "Yeah, sure. 'Round seven?"

Marty pulled into the dirt driveway leading to Dwayne and Ramona's single-wide. They lived in the middle trailer of five, all lined up back-to-front. A row of mailboxes across the dirt road had corresponding numbers. "Sounds good."

Dwayne hopped out and Marty watched him carry his toilet paper to his lovely Ramona. A potted plant long ago dead sat on the front steps looking bleak. A sign of things to come? As he turned the big Buick around, Marty wondered if plants could catch the damn virus. Everything else was dying from it. Why not plants?

When he got home, Sharon was in the kitchen fixing supper. He went to give her a peck on the cheek but she pulled away. "Oh gag. You've been with Dwayne again. Go change clothes before supper." She waved her hand like she was shooing away a fly.

Marty did as he was told and for a brief moment, wished she didn't boss him around quite as much as she did. She was a good woman. Bossy, but good.

They ate supper in the living room on TV trays while watching the news. 1,456 new cases of the virus in their region. Was that confirmed or suspected? Marty looked down at his supper plate. He'd rather look at the burnt pork chop and sad potatoes than the news. With all their fancy graphs and statistics and medical talk, no one knew what was going to happen. He'd never admit it to Sharon or to even Dwayne but this shit scared the hell out of him. He was one of the *vulnerable* ones according to the news.

The next day, Marty carried two camo hunting masks to the car then left to go get Dwayne. During their planning the night before, they'd decided the lunch hour would be a good time to make their move. And here they were, getting ready to do it. Elephants stomped around in Marty's gut, not because he was scared but because it was lunch time. He cussed himself for forgetting to eat a little something before leaving the house. Keeping his blood sugar regulated was important. And not having his stomach growling like a grizzly during a heist was equally important.

He parked the Buick as close to the front as he could then killed the engine.

Dwayne coughed into his fist then wiped his hand on his worn-through jeans. He looked a little flushed. "We gonna do the self-check lanes, right?"

Marty nodded. "Right. We wait 'til there ain't that many folks checking out, then we act like we're buying a pack of gum or something."

"Can it be some Tic-Tacs? I can't do gum with my teeth and all."

Marty lowered his brows, scrunching his nose like he got a whiff of shit or something. "Don't matter what the fuck you buy, Dwayne. The point is to get the little gal helping in that area to come over there."

"What if it's that battle ax who thinks I don't know how to ring up my own bananas? I'd like to show her a banana." He coughed again, this time forgetting to cover his mouth. He tried to suck in a deep breath but stopped mid-gasp.

"The battle ax don't work on Thursdays," Marty said. He knew her schedule and purposely avoided shopping those days. "So, we call the little gal over and that's when we make our move. Got it?"

Dwayne nodded. Coughed again. Marty was growing a little concerned. He handed Dwayne a mask then pulled his own down over his face. He reached into the glove box and took out the .22, slipping it into the waistband of his jeans. Just in case. He pulled his shirt tail out and let it hang loose.

"It's Showtime," Dwayne said.

They walked together to the entrance of the store. Yellow tape roped off sections of the sidewalk so foot traffic could only go one way in and one way out. None of the entering through the exit shit. A gal with a blue vest and a notepad stood between the entrance and the exit. When someone would come out, she'd let someone go in. Just as he was ready to step in front of Dwayne, the girl motioned for Dwyane to go in.

Dwayne jerked around and stared at Marty. "What do we do?"

A fat lady behind Marty said for Dwyane to move on. Then she said, "You his emotional support animal or something?"

Marty wanted to knock her over to see if she'd bounce. Instead, he motioned for Dwayne to go through and prayed the idiot would wait for him.

The gal in the vest said, "You going in?"

Dwayne gave Marty another panicked look then shuffled on through.

Five minutes passed. No one came out. Marty eased forward a little, just to see inside, but the girl in the vest shooed him back. "Six feet, sir. Step behind the blue arrow."

Marty took a step back and cussed under his breath. Sweat beaded on his scalp under the mask. For a moment, he started to take it off while just standing there but thought better of it. He glared at the girl in the vest.

Ten minutes. The fat lady behind him leaned against one of the cement poles. Huffing.

Marty spoke to the vest girl. "Can I just go check on my buddy? He don't do too well by himself."

To Marty's surprise, Dwayne came out the exit toting a plastic Walmart bag. He motioned for Marty. "You ready?" Dwayne wasn't waiting for an answer. He made a bee-line for the Buick.

Marty stumbled past the fat lady and hurried to catch up with his partner. "Dwayne—what's going on?"

"Hurry up, Marty. I 'magine the cops gonna be whipping in here any minute." He coughed so hard Marty knew he broke a rib. Dwayne doubled over, clutched his knees for support.

Marty rushed over to him and helped him the rest of the way to the car. He opened the passenger side and eased Dwayne into the seat then hurried around to the driver's side. Two black-and-blues skidded into the parking lot just as Marty pulled away.

He ripped off his mask off, laughing more than he laughed when ol' Dwayne got sprayed by a skunk. Driving with one hand, he opened the bag and peered in at the mounds of cash.

"Good God! You did it! You did it, man."

Dwayne peeled his own mask off. Marty did a double take. Dwayne's face looked like it was on fire. Sweat rolled over his cheeks. He coughed so hard, Marty thought his eyes were gonna pop out of their sockets.

"Ah, shit, Dwayne. You got the virus, don't you?"

Dwayne nodded, wheezing, gasping for breath.

Marty slammed his hand against the steering wheel. "Damnit! Ah, fuck, Dwyane. Why'd you have to go and get sick?" His heart hurt so bad for his partner. They'd been together since third grade. The dumbass didn't have sense enough to do anything on his own. Except rob the Walmart.

Marty pulled to the side of the road. He put the Buick in park and turned to Dwayne. "What do you want me to do?"

"Hos…pit…al," Dwayne said, struggling for every breath.

Marty patted Dwayne's shoulder. "Ok, buddy. Ok. I'll drop you off at the E.R. I'll call Ramona and let her know."

Dwayne nodded, his head moving in a herky-jerky motion. Marty floored the gas, heading to the hospital. He then thought better of it and eased off a bit. He didn't want to get pulled with a bag full of stolen money. Dwayne reached over with a shaky hand and turned the heat on full blast. His whole body shook with the shivers.

What seemed like two hundred miles was actually only five as Marty turned into the E.R. side of the hospital. He pulled to the patient drop off as someone in what looked like a Hazmat suit came out with a wheelchair.

"Dwayne Seeders," Marty told the spaceman as they wheeled Dwayne into the hospital. He felt bad about not hanging around but from everything he'd seen on the television, they wouldn't let him, anyway.

He peeled the tires against asphalt as he got the hell out of there. He knew Dwayne had the damn virus. He knew it. The cough was different. He slammed his hand against the steering wheel, cussing. One thing. That's all he asked for to go right.

Dwayne was a tough 'ol bird, though. He'd pull through. He didn't have the *underlying conditions* that Marty did.

Marty drove home and was relieved to see Sharon's old Toyota was gone. Not that he didn't want to see her, but he'd prefer to count the money when she wasn't around. He carried the Walmart bag inside, impressed with the weight.

He sat the bag on the table then poured himself a glass of sweet ice-tea. After the first wonderful sip, he sat down and started counting. There had to be a couple thousand in the bag. Sweet Jesus. Maybe just once, something did go right for him.

Marty coughed.

THE END

Lynn Chandler Willis is a Shamus Award finalist and Winner of the Grace Award for Excellence in Faith-Based Fiction. She is the best-selling author of true crime, *Unholy Covenant*, now being featured on the ID Channel's *If I Should Die* series. As a former newspaper owner and publisher, she turned the experiences of a small-town newspaper into the Ava Logan Mystery Series. She is a member of ITW, MWA, SEMWA, and serves as President of Piedmont Authors Network (PAN). She lives in North Carolina with a border collie rescue named Finn and a mischievous feline named Jingles. Visit her website at lynnchandlerwillis.com

MOPE

Warren Moore

One of the good things about living in a small town is one-stop shopping. Most of the stuff you need to buy, from groceries to house paint, you go to Wal-Mart. If you can't find it there, you probably don't need it, which is good, because it's pretty much the only game in town, unless you want to drive an hour or so to get to the big stores.

It's the same way for government services here in Greensburg. We've got the courthouse, and well, that's pretty much it. If you need a building permit? Go to the courthouse. Pay your property taxes? At the courthouse. Murder a busload of nuns? Not only will they try you at the courthouse, but that's where they'll be keeping you before the trial as well. At least I reckon so—I know that's where they keep the drunks, and I'd have to figure there are some other cells in that wing.

Me? I have to get a fishing license. Kody wants to go fishing with his grandpa—that's me—and while he doesn't need a license, being as he's eight, we adults have to shell out fifteen bucks for the privilege of going after bluegill in a local farm pond. It's not that bad, really—the license is good for five years, so at three dollars a year, it's worth it for the time I get to spend with Kody.

His name's Dakota, actually, but we call him Kody, or I do, anyway. Calling him Dakota just reminds me of pickup trucks that don't run half the time, and we see enough of those around here. But he's a good kid, and Bob and Cindy are good parents, even if their taste in names isn't that great. I guess that means I did a pretty good job with Cindy.

So I get to the courthouse parking lot, and as I'm walking toward the building, I see a mope leaning against an F-150. I don't know him, but he looks like a Darrell or a Ronnie. Not real tall, skinny as a stream of piss, scraggly goatee, muscle shirt though there's not a muscle to be seen, Atlanta Braves ball cap with the store sticker still on the flat bill. He's not meth-skinny, more like Shaggy from *Scooby-Doo*. He's got tattoos on his arms, like a lot of the kids do, but it looks like he would have done better spending the money on some Bondo for the Ford, because it looked like the hunting and fishing decals were what held the damned thing together. If he were Mexican, I'd figure he worked at the chicken processing plant. As it is, maybe janitorial staff at the hospital.

But he's standing there with his skinny ass against the driver's sidewall of the truck bed, and he's holding one of those fruit baskets like I see in the Edible Arrangements commercials. He might've gotten it at Flowers 'n' Showers downtown—I don't know if the Wal-Mart does that, although they'll make a pretty nice sandwich tray to take to a graduation party or a funeral home, or whatever. Or maybe he got it at the hospital gift shop. Probably there.

But there he is, with the basket and red cellophane and I can see a couple of bananas and oranges and some grapes and what might be a cantaloupe or something, and I nod to him as I walk past and he nods back, and then as I'm heading up the steps to the courthouse, a blue Nissan rolls into the lot, and three women get out. One's a lawyer, or maybe a social worker—dark skirt, white blouse, dark jacket, and briefcase. The other two look local, like you might see working at a hairdresser's or the state liquor store. They're dressed up a little more than most, but you can tell they're not used to it really. They walk fast to the courthouse, and they've started at the other side of the parking lot from the mope.

He starts moving toward them, though, holding the basket in both hands. One of the women—not the lawyer—hollers, "No, Darrell." Got the name right, I guess. It's not a scared kind of *No*, more the way you might say it to your kid when he won't shut up about wanting to stay up late and play video games. They go in. I go in. Darrell's still coming on with his basket.

When you get in the courthouse, there are a couple of deputies at the front desk, and you have to walk through a metal detector and put your bags through an x-ray conveyor thing like they have at the airport. The women drop their purses on the belt and walk through the detector. I put my wallet and keys in a little plastic basket and send it through. I'm walking through the detector and here comes Darrell. His Adam's apple starts bobbing in his scrawny neck, and he says, "Sharon, please—just wait a minute. Let me talk."

One of the girls turns away and starts walking a little faster toward the courtroom. She must be Sharon. The other one puts her arm around Sharon's shoulders and tries to match her stride. I don't know if she's Sharon's sister, or girlfriend, or what, but she's pretty clearly moral support.

The lawyer speaks to the deputies, "We're going to get a restraining order. He isn't breaking the law yet, but she doesn't want to talk to him." And off they go down the hall. I'm getting my stuff out of the tray as Darrell is trying to find a place to set the damn fruit so he can put his stuff in another tray. He finally puts the basket on the table next to the detector and empties his pockets. The women have disappeared.

I see what he puts in the tray: wallet with one of those World War I German crosses, pack of L&M cigarettes, twenties in a money clip—or maybe just the outside bill is a twenty for show—and truck keys. He walks through the detector. *Buzz.* I start to walk away as they make him walk through again. *Buzz.* One of the deputies reaches for the wand. I hear the words "belt buckle" as I go to the license office. Another deputy is putting the fruit on the conveyor belt.

Not much of a line, so when I come out ten minutes later and fifteen dollars lighter, Darrell's standing there with the deputies, near a portrait of an old judge on the wall. They're telling him he probably just ought to forget this whole thing, when here comes Sharon and her friend and her lawyer.

Darrell grabs the fruit basket, and gets the girl's name out of his mouth, when she says, "Darrell, it's done. I've got the order. You have to leave me alone."

"Come on, honey, you know I love you," he says. "I got your favorite." Sharon starts crying a little, moving away from Darrell, toward the door. He steps toward her.

A deputy says, "I don't think she wants to talk to you, sir."

"Aw, man, I just need a chance!" Then he yells to Sharon, "Please, baby. Just a minute." His voice breaks on the last word. He takes another step—the other deputy puts a hand on Darrell's arm. Darrell jerks away, "Fuck, man!"

Bad decision. Both deputies grab him and spin him around. I don't know if they're enjoying this, but maybe they're excited for the action, because they spin him pretty damned hard. The basket falls to the floor; the cellophane rips and apples, oranges, and pears scatter across the tiles, a couple rolling under the table. Sharon sees it and her eyes get big, but her friend steps into her line of sight and she and the lawyer steer Sharon out the door as Darrell tries a backwards kick and gets slammed to the ground for his trouble. They slap the cuffs on him and they're hauling him off to that wing I mentioned earlier, where they keep the drunks. Darrell's still yelling that he just needs a minute, but the sound's getting fainter, and there's nobody interested in how much time he thinks he needs. I turn around, and Sharon and her lawyer and her friend are standing by the Nissan. There's a group hug, and the lawyer gets into the driver's seat as the other two women get in the back.

The car backs out, and pulls out of the lot. I don't see which way they're going, but it seems like pretty much any direction is going to take them farther from Darrell, because he won't be going anywhere for at least the next few hours.

All of a sudden it's just me in the empty lobby with a bunch of fruit. I pick up a couple of apples near the table leg as I get ready to go home. They'll make good snacks for Kody and me this afternoon at the pond.

THE END

About Warren Moore III -- Born in Nashville and raised in the burbs of Nashville and Cincinnati, he is a Professor of English at Newberry College in Newberry, SC. Along the way, he has been a journalist, tire salesman, stand-up comic, advertising copywriter, magazine editor, and drummer in a variety of unsuccessful bands. He finished tied for 105th in the 1979 National Spelling Bee and holds a Ph.D. in English from Ball State University with a specialty in medieval literature, and has taught courses covering topics from the Seven Deadly Sins to film noir.

BROKEN GLASS WALTZES, his first novel, was published in 2013, and he has published short stories in print and online venues since then. He also plays drums in a 60s-style garage band, and lives in Newberry with his wife and daughter.

The Ghostwriter

Jonas Saul

It was the scariest day of my life, yet the most beautiful.

I'll never forget it as long as I live.

I'm a writer of autobiographies. I meet with men and women in old age homes and write their stories as they narrate them to me. I'm quite successful at what I do. Not many people are in this line of work, so competition is small.

On this particular day, I was directed to room 213 where my client was resting. His name was Markus John. He's supposedly ninety-six-years old and ready for a lift to the ever after. I was excited to talk to him because I understood this man had a fantastic story about the second world war. He was in some kind of elite group and he wanted me to write about how it affected his family life.

There are times I only get drivel from my clients. Half of them experience difficulty remembering things. I've even had a few who were so lost with Alzheimer's that we couldn't go on—dementia, too. Sad, I know, but I try. I always try.

The blonde attendant stopped in front of room 213 and waved me in with a flourish of her arm. As I entered the room, my eyes glanced at her name tag.

"Thank you, Rebecca," I whispered as I stepped into the room.

After a moment, I turned back to smile at her, but she was gone. She was, no doubt, off to perform other duties that involved the frail, the old, the sick. How noble.

A large man lay in the bed, covers neatly wrapped around him, stopping just short of his neck. His eyes were closed. I hesitated. Maybe this wasn't a good time. It was set up yesterday by phone. We agreed I'd come for 1:00 p.m. I'd leave by 4:00 p.m. He needed his rest. We'd just try to get as much done as possible in that time.

A table and chair were set up by the bed. I placed my laptop down, booted it up, and sat in the chair. When he awoke, I wanted to be ready.

"I am ready," he mumbled.

I jumped. He'd startled me. I didn't expect him to talk or read my mind. At least that's how it felt to me in that moment.

"I'm sorry, I didn't know you were awake."

"My eyes aren't open, but I'm awake." He spoke with a raspy voice, his throat weakened with age. "My time is short. Are you ready?"

"Yes, of course. Do you feel up to starting now?"

"I don't have much choice. I will be brief. Please pick up what you can. Then piece it together later. You'll understand."

His voice had an tone I couldn't place. Not that I'm musically inclined, it's just, I've never heard a voice sound that way. Like it was coming out of a flute with a reed for a voice box. Yeah, as if a flute was talking to me, but deeper.

Markus John told me everything he felt he needed to in his clipped sentences and resonant voice. The way he talked with his eyes closed made his story one I'll never forget. This man had seen war, death, loss, and saw it all with bravery. He'd been shot twice and stabbed once. He'd seen more than most in his time. More than I would ever dream of seeing or want to. This man, Markus John, humbled me. I wanted to hug him, tell him it would all be okay. I only wished I had a father half the man Markus was.

Actually, I wished I had a father. My father left us when I was eight years old. I never heard from him, nor saw him again. My mother forbade the use of the word *father* in our house. There could be something to why I do this job after all. Maybe a part of me is searching for the story of a decent old man, one I can hold on to and not let go.

Markus surprised me an hour into his tale. He opened his eyes. He had one glass eye, and a soft blue tinge surrounding a green outline for the other. His good eye pierced me. It felt like he could look right through me. I seemed to recall my dad had a glass eye, too.

After a time, Markus spoke about his daughter. He explained that the story we were preparing was for her, and only her. He would explain at the end how I was to get this story to his daughter, and she would understand everything when reading it.

His goal today was forgiveness. He displayed compassion like I'd never seen. It was an honor to ghostwrite his life. I took notes, scrolled every bit of pertinent information, and while I listened, I was taken aback by this man, hour after hour.

As he talked about his connections with an underground organization, I almost got lost. I listened, I typed, but I wasn't there anymore, in the old age home. I was in his story, lost, floating through it. The things he had done in his life took my breath away. I had been doing this professionally for over four years, and no one had ever brought the level with vigor and humility as this man did. I think what I related to the most was how he had to leave his family to fight in the war, and the pain that had caused him.

Because after the war, he could never return home. His presence was too dangerous for his family.

"I was part of an elite group," he whispered, starting to fade after several hours of talking. "We infiltrated levels of government ... in more than one country."

His eyes were closed again. He paused, coughed, then continued.

"My name has been changed, my face altered. I've been on the move, going from one country to another, since the war. There was always someone after me. But that's over now. They're all dead."

It was past 4:00 p.m. He was tiring as he tried to finish. A half hour later, he said he was too tired to continue. With his eyes closed, he talked a little more.

The last thing he said stopped me as I closed my laptop. A chill coursed through me and I fixed my gaze on him.

"What was that, Mr. John?" I asked.

"I said, I died years ago." A single tear descended his cheek. And then his breathing was louder than his voice. I could tell he'd fallen asleep.

I gathered my things and left the room with a deeper understanding of what he meant by his last comment. He'd died years ago because of the loss of his family, the war, the loss of people he knew and loved. He'd died years ago by the inequality of life, the emotional scars we all bear.

Someone once said people weep when we're born, they weep when we die, and in the middle, we try to hold it together. But sometimes the pain we bear seems insurmountable, unfair even. I understood this man more than I wanted to. I only wished I had a daddy like Markus John.

When I left the building, it hit me that I didn't get to figure out how to get it to his daughter. He'd said this project was for her and that after we were done, I would be able to get it to her.

I decided to come back tomorrow for more details.

When I got home, I couldn't stop thinking about Mr. John. It inspired me to open up the old photo albums my mother had left me after she died fifteen years ago.

The photo albums were in the attic right where I left them after my mother's funeral. I brushed off the dust and opened the first one. It was only 8:00 p.m. I had a glass of wine, and all night to reminisce. I got through one book and opened the second one. That's where I saw a couple of pictures had been slipped in behind others. I pulled a few out. A faded photo with a man sitting and a woman standing beside him caught my eye.

I set my wine glass down and stared. Even though the picture was quite faded, I could tell it was my mother, but the man was hard to discern. I pulled and yanked picture after picture, until I came up with one that was better.

This time I was shocked. There were three people in this picture; my mother, me at around seven-years old, and my father, who looked remarkably like Markus John. My father's name was Joseph Hardy, though. He had a patch over the eye that would receive glass as a replacement just as I had remembered him.

It was the same eye as Markus John's.

I was up and out of the house in less than five minutes. I drove like a maniac and got to the retirement home in twenty minutes flat. Rebecca wasn't at the front counter. I approached a random woman and asked to see Mr. Markus John.

"Hold a minute, ma'am," the woman said. "I don't recognize that name."

I checked her name tag. "I was here this afternoon, Samantha," I said. "Mr. John dictated his autobiography to me. We agreed to meet now, at 9:00 p.m." I was lying, but I couldn't help myself. I had to meet Markus again.

My heart was racing. I found it hard to breathe. I had to get in—I needed answers.

A binder was open in front of Samantha. Her slow and nonchalant way of turning the pages was driving me crazy. *Come on*, I shouted in my head.

"It appears that there is no one here by that name."

I couldn't believe what I was hearing. She had no idea how to do her job.

"I was here earlier," I said, steadying my voice. "Markus John related his life story to me. I'm an autobiographer. He was in room 213. Rebecca was the woman behind this counter. She showed me down the hall. Please check your books again."

Samantha cracked a smile. I was incensed by how rude she was being.

"I'm one of the staff supervisors. I can assure you, we don't have a Rebecca on staff. This entire complex is one level. There is no room numbered 213. I'm afraid you must have the wrong building, ma'am."

Absolutely absurd. No way. I wouldn't believe it. I could see the room I was escorted to earlier. It was down the hall on the left. I turned from Samantha and strode toward the door.

Samantha protested behind me, threatening to call security.

I got to the room and looked inside.

My hand went to the doorframe to steady myself.

The room was a small cafeteria for the employees.

There was no Markus John. No old man sleeping. No bed.

I glanced around, ignoring Samantha. I knew I was right on this. I was here only four hours ago.

"The woman earlier," I whispered. "Her name tag said Rebecca. Can you re-check your staff names?"

"It's not necessary. I do all the hiring. We do not have a Rebecca on staff. Now, if you please, leave the building. I don't want you upsetting our residents."

I walked away in a daze. This wasn't happening, couldn't be happening. I don't take drugs, I don't hallucinate. I was here, and so was Markus John.

I stood by my car trying to piece it all together. I remember one thing clearly. He said he'd died years ago. I had thought he meant emotionally. Could he have been speaking literally?

Movement caught my eye. A man was standing by a tree about a hundred yards away. A woman stood to his right.

I squinted in the light of dusk. The man waved and turned away. The woman followed. When he turned from me, one sharp ray of summer sunlight caressed his back.

It was Markus John and Rebecca. There was no doubt in my mind. Then they were gone. I have no idea where they went or how it was possible to disappear like they did, but they were just gone.

It took me a few weeks to get over it. I cried. I grieved. I couldn't write for a month.

Not many people get the chance to meet their parents after they've departed this plane, but I did. I got to, because my dad was amazing.

According to the life he lived, the story he recited, he'd done it all for us. My daddy was my hero.

It took me another month to know who Rebecca was.

A search online, a family tree, and hours of labor revealed the answer.

I found an old picture of my mother before I was born, from her high school days. Rebecca was my mother's middle name. She was just as beautiful as the day I met her at the retirement home.

I can't seem to stop crying.

Goodbye Mom and Dad ...

THE END

Jonas Saul is the bestselling author of the Sarah Roberts Series and has written and published over thirty thrillers. After selling more than two million books, he signed with the Gandolfo Helin & Fountain Literary and Dramatic Rights Management.

Saul has traveled extensively throughout the world to scout settings for his thrillers, spending several years between Greece, Italy, Denmark, and Hungary. He is regularly invited to be a guest speaker, teacher, or workshop presenter at international writing conferences.

"Sarah Roberts is one in a million. If you're her friend, she'll crawl through Hell to protect you. If you're her enemy, she'll send you there." – Reviewer. www.jonassaul.com

TEST DRIVE

Ross Cavins

Jerry Spivey literally kicked the tires of the Dodge Charger as he walked around it, studying the vehicle the same way he'd studied the Colt 45 he had firmly wedged in the small of his back under his jacket.

The air frosted his breath as he spoke in a thick Southern accent, "And yer sure she's fast? Used to be a po-leece car, you say?"

"Yep," said the salesman. He'd introduced himself as Harlan as soon as Jerry stepped out of his pickup truck. Harlan with no last name. Jerry shook his hand and didn't say his own name.

Harlan the salesman said, "It's got a six-point-eight liter—"

"That's all a bunch of gibberish to me. Don't mean nothing." Jerry waved his hand as he spoke. "Alls I need to know's is she fast? She handle good?"

Harlan patted the hood. "Anti-lock brakes, rack and pinion steering, independent suspension—"

"Them's just a bunch of fancy words. You ain't listening to me, son. Can she go like the wind or not?" Jerry stared at the salesman, face to face.

Harlan fingered his comb-around and smiled big enough to give his new veneers some sunlight. He tugged at his dress slacks but they were snug in place and didn't move. "Sir, this baby right here'll leave your dog behind if he ain't strapped in tight."

The dog, hearing his name, Dog, clamored to the edge of the truck bed to get a better look at the guy who called him. Harlan kept his smile but backed up a step as Dog sniffed at him.

"I ain't crazy about the color," Jerry said, removing his cap so he could scratch his balding head. "I mean, if yer gonna paint a car red, paint it red, for Christ's sake."

"They call this color, Claret. Like the wine. Claret wine?" Harlan attempted a smile but it was lost on Jerry.

Jerry strolled around to the passenger's side, peering in the window. He leaned forward and cupped his hands over the glass to cut the glare of the sunless sky. The weatherman had said there was a thirty percent chance of flurries that day. Jerry always wondered if they guessed at that, thirty percent or maybe forty, depending on what the guy wanted, or did he use a fancy computer that told him all the answers, and if he used a computer, how come the percentages were always rounded and why not something like twenty-eight or thirty-one?

Jerry straightened and stretched out his arms, interlocking his fingers and popping them loud enough Dog glanced at him with a huff. "Well," he said. "You gonna let me take her on a test ride or you gonna jabber on some more?"

"Uh, yes. Yes sir." Harlan held up a finger. "Just let me get the keys. You move your truck down here to this empty spot, and I'll be right back."

Jerry parked his truck as Harlan waddled off to the little brick building at the back of the gravel lot. Jerry strolled back to the car and waited at the driver's door for the salesman to return. He studied the sky; he put it at more than forty percent chance himself. Maybe forty-two.

Harlan fast-walked back and unlocked the doors with the clicker before tossing the keys to Jerry. Harlan slapped a magnetic dealer's plate on the back as Jerry opened the door. Harlan scurried to the passenger's side. Jerry whistled toward his truck and Dog, a Doberman-Rottweiler mix with a small head, leapt over the truck gate and bounded toward him.

"What are you...?" Harlan began as Dog hopped into the Charger. Harlan waved his hands and said, "You can't take that dog on a test drive."

Dog settled himself into the passenger's seat and watched Harlan through the glass window.

"Why not?" Jerry stared at the salesman over the roof of the car.

"He... he's a dog."

"He'll be riding in it, too. You don't think his opinion counts?"

Harlan shook his head. "But he's a dog."

Jerry studied Harlan, a scowl taking over his face. "You got a cat, don't you? You look like a cat owner."

"What ... yes, I have a Himalayan mix named Romeo." Harlan beamed. "He just turned six in August."

Jerry cleared his throat and shook his head as he turned to the side and spat a glob of mucus over the open door. "Figures." He crouched and slid into the driver's seat.

Harlan opened the side door, but Dog swiveled in the seat and growled at him. He held the door open a crack and Jerry asked what he was doing.

"Coming on the test drive," Harlan replied.

"Why the hell'd you wanna do that?"

"It's company policy. I have to go on the test drives."

Jerry muttered and said, "Well git on in then." He pulled the cardboard price sign out from the windshield and shoved it in the back.

Harlan hesitated, then said, "Can you tell your dog to sit in the back?"

This made Jerry laugh.

"You tell him."

Dog had stopped growling and now sat on his haunches facing the front.

Harlan eased the door open all the way and shooed the dog without touching him. Dog studied the portly man with curiosity, tilting his head to the left. Harlan moved closer to the dog and Jerry said, "I wouldn't do that. Don't let his small head fool you. Them teeth's sharp, and when he clamps down on something, it can take a while to coax him loose. Had a cousin tried to move Dog out of his recliner once. Dog lunged out and clamped down on his boys." Jerry shuddered and Harlan slowly withdrew his hands. "It took an hour and a pound of bacon to get Dog to let go. Dale lost his left ball and to this day has to twist his pecker around to hit the toilet."

Harlan's hands covered his boys. "Well, what do I do?"

Jerry shrugged and jerked his head. "Hop in back if you're coming."

Harlan screwed his face up, then closed the door and got in back through the rear passenger door. He hadn't gotten settled before Jerry started the engine and began backing out of the parking spot.

"Seatbelt, please," Harlan said, struggling to get his own on.

"Seatbelt?"

"It's the law."

Jerry huffed, yanked the seatbelt across his body, and clicked it in as he spun the wheel. He shifted into drive and caught some gravel before he let off the gas.

"She's touchy," Jerry said.

"Lot of horses under the hood."

Jerry nodded as if that was to his liking.

"Okay," Harlan said. "How about you take a right out of here?"

Jerry hung a left.

Harlan leaned forward as far as his seatbelt would let him. "We have an approved route we always go when we take test drives."

"Another company policy?" Jerry asked.

"Yes."

Jerry eyed Harlan through the rearview mirror.

"That's okay," Harlan chirped. "Just take a right up here on Patterson."

Jerry passed Patterson without taking his foot off the gas.

"Okay," Harlan said, fidgeting a little. "We can still pick up the route if you take a right on Forest Boulevard. That's the next light, right here ... "

Jerry passed Forest Boulevard at five miles over the speed limit and this time didn't meet Harlan's eyes in the rearview mirror. Harlan undid his seatbelt and pulled himself forward by gripping the front seats. Dog turned to study him for a moment before looking back out the front window, disinterested.

"Where are we going?" Harlan asked after a moment.

"Don't worry about it," Jerry said, still not looking at Harlan.

Harlan sat that way for a while, head stuck between the front bucket seats, before exhaling and sliding back in the seat. He finally said, "She handles real nice, don't you think?"

Jerry said nothing so Harlan continued, "She's only about three years old. Got a lot of miles on her, but I was assured she was tuned up once a week. Makes sense though, doesn't it?" No comment from the front seat. "I mean, the cops would need this baby in top shape all the time, you know. Chasing the bad guys and whatnot."

When there was no reciprocation from Jerry or Dog, Harlan relaxed and started looking out the windows. He continued, "You know why I heard they closed down that Taco Bell?"

Harlan pointed as they passed the restaurant. The landscaping was brown and unkempt, posters for the Gordita still stuck in the windows. "I heard they found this huge roach nest in the ceiling. Said the exterminator went up there to spray, and they didn't scatter. Instead, they attacked him. Huge things. Gouged an eye out before he fell down the ladder."

Jerry made a few tight turns, tires squealing, rocking Harlan around the back seat, and finally pulled into the New Community Bank. He backed into a parking spot and shoved the gearshift into park. He glanced left, then right, then eyed Harlan through the rearview mirror, saying, "I'll just be a minute."

✳✳✳

Harlan watched as the guy got out of the car, leaving it running, and walked around back. Harlan tried to turn around to get the guy's attention, but the two double cheeseburgers he'd had for lunch were still sitting heavy in his belly. The guy came around to Harlan's door and made the motion to roll the window down.

Harlan hit the button, but it wouldn't budge because the window locks were on. Frustrated now, the guy yanked the door open and threw the dealer plate onto Harlan's lap.

"What's this for?" Harlan asked.

The guy grinned and said, "It was falling off."

"Really? I thought I had it on good." Harlan struggled to get out and the guy shoved his hand through the door.

"Don't worry about it," he said.

"I just want to get it on good. We can't drive without it." Harlan rocked to get turned and the guy put a hand on his shoulder.

"Do me a favor," he said, his voice taking on an edge. "Stay right there. I'll take care of the tag in a minute." The guy flashed a toothy grin. "You just hang out a minute."

Harlan started to protest, and the guy looked up front, saying, "Dog."

The dog turned in his seat and stuck his square head over the headrest.

The guy said, "Stay." The dog huffed a short response. Then he pointed at Harlan and said, "Stay." The dog answered with a quick growl and leveled his gaze at Harlan.

Harlan's breath stopped.

The guy laughed, then slipped on some tight leather gloves and pulled a knit cap from his jacket pocket. He looked at Harlan and winked. "I'd suggest you take it real easy for a little bit."

He closed the door, and Harlan watched as the guy pulled the cap over his head and down his face. It was a ski mask with mouth and eye holes.

As the guy strolled into the bank, Harlan began to wish he'd been a little more forceful about following the approved test drive route. Or about the company not allowing dogs on the test drives. Or at least maybe he could have insisted on seeing a driver's license before the test drive.

The guy had controlled the whole situation from the beginning. That was exactly the opposite of what Harlan had been taught at the sales seminar he attended last month at the Koury Convention Center: Strong Sales and Strong Men Make Strong Salesmen. It had cost him a hundred bucks after his boss, Freddy, split the cost down the middle.

Strong salesmen control the sales encounter; they direct the conversation and cover the points they need for the sale. Strong salesmen assert themselves and demand to be heard, in a nice and leisurely manner. Strong salesmen say just enough to sell the product, and not a word more. Strong salesmen make the sale, because the customer is there to buy, and all a truly strong salesman has to do is find out the one thing that will sell the product to that customer.

Sometimes it's price. Sometimes it's convenience. Or quality. Nostalgia. Utility. Color. No matter who the customer is, there's always an overriding factor that will sell them.

With this guy, Harlan had discovered it in less than half a minute.

Speed. He wanted speed.

And now Harlan knew why.

Harlan wondered if he could squeeze out of the car before the dog got him. He looked at the beast. It hadn't moved since the guy pointed at Harlan and said to stay.

Harlan edged his hand toward the door handle. The dog stared. He gripped the handle and flicked it. Nothing. Damn, he thought, the child locks thingee was engaged. Maybe not the other door.

Harlan eased over the back seat toward the driver's rear door. The dog growled just before Harlan reached it. Harlan paused but the dog kept growling. Harlan pulled back and the dog stopped.

Harlan reached again. Growl. Pulled back. No growl.

He was about to try it once more when the guy came strolling out of the bank shoving something behind his back. He was swinging a bulging plastic grocery bag and whistling, nodding at an older lady passing him like nothing was wrong. He was still wearing the ski mask.

The guy hopped in the Charger and started it. He ripped off the mask and said, "You should really put that seatbelt on." He glanced over his shoulder. "It's the law, you know."

He laughed as he stomped the gas and peeled out of the parking space. The car hopped the curb, plowed over some small bushes, and merged into traffic, narrowly missing a bread truck in the second lane.

They headed the opposite way of the car lot, speeding past cars like they were standing still. The guy hooked a left against oncoming traffic and rolled Harlan so he was flush-faced against the window.

Harlan tried to scream at the cars barreling straight at him, but it only came out as a gurgle.

Then the guy yanked the Charger into a quick right just as soon as Harlan straightened himself. Harlan rolled over to the left side, his face planting into the seat as he felt the car lift to two wheels momentarily.

Harlan was tossed around the entire drive until the guy slid the car into the gravel lot of Freddy Joe Autos—barely missing a Mazda Miata and Pontiac Sunfire parked on the grass near the entrance—and came to the stop in a roil of dust.

The guy clicked the electric locks and Harlan stumbled from the car. He shook his head, steadying himself and waiting for the air to clear. He was glad to be on solid ground again. He didn't like roller coasters as a child, and now he knew he still didn't care for them. Those two cheeseburgers were making their way topside something fierce.

Harlan swallowed hard and ambled over the driver's side, ready to demand the keys right that instant, until he remembered the guy had something shoved behind his back. It didn't take much imagination to figure out what it was.

Instead, he smiled and waited for Harlan to roll down the window, then said, "I told you she was fast, like gliding on air. What did you think of the—"

"That the price you gotta have for it?" The guy threw his thumb over his shoulder, indicating the cardboard sign behind his seat.

Harlan did a double-take. His Strong Salesman training kicked in. He had his fish on the hook. Now all he had to do was reel him in.

"Ah, well, you see ... it did used to be a cop car and the engine's been completely rebuilt." The guy started waving his hand and reaching beside him. Harlan got nervous and began talking faster. "And I know it's got a lot of miles but the tires are practically new and Juan changed the oil just last week and—"

"Jesus Christ," the guy said, waving two bundles of cash out the window. "You think that'll cover it?"

"Uh..." Harlan snatched the money from the guy's hand. Each bundle was marked "10k" and Harlan was speechless.

The guy nodded and said, "Yeah, that oughta cover taxes and stuff. Plus a little left over for you and the missus." He winked.

Harlan didn't have a missus but didn't correct him. What he did say was, "We need to sign paperwork."

The guy shook his head. "No, we don't."

He started to pull away, and Harlan yelled, "What about your truck?"

The guy yelled back, "I'd get rid of it if I were you. It's stolen."

Harlan watched as the Charger pulled out of the lot and squealed away. He shook his head and strolled toward the truck. As he ran the whole encounter through his head again, a plan began to form.

He was the only person at the lot today besides the accountant, Sherry, and when Harlan had popped in to get the Charger's keys, she'd been so engrossed in Facebook she hadn't even looked up. Odds were she wouldn't know how much time had passed.

Nobody at the bank had seen him in the car. He knew because he'd not seen a single person himself except the old lady when the guy was coming out, and she was staring at the guy.

Add that to the fact the guy hadn't signed a single paper and Harlan had a plausible story forming.

Maybe what had happened was that the guy had stolen the car outright, *without a test drive*. He'd come to the lot in his truck, which the cops would later find out was stolen. He'd wanted a test drive, then stole the Charger outright.

As sirens approached, it began to click together in Harlan's mind.

Sure his DNA would be in the backseat; he'd shown the car yesterday. Of course, his DNA would be in the car.

He'd tell the cops the guy had shown up in a hurry, looked nervous, like he was on drugs, had beady eyes and a strong accent. Harlan hadn't trusted him from the beginning, knew something was off, and when he asked to see the guy's driver's license, the guy took the keys and stole the car. Just like that.

Harlan could sell it that way exactly. After all, he'd gotten the Platinum Steel Salesman rank at the convention after scoring a 93 on the test the last day. He was now a certified Strong Salesman, the strongest he knew. He could do this. For twenty grand, he could do it with a smile and a twinkle in his eye.

He finger-combed his hair one last time as the flashing blue lights reflected off the insurance building across the street. He straightened his jacket, and just before he slipped the cash into the jacket's inner pocket, he thumbed through the two stacks and sniffed them like he'd seen gangsters do on TV. And that's when the dye packet blew.

THE END

Ross Cavins is the author of the award-winning book, *Follow The Money*, the Claymore Award Finalist, *Barry vs The Apocalypse*, and *The Walk-On*. A self-appointed disciple of Elmore Leonard, his sense of humor is sort of like Disco; you dance to it even if you don't admit it. You can find him at RossCavins.com and RCGPublishing.com.

BLUE DEATH

Agnes Alexander

It wasn't unusual to find discarded furniture and other household items emigrants had removed to lighten their wagonloads on the Oregon Trail. But it was unnatural to see a lone covered wagon left behind unless it had been attacked and was disabled.

After a rough track-down of a gang of bank robbers, U.S. Marshall Andrew McKinsey decided to visit his parents on their Wyoming ranch for a needed rest. The last thing he expected to do was to come upon an unhitched wagon that had been pulled to the side of the trail. Though it appeared to be in good shape, he didn't see anyone around it. Slowing his horse to a walk, he approached with caution. He wondered what could have caused the occupants to desert their transportation, if that had been what happened.

Dismounting and ground-hitching his horse, he placed his hand on his holstered gun as he approached the back of the wagon. The first thing catching his eye was the fact the wagon had a lived-in look. A mattress occupied one side and boxes of supplies filled in the back and the other side. Utensils and clothing were scattered about, though they looked clean.

Frowning, he moved to the other side, where he found a campfire had recently burned. A kettle hung over the dead fire and a small pot rested on one of the surrounding rocks.

Somebody was camped here. But why had they stopped in this lonely area to set up, and where were they now? And where were the animals they used to pull the wagon?

He turned and looked toward the grove of mesquite and wild bushes growing near a creek that ran through the area. It was then he saw the woman. Her long brown hair fell around her face. He noted that from the distance, she appeared to be attractive. He watched as she rose and wiped her hair back with the back of her hand. She then bent again, and it appeared she was digging in the hard ground. She was oblivious to his presence.

With his hand still on his gun, he walked toward her. Hoping not to frighten her, he said, "Hello, ma'am."

When she ignored him and continued to dig, he spoke again.

This time she turned and looked at him. She didn't appear to be frightened, and in a flat voice, she said, "Don't come near me. You'll catch it."

He was now close enough to see the haunted look on her face. Not sure what she was talking about, he kept his voice calm. "Catch what, ma'am?"

In an emotionless voice, she said, "The Blue Death." Ignoring him, she then turned and resumed her digging.

He'd heard people called Cholera the Blue Death because a person with the disease often turned blue near the end of their life. He eyed the four fresh graves beside the hole she now dug and wondered if Cholera was how the people in them had died. He didn't want to think this pretty young woman had killed and buried four people, but in his line of work he'd learned anything could happen. As a law officer he felt he had to ask. "Who is buried here?"

She looked at him again. "I told you not to come close to me."

"I'm strong. I'll be fine."

"Daddy was strong, but he died."

"What killed your daddy?"

She glared at him. "The Blue Death, of course. It killed all my family."

"Are these people your family?"

She nodded then turned again to her digging.

"Whose grave are you digging now?"

She turned her head and her brown eyes seemed to bore into him. In an almost whisper, she said, "Mine."

He was amazed at her calmness and wondered if she was touched in the head. "Why don't you sit and rest a while and tell me about your family."

"But I want to get my grave dug while I still have the strength to do it."

"I'll help you dig it after you rest. Maybe you'll give me a cup of coffee."

She shrugged, dropped her shovel and headed to the firepit.

He fell in step beside her. "My name's Andrew McKinsey." When she said nothing, he added, "What's your name, ma'am?"

"Joanna Tyson."

When they reached the fire pit, he started the fire, then moved his horse to the grassy area so she could graze.

Joanna had the coffee pot on the rocks when he returned. She turned and took a seat on one of the two camp chairs she'd taken from the wagon and placed several feet apart. "I poured out the lemonade Mama made, or I would have offered you some."

He took the other chair. "You don't like lemonade?"

"No. I've never cared for the taste of lemons. While the rest of the family drank it, I boiled some water and made myself a cup of tea. It was such a fun night." Tears came to her eyes.

Though in his work he'd seen a lot of women cry and he considered himself tough when it happened, something about Joanna's brown eyes filling with tears touched him. His voice almost cracked as he asked, "Want to tell me about it?"

She nodded. "The train had come through a hard time and we had several wagons that needed repair. We found a stream where it looked like buffalo hunters or Indians had camped and butchered their kill. The wagon master said it wasn't the usual place for emigrants to stop but we didn't have a choice."

"I've come upon such areas before."

"After the wagons were repaired, we moved on, and the next time we camped we had kind of a special night. There was music and dancing and my family had the special lemonade made from the water we'd brought from the other stream. But as I said, I made myself hot tea. We all went to bed happy and expecting good things for the next few days."

She took a deep breath. "But it didn't happen. Just before daylight, my little sister woke up deathly sick. At first, we thought she just had a stomach upset, but as the day wore on, she continued to get worse. That night, we camped here and the wagon master came to check on Molly. He got all upset and told us Molly had Cholera and none of us were to leave our wagon. Even those close to us pulled away and we were left out of the circle. The next morning, we were told we weren't allowed to travel with the train any further. He said we could wait a couple of hours and follow it. Two hours later, Molly was turning blue, my father and mother were both sick, and we decided to wait until they were better."

She stopped for several minutes, and Andrew wondered if she was going to say anything else.

Then she went on. "Molly died that afternoon. She was only fifteen years old. My brother, Hank and I dug her grave. Daddy helped a little, but he was getting worse. He and Mama both died the next day. It took Hank and me hours to dig their graves because he was getting weaker. Hank lasted two days more. I dug his grave and buried him yesterday."

"I'm so sorry, Joanna."

Jumping up, she moved to the fire. "The coffee should be ready. I know you don't want to use my utensils. Do you have your own cup?"

"I do. I'll get it."

When he returned, she'd taken her seat and he went to the fire and poured his own coffee. "Aren't you having any?"

"I'll make some tea in a little while."

Taking a swallow of coffee, he looked at her. She was too young to have suffered what she had with this awful disease. What was she going to do and where was she going to go now?

She interrupted his thinking. "Whenever you finish your coffee, I don't expect you to finish my grave, but I would appreciate it if you would dig a little on it. I get so tired."

"May I ask you something, Joanna?"

"Yes."

"You seem to be in good health, so there is an off chance you may not get the disease. Therefore, why do you bother digging the grave?"

"Are you trying to get out of helping me?"

"Not at all. I was just wondering."

"Well, I know the Blue Death will kill me. My folks were fine, then in an instant one by one they started dying. I figure the same thing will happen to me and I have it all planned out for when it does."

Andrew lifted an eyebrow. "What have you planned?"

She shrugged. "I don't see any reason not to tell you. I figure I'll get the grave dug. Then when it gets so I can't take care of myself, I'll go lie in the grave and die. I might even cover myself up to my neck if I have the strength to do it. If not … well, it won't matter anyway."

Andrew frowned. How could this beautiful young woman think this way? She might get the disease, but there was an off chance that she wouldn't. "So, you plan to simply camp out here until you die?"

"What choice do I have? I can't follow the wagon train because I turned the animals loose knowing they wouldn't survive being hitched up to the wagon. I had my hands full looking after my family. I didn't have time to worry about taking care of the livestock."

"Let me ask you one question, Miss Tyson. What do you plan to do if you don't die?"

Joanna stared at him as if he'd lost his mind and tears formed in her eyes. "But I will die. I have to. I've lost my whole family and I don't want to go on without them."

Andrew was in a quandary. He wanted to get back on the trail home, but what if she were right? What if she was infected? In that case, there was no way he could take her into a town and put others in danger. Yet how could he leave this defenseless woman alone? On the other hand, he couldn't stay here with her. To top it all, since he'd had contact with her, he might be infected himself.

Before he could come up with anything to say, he heard the sound of a horse's hoofs. She frowned. "I've been alone here for a week. Then today you show up and now there's someone else coming."

He stood and put his hand on his gun as a rider appeared in the distance. "Looks like he's alone but to be safe how about you heading to the wagon."

"No."

"Suit yourself."

The rider reined up. "You folks having trouble?"

Andrew ignored his question. "Where you headed, mister?"

"I'm the scout for the wagon train coming this way. Came looking for a good place to set up camp. Name's Buck Sommers."

"Andrew McKinsey, US Marshall. I'm headed home after a long and hard capture of some bank robbers."

Buck frowned. "In a covered wagon?"

Andrew had to chuckle, but before he could answer, Joanna said, "The wagon is mine. Mr. McKinsey came upon me just as you did."

"What in the world are you doing out here, Miss?"

"The wagon train we were with left us. They said we could follow or wait for the next one."

"Maybe you can join up with us. Where's the rest of your party?"

"Buried up there on the hill."

He frowned and looked at Andrew. "What is she talking about?"

"Her family came down with Cholera and the train left them behind. Miss Tyson is the only one still living."

After this information, Buck took a quick leave, explaining she wouldn't be allowed to join his train either.

When night fell, Andrew tossed out his bedroll on the hill, but near enough to her wagon that he could hear her if she called. As she climbed inside into the wagon's bed, he said, "If you need me, just yell."

She nodded but didn't reply

As he was going to sleep, his mind went in all directions. Why didn't he continue on his way to his ranch? Why did he feel he had to help pretty Miss Joanna Tyson?

When this thought crossed his mind, he knew why. The woman was probably no more than eighteen years old and his upbringing wouldn't permit him to leave her stranded. Even if she did develop Cholera, she needed somebody to help her to the end.

"I wish I'd gone to Denver and taken another job instead of heading home for a rest. That way I wouldn't have to worry about her," he muttered to himself.

A distant rumbling noise interrupted his thoughts and he sat up. He knew the noise was made by running horses. As he peered into the dark, he realized one of the riders carried a torch. At first, he thought it might be a group of hunters. They often carried a torch when they hunted their prey at night. But what could such a group be hunting in this area?

He got out of his bedroll, strapped on his gun and moved to the wagon. "Miss Tyson, you might want to get up. It looks like we're going to have company again."

By the time she climbed out of the wagon and joined him, the riders reined in their horses but kept a distance, though they stayed close enough to talk. Andrew figured there were ten or twelve of them. He recognized Buck Sommers.

"Stay behind me, Joanna," he whispered, then to the men he added, "What do you men want?"

A man with a long beard said, "We want you and that gal gone from this trail. I don't intend to bring my train this way with that contaminated wagon setting here in the open."

"What do you plan to do about it?"

"We're gonna burn it," one of the men said.

"And if'en you don't get off this trail, we'll burn you and her, too," another voice added.

When Andrew went for his gun, Buck leveled his rifle at Andrew's head. "Don't do it, McKinsey. I don't think you want to get shot, and neither does that woman you're protecting."

"Go to it men," The bearded man said.

Some of the riders produced torches and lit them from the already lighted one.

"Please, don't burn it. Everything I own is in this wagon," Joanna cried.

"What does it matter? You're dying." Someone shouted.

The first torch went into the canvas cover and in a matter of minutes, the entire wagon was in flames.

The bearded man looked at them and said in a stern voice, "Buck will come back in the morning to make sure you're gone. If you ain't, both of you will be shot. We ain't gonna have nobody carrying Cholera near our train." He turned his horse. "Let's go, men. We don't want to get close enough to them that we catch the thing."

Joanna fell to her knees sobbing. "What am I going to do now?"

Andrew pulled her to her feet. "Get hold of yourself, Joanna. You're going to leave here with me. I'll saddle my horse and we'll head out tonight. They weren't kidding when they said they'd kill us."

"But I can't leave my family."

"You have no choice. While I get things together, you go say goodbye to them. I'm sure they loved you and they'll understand why you have to go."

A few minutes later, without saying a word, he climbed into the saddle and he pulled Joanna up behind him. Though their future was unknown, they headed in the direction of his parents' ranch. For some unexplained reason, Andrew had a strange feeling Joanna was his future.

THE END

Author's Note: Cholera is a disease caused by unsanitary conditions and/or ingesting unpurified water. Today Cholera is found mostly in underdeveloped countries where hygiene is not part of life. It is almost non-existent in the United States today. That wasn't the case in the 1800s when emigrants settled the West. It plagued the wagon trains and almost 100% of the people who contracted the disease died. Because of the agonizing deaths, people feared it more than any other hardship on the trail. Because they didn't know of or didn't believe in germs, they believed the disease was contagious and when someone came down with the Blue Death they were avoided at all cost. (It was called the Blue Death because the victim often lost so much bodily-fluid they turned blue near the end of their life).

Agnes Alexander is the penname of Lynette Hall Hampton. Under the AA name she writes mostly Western Historical Romance and an occasional mystery. She writes for Harlequin under the LHH name. She has had over 50 books published and says she'll have to live to be 150 to write all the books she has in her head. A lifelong resident of NC, she has always had a passion for history, especially of the way the US was settled. She loves to travel for fun and research and has visited 48 of the 50

states. She lives with her cat, Victoria and when asked what her favorite thing to do is, she doesn't hesitate to say, "I have one wonderful child and she gave me two precious grandchildren. It doesn't get any better than spending time with them."

COVID-19 ANTHOLOGY ESSAY

Alexia Gordon

A crisis, unlike any endured for a generation, grips the world. Fears of contagion, death, and the unknown have combined with disruption of routine, social isolation, economic instability, debilitating illness, and massive loss of life to amp anxiety to levels unimagined by many. In our social media era, the anxiety spread faster than a viral tweet, leaving many wondering if—fearing that—everything they held dear had come to an end. But, as awful as things seem now, this isn't the End Times. Humanity has survived worse than COVID-19. We will survive this.

Full disclosure—I live by the motto, "Keep calm and carry on." More disclosure—COVID-19 isn't the worst thing to happen in my life in 2020. My dad died March 23. That was the worst thing. Not that 2020 had been going all that well for me, anyway. Since January, my publisher dropped me, I suffered a five-week-long bout of sinusitis (mostly while traveling for work with no time to be sick), and a man smashed my car because grabbing the last parking space was more important than looking to see who was behind him. The coronavirus pandemic feels like one more cosmic slap in the face from a universe intent on reminding me just how little of a shit it gives. By the time the pandemic hit the US in full force, I felt numb. Thank you, sir, may I have another? I'm also an extreme—as in literally off the chart when I take those work style/personality inventory tests where you place a dot representing your score on a grid—introvert, so social distancing measures have had little impact on my life. I was social distancing before social distancing was cool, as the t-shirt says *Avoid other people*? since I was twelve. Grocery delivery? Already doing it. Household supply delivery? Charter member of mail order subscription services. Meal delivery? Delivery service apps are pinned to my home screen. Telework? Yes, please. Please? Pretty please? Virtual church? You mean I can worship in my pajamas? Amen. My only beef is that extroverts discovered they could host virtual happy hours on Zoom. Now I've got to adapt my excuses for dodging in-person meetups to use to skip out on virtual ones. And, although I'm not immune to anxiety, my anxieties don't center around contagion. I also don't believe in giving in to anxieties. That's not how I cope.

I'm not suggesting fear of contagion isn't a real thing. Its most severe form has a medical name, mysophobia, fear of contamination. It's just not one of my anxieties. Worries about violence and about failure are what knot my stomach and tighten my throat. Germs don't bother me so much; maybe because as a physician, I've been surrounded by them—hepatitis, dengue, HIV, influenza, staph aureus, rhinovirus, coronavirus, herpes, et. al.—for almost two decades. I'm also not suggesting one coping strategy beats another. The best strategy, as long as it's legal, moral, and not harmful, is the one that works for you.

What works for me? Adopting the attitude espoused by novelist Ben Okri, in an opinion piece for *The Guardian*—be aware of the problem, respect the significance of the problem, be conscious of what needs to be done to mitigate the problem, but remain calm. Don't panic[1].

Be aware, but don't panic. I know, not easy for most, impossible for some. Okri recounts stories of friends who developed physical symptoms, severe enough to send them to the doctor, after reading too much about the pandemic[2]. However, for me, "don't panic" is my go-to method for coping with the crap life flings my way. Calm down, take a deep breath, don't panic, carry on. Maybe this is because I belong to Gen X, the oft-overlooked generation that "survived Reagan, the crack epidemic, the AIDS epidemic, the War on Drugs, mass incarceration, the S&L collapse all the while living on nothing but PB&J and ennui.[3]" Yes, this tweet, quoted in multiple media outlets[4, 5], conveys an in-your-face undertone but there's truth to it. Generational differences in the pandemic response exist.

Or, maybe I adopt the "remain calm" approach to coping because I fall into that subset of anxiety sufferers Laura Bradley describes in her Daily Beast essay[6]. "The anticipation of the unknown" is what haunts me, not the "terrible thing" itself. So, once the worst has happened, I can exhale, square my shoulders, and figure out what to do next.

If you've kept with me this far, either because you're hate-reading or because you read something you identify with or, at least, understand, you may be asking, "What do you do next?" How do you find sense in nonsense, impose order on chaos? You're calm; how do you carry on? I keep going by being useful.

Useful? Yes. Useful how? By offering care and comfort? By empathizing with the trials of others and taking on their pain? Honestly, no. Go back and read what I wrote about being a solitary introvert. Warm and fuzzy and invested in the emotional well-being of others isn't me. (Of course, I've learned to compensate for my stand-offish, cold-blooded nature. I've had to, to function in society as a reasonably well-adjusted adult. I've worked hard not to become a certified sociopath. Don't laugh. Socio- or psychopathic traits, including "resilience to chaos[7]," are often associated with success. However, they're also often associated with long prison sentences[8]. I hate jumpsuits, and neither orange, beige, nor horizontal stripes look particularly good on me. Therefore, with apologies to Dr. Jung for half-remembering his readings from my college psychology classes, I embraced my shadow and consciously worked to compensate for it.) How do I make myself useful, given my deep-seated tendency toward anti-socialness? I leave the succoring to those who have the heart for it (thank God for empaths) and turn to what I have a taste for—information gathering and sharing.

I'm task-oriented. I'm most content when the tasks I undertake have a purpose. Busy-work—sitting in the corner quietly coloring—frustrates me like not much else. If I do something, I need a reason to do it. I feel accomplished when I find purpose in what I do. I'm happiest when I'm contributing to the greater good, even if only in a tiny way. I also find contentment in data. Facts. Evidence. Information. Knowledge is power and information—accurate information—is the key to knowledge. This trait lies at the root of my interests in both medicine and crime fiction.

A friend once expressed surprise that a physician would score high on introversion scales, thinking, I assume, of the image of a kind and caring family doctor holding her patient's hand as she shepherded them through a health crisis. But there's another side to medicine, the inquisitive, problem-solving side. The side that likes to fix things. The desire to understand how things work, why things go wrong, and how to correct them when they do is the characteristic that lands "doctor" on the list of careers you'd be suited for on job aptitude tests. The desire to help others, by itself, does not. (That trait is usually associated with worthy careers like social work and counseling[9,10].) My inquisitive, problem-solving nature, my urge to fix things, drives me to figure out why John has a fever, what's causing Jane's rash, and how I can make them both go away. (The fever and rash, not John and Jane.) It also drives me, in writing and reading mystery fiction, to figure out whodunit and how and to see if the sleuth will solve the puzzle before the murderer escapes. Inquisitiveness and problem-solving help me deal with COVID-19 by driving me to seek out and share accurate information about the novel coronavirus and the disease it causes, as well as historical information about past pandemics and (inter)national disasters. I make myself useful by counteracting rumor and misinformation and by putting the current situation into perspective. I remind people this isn't our first, nor our worst, pandemic. We've been through this before[11]. We will, eventually, go through this again. And we'll survive. Humanity will survive.

I hope you find my essay on how I'm dealing with the pandemic and its impact and why I'm coping this way useful. If not, if my coping strategy is so far removed from your worldview that you glean nothing from it at all, at least consider it an explanation for some of my social media posts. And if fear—of death, of illness, of isolation—and hopelessness threaten to overwhelm you, let me be of use to you by sharing information that might help you take a step from the COVID-19 Fear Zone toward the Learning Zone[12,13].

THE END

A Brief Primer on Viruses and a History of Pandemics.

Disclaimer: I'm a Board-certified Family Physician, not an infectious disease specialist. My current medical practice is mostly administrative. I am not writing as a representative of the Government or any other agency. Opinions are my own. I am not giving medical advice. For medical advice, contact your health care provider.

Viruses are small (0.02-0.3 micrometers; 1 inch=25,400 micrometers) proteinaceous, DNA- or RNA-filled parasites that lie dormant outside of living cells. They invade living cells, take over the host cell's metabolic machinery, and reproduce. These copies either rupture out of the host cell or bud off from it[14, 15].

Millions of viruses that exist; approximately 320,000 infect mammals[16, 17]. Hundreds of these 320,000 are coronaviruses, a strain first discovered in the 1930s in poultry[18, 19]. Only seven of the coronaviruses infect humans; three of the seven are responsible for pandemic pneumonias in the 21st century[20]. The 2019 novel coronavirus, now officially named SARS-CoV-2, is one of these three[21, 22]. (The other two are MERS-CoV and SARS-CoV[23].) COVID-19 is the official name of the disease caused by SARS-COV-2[24].

The first recorded pandemic occurred in 430 BC. It spread from Libya, Ethiopia, and Egypt to Athens where it killed two-thirds of the population and helped Sparta defeat Athens in the Peloponnesian War[25]. Next came the Antonine Plague. From 165 AD to 180 AD, it traveled from Huns to Germans to Romans, killing Emperor Marcus Aurelius on the way[26]. Numerous plagues followed, including the

Black Death in 1350, which wiped out one-third of the world's population, the Great Plague of London in 1665, the first cholera pandemic in 1817 (followed by six more in the next 150 years), and the 1918 influenza pandemic, estimated to have killed 50-100 million people worldwide[27, 28]. 1981 brought the HIV/AIDS pandemic, still going on[29]. 2003 saw SARS, caused by the coronavirus SARS-CoV, closely related to the current pandemic culprit, SARS-CoV-2[30]. In 2009, a new strain of influenza, H1N1, appeared in the US. Dubbed "swine flu," it caused the world's fourth influenza pandemic (in addition to 1918, 1957-58, and 1968), resulting in almost 600,000 deaths in some estimates, eighty percent in people younger than 65[31].

Finally, some definitions. Epidemic: "an increase, often sudden, in the number of cases of a disease above what is normally expected in that population in that area[32]." Pandemic: "an epidemic that has spread over several countries or continents[33]."

Endnotes:

[1] Ben Okri, "Fear of COVID-19 is a mental contagion—and that's something we can fight," *The Guardian*, March 26, 2020. https://www.theguardian.com/commentisfree/2020/mar/26/fear-of-covid-19-is-a-mental-contagion-ben-okri. Accessed May 12, 2020

[2] Ibid.

[3] Megan Gerhardt. "Coronavirus Quarantine? Gen X was made for this. Boomers and Gen Z, not so much," *Think.* nbcnews.com, March 25, 2020. https://www.nbcnews.com/think/opinion/coronavirus-quarantine-gen-x-was-made-boomers-gen-z-not-ncna1168021. Accessed May 12, 2020.

[4] Ibid.

[5] Hillary Hoffower. "'We'll be the only ones left.': Gen X says they're better prepared for the coronavirus pandemic than any other generation," *Business Insider*, April 7, 2020. https://www.businessinsider.com/gen-x-prepared-coronavirus-pandemic-versus-boomers-gen-z-2020-4. Accessed May 12, 2020.

[6]Laura Bradley. "The coronavirus pandemic is a devastating mass trauma—but some people with anxiety and depression have seen their symptoms improve," *The Daily Beast*, April 5, 2020, updated April 27, 2020. https://www.thedailybeast.com/coronavirus-is-making-a-lot-of-people-anxious-and-depressed-but-some-sufferers-actually-feel-better-now?ref=scroll. Accessed May 12, 2020.

[7]Lindsay Dodgson. "Here's why CEOs often have the traits of a psychopath," Business Insider, UK, July 7, 2017. https://amp.insider.com/ceos-often-have-psychopathic-traits-2017-7. Accessed May 12, 2020.

[8]Tomas Chamorro-Premuzic. "1 in 5 business leaders may have psychopathic tendencies—here's why, according to a psychology professor." Make It. cnbc.com, April 8, 2019, updated April 9, 2019. https://www.cnbc.com/2019/04/08/the-science-behind-why-so-many-successful-millionaires-are-psychopaths-and-why-it-doesnt-have-to-be-a-bad-thing.html. Accessed May 12, 2020.

[9]Vernon G. Zunker. *Career Counseling: A Holistic Approach*, 8th ed. 2011. Cengage Learning. p. 311.

[10]Vernon G. Zunker. *Career, Work, and Mental Health: Integrating Career and Personal Counseling*. 2008. SAGE. p. 187.

[11] Fred Guterl. "Fear of Contagion," *Psychology Today*, June 14, 2012. https://www.psychologytoday.com/us/blog/the-guest-room/201206/fear-contagion#_=_. Accessed May 12, 2020.

[12]BC Epilepsy Society. "Empowering Yourself During COVID-19." April 17, 2020. http://bcepilepsy.com/blog/empowering-yourself-during-covid19. Accessed May 12, 2020.

[13]Winston & Strawn, LLP. "Focusing on Resilience." April 13, 2020. https://www.winston.com/en/thought-leadership/focusing-on-resilience.html. Accessed May 12, 2020.

[14]Samuel Baron, et. al. "Chapter 45: Viral Pathogenesis," in *Medical Microbiology*, 4th edition, 1996. S. Baron, ed. Galveston, TX: University of Texas Medical Branch at Galveston. Accessed May 12, 2020. https://www.ncbi.nlm.nih.gov/books/NBK8149/.

[15]M. Drexler. "How Infection Works," in *What You Need to Know About Infectious Disease*. 2010. Washington, DC: National Academies Press. https://www.ncbi.nlm.nih.gov/books/NBK209710/. Accessed May 12, 2020.

[16] Vincent Racaniello. "How many viruses on Earth?" *Virology Blog*. September 6, 2013. https://www.virology.ws/2013/09/06/how-

many-viruses-on-earth/. Accessed May 12, 2020.

[17] Mindy Weisberger. "Billions of Viruses Are Falling to Earth Right Now (But That Isn't Why You Have the Flu)," *Live Science*. February 07, 2018. https://www.livescience.com/61689-viruses-fall-from-sky.html. Accessed May 12, 2020.

[18] Carly Vandergriendt. "What Is a Coronavirus?" *Healthline*. March 31, 2020, updated April 29, 2020. https://www.healthline.com/health/coronavirus-types. Accessed May 12, 2020.

[19] Matthew E. Levison, MD. "COVID-19: What We Know About Coronaviruses," *Merck Manual: Professional Version*. February 26, 2020. https://www.merckmanuals.com/professional/resourcespages/covid-19-what-we-know-about-coronaviruses. Accessed May 12, 2020.

[20] Ibid.

[21] Ibid.

[22] World Health Organization. "Naming the coronavirus disease (COVID-19) and the virus that causes it," Coronavirus Disease 2019: Technical   Guidance. https://www.who.int/emergencies/diseases/novel-coronavirus-2019/technical-guidance/naming-the-coronavirus-disease-(covid-2019)-and-the-virus-that-causes-it. Accessed May 12, 2020.

[23] Matthew E. Levison, MD. "COVID-19: What We Know About Coronaviruses," *Merck Manual: Professional Version*. February 26, 2020. https://www.merckmanuals.com/professional/resourcespages/covid-19-what-we-know-about-coronaviruses. Accessed May 12, 2020.

[24] World Health Organization. "Naming the coronavirus disease (COVID-19) and the virus that causes it," Coronavirus Disease 2019: Technical   Guidance. https://www.who.int/emergencies/diseases/novel-coronavirus-2019/technical-guidance/naming-the-coronavirus-disease-(covid-2019)-and-the-virus-that-causes-it. Accessed May 12, 2020.

[25] History.com Editors. "Pandemics That Changed History," History.com, February 27, 2019, updated April 30, 2020. A&E Television Networks. https://www.history.com/topics/middle-ages/pandemics-timeline. Accessed May 12, 2020.

[26] Ibid.

[27] Ibid.

[28] Fred Guterl. "Fear of Contagion," *Psychology Today*, June 14, 2012. https://www.psychologytoday.com/us/blog/the-guest-room/201206/fear-contagion#_=_. Accessed May 12, 2020.

[29] History.com Editors. "Pandemics That Changed History," History.com, February 27, 2019, updated April 30, 2020. A&E Television Networks. https://www.history.com/topics/middle-ages/pandemics-timeline. Accessed May 12, 2020.

[30] Ibid.

[31] Centers for Disease Control and Prevention, National Center for Immunization and Respiratory Diseases (NCIRD). "2009 H1N1 Pandemic (H1N1pdm09 virus)," Pandemic Influenza: Past Pandemics. June 11, 2019. https://www.cdc.gov/flu/pandemic-resources/2009-h1n1-pandemic.html. Accessed May 12, 2020.

[32] Deputy Director for Public Health Science and Surveillance, Center for Surveillance, Epidemiology, and Laboratory Services, Division of Scientific Education and Professional Development. "Lesson 1: Introduction to Epidemiology, Section 11: Epidemic Disease Occurrence," DSEPD: Principles of Epidemiology in Public Health Practice. May 18, 2012. https://www.cdc.gov/csels/dsepd/ss1978/lesson1/section11.html. Accessed May 12, 2020.

[33] Ibid.

Alexia Gordon is a member of Mystery Writers of America, Sisters in Crime, International Thriller Writers, and Crime Writers of Color. She blogs with:

Miss Demeanors (https://www.missdemeanors.com/)
Femmes Fatales (femmesfatales.typepad.com/my_weblog/)
Killer Characters (https://www.killercharacters.com/).

She also hosts The Cozy Corner with Alexia Gordon, the podcast focused on cozy and traditional mystery authors. Listen on AnchorFM (https://anchor.fm/alexia-gordon), SoundCloud (https://soundcloud.com/authorsontheair/sets/the-cozy-corner-with-alexia-gordon), or your favorite podcast listening platform. A new episode premieres every other Wednesday.

Find me on social media (Facebook: AlexiaGordon.writer, Twitter: @AlexiaGordon, Instagram: @DrLex1995) and visit my website (www.alexiagordon.net) to sign up for my newsletter. Her honors include:

2017 Lefty Award for Best Debut Novel
2016 Agatha Award nominee for Best First Novel

Suspense magazine "Best of 2016" selection in Debut Novel category

Runner-Up, 2017 Lone Star Bloggers' Choice Awards, Best Mystery/Suspense

Short List, 2017 Lone Star Bloggers' Choice Awards, Best Series

Winner, 2018 Lone Star Bloggers' Choice Awards, Best Series

Winner, 2018 Lone Star Bloggers' Choice Awards, Best Mystery/Suspense/Thriller

Winner, 2018 Lone Star Bloggers' Choice Awards, Best Fantasy/Paranormal/Alt History

Starred review, *Publishers Weekly*, January 29, 2018

2019 Silver Falchion Award Finalist, Best Mystery

FAITHFUL

Beth Terrell writing as Jaden Terrell

The morning of the apocalypse, I was running late for Zumba. There was nothing unusual about that. Seemed like I was always running late for something. I pulled on a pair of 2x tights and a baggy T-shirt, then hurried down the stairs and grabbed my Monday bag from the line of polyester duffels in the hall. Monday's duffel had a change of clothes, two pecan pies for the town picnic, and the supplies for my classes on Native American beadwork and Chinese brush painting.

I snatched a handful of dried corn from a bowl on the foyer table and tossed it to my hen, Isabella, on the way to the car. She stopped scratching in the grass, scuttled past the double-decker luxury henhouse our friend and local handyman Wallace Dufrene had built for her, and hurried over to peck at her snack.

"Bye, Izzy," I called as I peeled out of the driveway, spewing gravel. She didn't even bother to lift her head in reply.

My best friend, Trini, intercepted me in front of the gym doors. She wore an oversized lace blouse over a lavender sports bra and leggings. Her hair was pulled back into a neat pony tail, and her glasses were shoved up onto her head, the red frames accenting her blonde strands.

"I have terrible news." She put a hand on each of my biceps. Okay, so they're a little more like water wings. But I'm sure there are biceps under there somewhere.

When the suspense became too much, I said, "What news?"

"I don't know how to tell you this, Maudie," she said, "so I'll just come right out and say it. Wallace Dufrene is dead."

I forgot all about my water wings.

"What do you mean, dead?" I thought of all the ways a man could die and could reconcile none of them with the handsome young jack-of-all-trades who kept my car running and my grass mowed. "The man is all of thirty-five."

"He was cleaning out the gutters of that new church," Trini said. "The Fellowship of the Faithful. And he must've slipped and fallen off the ladder."

I shook my head. "Wallace didn't fall off any ladder. The man has the balance of a mountain goat."

"Anybody can have an accident." She reached into her purse, which was about the size of a postage stamp, and pulled out a tiny digital recorder with a built-in camera. "Anyway, I'm writing it up for the *Clarion*, and I need you to come with me."

"Come with you where?"

"The church, silly. I can't go there by myself. Not where someone's . . ." She gulped down a deep breath. "Where someone's *died*."

I shifted my bag to my other shoulder and looked down at my T-shirt, which had a picture of Horton the elephant with his motto beneath: *An elephant's faithful, one hundred percent.* If Horton could withstand the derision of his friends to hatch the egg of a derelict bird and later save a tiny civilization living on the head of a clover, I could accompany my best friend to the scene of a tragedy. Trini needed me.

Besides, I owed it to Wallace.

We took my car, a Honda so ancient the primer peeked through the paint like a thousand tiny freckles. Trini shoved a Cinderella rod puppet I'd made in puppetry class off the passenger seat and slid in, adjusting the seatbelt to its smallest setting. Nudging the puppet aside with the toe of her sneaker, she snapped the belt shut over her tiny tummy and settled in.

***

The church was on the outskirts of town, in a quaint-looking white building with a steeple and bell tower, no cross. It had once housed a congregation of Free Will Baptists, but the Baptists had swelled beyond its limits and now worshipped two towns over in a superchurch that streamed its Sunday sermons to a YouTube channel for the benefit of shut-ins and anyone too lazy to get out of their pajamas.

We pulled into the empty lot and parked beside a sign that said simply *The Faithful.* It had been a short drive, but Trini pushed her fists into the small of her back and stretched while I closed my eyes and used my Gift to scan the grounds for the confused energy that often surrounds a place of sudden death. I felt it at once, a befuddled sadness centered on the west side of the building. I opened my eyes and, with Trini at my heels, followed it around to find the ladder still propped against the outer wall.

It looked sturdy. But maybe a rung was loose. That was the only reason I could think of for a man like Wallace to have fallen from it. I gave the thing a wary look and took a deep breath. I'm not a small woman, and if the ladder hadn't held for Wallace, there was no reason to think it would hold me.

"You aren't going up there," Trini said, her voice thin.

"Yes I am." I put a foot on the bottom rung and bounced a little, testing it. It still seemed sturdy, so I climbed on up, holding my breath and clutching the sides for dear life. The steeple stretched high above me, a white spike against a span of blue.

Trini fanned at herself with her hands. "You be careful up there, Maudie."

"I'm *being* careful," I said, but just at that moment, a feeling of vertigo swept over me. I swayed at the top of the ladder, then teetered backward and felt the ladder pull away from the wall.

I'm a goner, I thought. *Wallace, I'm coming.*

Then strong hands wrapped around me from behind. I caught a whiff of Wallace's aftershave, a spicy, woody blend that made me think of a John Denver song, and the top rails of the ladder thumped back against the building.

I squeezed the ladder with shaking hands and pressed my suddenly sweaty forehead against the top rung.

Thank you, I mouthed.

A vision shot through my mind—the sudden shake of the ladder, the loss of balance and the tumble to the ground, the moment of stunned breathlessness followed by the flash of an arm and a fist clutching a rock. Then a burst of pain. Then nothing.

And finally a bewildered awakening, a feeling of uprootedness, and the slow realization of loved ones lost and plans cut short, of unfinished business and all that would never be the same.

Blinded by tears, I felt my way down the ladder.

Trini helped me down the last few rungs. "What is it, Maudie? Did you see something? I swear to goodness, I thought you were gonna fall for sure."

"Wallace didn't fall," I said, stifling a sob. "He was murdered."

After a moment of stunned silence, Trini cleared her throat. "Are you sure?"

"I saw it happen."

She frowned. "Like in a vision? Did you . . . did you see who did it?"

"No, just an arm and the rock that hit him." I wiped my sweaty palms on my shirt and said, "We have to tell Sheriff Tate."

She twirled her ponytail around one finger. "Maybe you should tell him, Maudie. It was your vision. Besides, I have to get home and type up something for the *Clarion*. I'll meet you at the picnic."

***

Sheriff John Tate was none too happy to hear that I'd had a vision of Wallace Dufrene's murder. Oh, he was polite enough, but he punctuated his sentences with sighs and rubbed his temples when he thought I wasn't looking.

"I can't take visions and hocus-pocus to court," he said. "The evidence all points to a fall."

"It isn't hocus-pocus," I said. "It's a gift. My mother had it, and my grandmother, and as far as I can tell, the women in our family have been using it since they were softening mammoth hides with their teeth."

"Maybe so," he said, pinching the bridge of his nose between two fingers, "but it's still not proof."

I stuck out my chin. "Don't you worry, Sheriff Tate. I'll get your proof."

But I had no idea how to do that. I hadn't seen the killer's face, and I didn't know why anyone would want to kill poor Wallace. His longtime fiancée, Amber, might know something, though, and I knew just where to find her.

I stopped off to change clothes in the ladies' room at Dabby's Donut Den. Of course, I had to order a couple of plain glazed for politeness' sake. I ate them on the way to the park, where I met up with Trini, who looked pert and perky in jeans and a ruffled blouse. We took my pecan pies and her strawberry delight to the dessert tent and found ourselves enveloped in a cloud of powdered sugar. Through the haze, I saw Amber Leibewitz in a folding director's chair, dabbing at her eyes and making polite sounds to the sympathetic cluster of women tut-tutting around her. She looked shell-shocked.

When she saw me, she launched out of the chair and flung herself into my arms. Fortunately, she's a waif-like girl, and it was like being launched at by a miniature poodle.

"Oh, Miss Maudie," she sobbed into my generous bosom. "What am I going to do without him?"

I patted her back until she calmed down. Then, with a meaningful glace at Trini, I said, "Let's go get some air. Okay, Amber? It's a little close in here."

Trini fanned herself and said, "Close? I'm suffocating. Was there some kind of explosion?"

Amber sniffled. "Glorybell dropped a whole bag of confectioner's sugar into the fan when she heard the news about . . ." She howled again, and I took her by the hand and led her out of the tent.

"Amber," I said, when her sobs subsided. "We need to talk."

She wiped her eyes with the heels of her hands. "I don't care what Sheriff Tate says. Wallace didn't fall."

Trini and I exchanged a look. I said, "What makes you so sure?"

"He told me there was something fishy going on at that church. That a group of important members were meeting there this morning, and he planned to listen in and see what they were planning." She blinked at me with wet red eyes. "He thought they were cultists."

Trini choked on a laugh. "Cultists?"

"Laugh if you want," Amber said primly, giving Trini a cool glance, "but he said he was going to expose them, and now he's dead."

"We believe you," I said. "But what made Wallace think the Faithful are cultists?"

She hunched a shoulder. "Oh, I don't know. Maybe it was all that talk about Hell gates and human sacrifice."

I shot another look at Trini, whose eyes gleamed with the sudden promise of a front-page by-line. Shoot, human sacrifice would probably put her above the fold. Especially in a town where a couple of college kids stealing mailboxes qualified as a crime spree.

"Is there anything else?" I asked Amber. "Anybody else who might have had a grudge against Wallace?"

She fingered the ring on her left hand. "You knew him, Maudie. He'd walk six miles in the rain to change a flat tire, and half the time he wouldn't even charge for it. Who could possibly have had a grudge?"

Her tears had given way to a quiet despair. There was nothing I could do to ease her grief, but I gave her a hug and whispered, "Don't tell anyone what you told us. If one of the Faithful did kill Wallace, there's no reason to let them know he told you his suspicions."

She nodded, and I followed the warning with a few words of protection. As we walked her back to the tent, I could see the faint glimmer of my wards, like glitter in her hair.

***

With Amber ensconced in her director's chair, Trini leaned in close and said into my ear, "We have to go back to the church."

I pointed across the park, where Reverend Baylor, the Faithful's head minister, was spreading a checkered tablecloth onto the ground. "Let's talk with Brother Baylor first. See what he says."

"What, are you going to ask him point blank if the Faithful are some kind of cult?"

I shrugged. I didn't know what I was going to ask him.

According to the gossip mills, Brother Baylor was forty-three, but he could have passed for seventy, an insectile man with long, thin limbs and skin so weathered it looked like a carapace. While we picked our way through a patchwork of picnickers, he knelt on the ground, smoothing wrinkles from his checkered tablecloth. A savory smell wafted from the basket on the ground beside him. Fried chicken and apple pie, I thought, and freshly baked bread.

"Terrible accident at your church this morning," I said to him.

He looked up with a long slow blink. "Yes, poor man. I suppose he must have been drinking."

"Wallace didn't drink," I said.

"No? Then perhaps he was simply overtired." He rubbed the tip of his nose with a bony finger. "I suppose we'll have to find someone else to do the gutters. May I offer you a piece of chicken?"

"No thank you," I said through gritted teeth, though my stomach was growling. For no good reason, I wanted to slap him. Instead, I spun away and headed for my car, with Trini hot on my heels. "*Now we go to the church.*"

This time we parked at an abandoned service station and walked almost half a mile through the woods to the church. It was locked, of course. I moved Wallace's ladder and, while Trini held it steady, climbed it without mishap. Then, carefully, huffing like a steam engine, I clambered onto the roof, crawled on my belly to the steeple, and hauled myself into the bell tower. A layer of dust covered the wooden floor, and the bell rope was frayed and filthy. The air smelled like pigeons.

As I knelt on the tower floor, gasping for breath and feeling for a trap door, Trini scrambled in after me and whispered, "What are we looking for?"

"I don't know," I puffed. My fingers found the edge of the trap door, and I flung it open. "We'll know it when we see it."

The trap door opened onto another ladder and a cramped upper level filled with crumbling hymnals and dusty organ pipes. A flight of narrow stairs led down into the sanctuary, where the pew cushions had been covered in black velvet and the cross in front had been splashed with red paint and turned upside down.

"Oh," Trini breathed, pressing so close into my back that I could feel her trembling. "Looks like Wallace was right."

We scoured the sanctuary, jumping at every noise and pausing every few minutes to listen for the sound of Brother Baylor's Nissan. Nothing there. Nothing in the baptismal pool but peeling paint and cobwebs.

"Here," Trini called softly, waving me over to a door behind the choir loft. "I think I found something."

The something she'd found was a library. Books lined all four walls, books with titles in Latin, books in languages I'd never seen, books with titles like *The Seven Secret Names, Blood Magic,* and *The Book of Reckoning.*

In the center of the room were a leather chair and a massive oak desk covered in papers. We approached it holding hands like children. I could feel Trini's heartbeat through her palm. Like we had when we were youngsters, we looked at each other and counted, "One...two...three."

I looked down at the topmost paper, a yellowed parchment illuminated with nightmare creatures, and a roaring started in my ears. In neat box letters, it read: *A Spell for Opening the Gates of Hell.* A list of ingredients, each followed by a check mark, topped the page. Beside "blood of a righteous man," someone had scrawled *Wallace Dufrene.*

As if from a great distance, I heard Trini moan, "Oh no, oh no, oh no."

I skimmed the spell. It was a nasty thing, full of curses and evil. And according to the calendar beside it, it was scheduled to take place that very night.

Trini said, "We have to stop them. There must be a counterspell here somewhere."

I scanned the room. Books upon books. "We'll never find anything in here. We have to get out before Brother Baylor gets back."

"I know, I know, but..." She gave her ponytail a nervous tug.

"You're the only one who can do it. The only one I know who has real magic."

"It's not magic," I said. "It's—"

"I know." She held up a hand. "It's a gift. But what good is a gift if you don't use it?"

She had a point there. My gran always said the Gift was a great blessing and a great responsibility. If you had it, you were obliged to use it in defense of Goodness, Love, and Light. Besides, if the Faithful managed to open a Hellgate, it would be the end of this cozy little town, of Zumba classes and tap shoes, of town picnics and lying on your back to watch the stars. Darkness would swallow us, and slowly but surely, it would swallow the rest of humankind as well. What else could we do but try?

At first it seemed like the books were filed randomly, but after a while, the groupings started to make sense. Trini found a section filled with defensive spells and counterspells, and a few minutes after she called me over, I found a book called *Gates: In and Out, Open and Shut.* As I pulled it from the shelf, a piece of ivory parchment fell out.

I picked it up, looked at it, and said, "I think this is it."

It was a potion for closing or preventing the opening of interdimensional gates. The ingredient list read:

Eye of Newt

Belladonna

Stinging nettles

Hand of glory

Hair of a black dog

A coffin nail

Hemlock

Sea salt

Lemongrass

A fresh chicken foot

We stared at the paper for a long moment. Then Trini said, "Oh, Maudie. You have to make this."

I groaned. "Where am I going to get all these things before tonight?"

She frowned and tapped her forehead. "Wait. I did a story once about the local occult scene, and—"

"We have a local occult scene?"

"There's a little shop out near Tater's Bend, has all kinds of ingredients like this. I bet you could find what you need there." She put a hand on my forearm and looked earnestly into my eyes. "You're the only one who can do it, Maudie. The future of humanity depends on it."

The hum of Baylor's Nissan made my breath catch in my throat. Without a word, Trini grabbed my hand, and we fled out the back door and into the woods. We were both breathless by the time we got to my car. As I pulled out of the service station lot, Trini said, "I think we should split up. You make the potion, and I'll get us some weapons and reinforcements. We'll meet back at the church a few minutes before midnight and catch them in the act."

As I dropped her off at her little blue Pinto, I gave her a mock salute. The irreverence made me feel a little braver.

****

While Trini went in search of weapons and allies, I drove to the shop she'd told me about. The minute I stepped inside, I knew it wasn't going to work. The shelves were filled with parchment packets, dusty jars, and the bones of little helpless things. The sharp-faced man behind the counter looked up, but before he could speak, I was out the door, my arms prickling with dark energy. I would have to try another way. You can't fight evil with evil.

I drove straight home and set about gathering the ingredients for the interdimensional gate-closing potion. Sea salt, check. Lemongrass, check. I plucked some stickers from the back yard for the stinging nettles and stopped by Old Sam Reynolds' place to pet his Rottweiler and capture a few black hairs. The coffin nail was harder. Ben Hardwick, who ran the funeral home, wasn't inclined to give me a fastener from an actual coffin, so I picked up a nail from the Home Depot. I figured it could be used for a coffin as well as anything.

On the way home, I stopped by Elm Creek and soaked my sneakers catching a salamander. I cupped him in my hands and felt his cool sliminess against my palms and fingers. Then I opened my hands a sliver and looked into his little eyes.

I couldn't do it.

I knew the fate of the known universe was at stake, but I just didn't have the heart to pluck out the little fellow's eye. Magic might require sacrifice, but I could only sacrifice what was mine to give. I went home and washed my hands and rummaged in the fridge until I found a jar of garlic-stuffed olives. They looked very eye-like, with the garlic cloves as pupils. Besides, garlic is noted for healing properties.

Now I was on a roll. I used basil for belladonna and turmeric for hemlock. Good, wholesome plants in place of poisons. Then I pulled out Gran's old soup pot, half-filled it with water, and turned the heat on low. The olives went in, then the lemongrass and spices, then the nail, dog hairs, and stinging nettle. The hand of glory stymied me. A hand of glory was the dried hand of a hanged man. We were fresh out of those.

I steeled myself and picked up my meat cleaver. My stomach did a slow flip-flop. Hold fast, I told myself. An elephant's faithful, one hundred percent.

Then I laid my left hand on the chopping block and lifted the cleaver. I cried out as it sliced through flesh and bone, then, tears streaming down my face, flipped the tip of my little finger into the potion.

Only one ingredient left. A fresh chicken foot.

I thought through my options as I ran cold water over my wounded finger and pinched it in a towel until the bleeding stopped.

Then I went out to the back yard and called Izzy.

She was a good hen and strutted to me when she heard her name. I picked her up, ignoring my throbbing finger, and carried her to the stove. Steam rose from the burbling concoction in the pot. I waved one hand over it until I found the ideal temperature—warm but not scalding—then picked up Izzy and held her over the steam.

She clucked a brief protest, then relaxed into my hands as I murmured magic words. They weren't the words on the page. I didn't know those words, but when I looked at them I knew they were guttural and cruel. A finger of doubt jabbed at my heart. Was I diluting the spell? Jeopardizing all of mankind for the sake of a newt and a little bantam hen?

Pushing my doubts aside, I finished my chant and set Izzy on the floor. She gave a few worried clucks and pecked at the tiles while I poured the rest of my orange juice into the sink and ladled the potion into the orange juice bottle.

The clock on the kitchen wall said it was time to go meet Trini. While I tucked the potion into a fabric shopping bag and grabbed my purse with the hand that wasn't missing part of a finger, Izzy wound around my feet like a cat, protesting with fretful clucks.

"Stay here, Izzy," I said, shooing her out the door and into the darkness toward her luxury henhouse. She fluttered back to me and tried to fly into the car as I climbed in.

"No, stay!" I said, but when I pulled out and looked in the rearview mirror, there was Izzy, head thrust forward, wings stretched behind her like a Boeing airplane, running after the car like a Labrador retriever. A high-pitched sound came from her throat, a sound I'd never thought could come from a chicken.

"Fine," I said, and pulled over to wait for her. "You can go, but you have to wait in the car."

The parking lot of the Faithful was almost full when I got there, and my heart did a little skitter as I grabbed my orange juice bottle and gently shut the car door, leaving Izzy in the passenger seat with the windows down. The night was cool and smelled of lilacs. I pointed a finger at Izzy and said, "Stay here."

Trini was waiting for me in the shadows by the front door, an anxious light in her eyes. She nodded toward the bottle in my hands and whispered, "Is that it?"

I nodded and whispered back as I unscrewed the top, "I hope it works."

We crept into the sanctuary, leaving the door slightly ajar. At the end of the center aisle, Brother Baylor and fifteen or twenty of the

Faithful stood in a semi-circle, chanting, while a shimmering portal appeared in front of the altar. Sickly colors swirled within its borders, and as we watched, the swirls began to coalesce. The swirls became formless shapes, then creatures with hunched backs, crabbed wings, razor claws.

My mouth went dry, my feet suddenly rooted to the floor.

Trini hissed, "Throw the potion!"

But I couldn't move.

Something shoved me from behind, and once again I smelled the woody spice of Wallace's cologne. With a high-pitched screech I'd meant to be a terrifying battle cry, I rushed the portal and sloshed the potion into it.

The creatures shrieked and recoiled. The gate began to shake. From behind me, Trini cried, "No! What have you done?"

I turned and saw my best friend charging toward me, her face contorted with rage. Brother Baylor and the Faithful kept on chanting, eyes glazed with religious fervor.

Trini thumped me hard in the chest with her fist. "You didn't do it right! I should have known you'd screw it all up, even though I practically *handed* you that potion. I even told you where to get the ingredients!"

I shook my head, confused. "What are you talking it about? It worked. The gate is closing."

"The gate is closing!" she repeated. "That spell isn't supposed to close the gate. It's supposed to hold it open."

I blinked, unable to process her words. "Hold it open? But…you…Why?"

"Look around," she said. "The world is a mess. The Big Guy in charge isn't doing that great a job. It's time to try new Management."

The portal pulsed and narrowed. Then a scaly, clawed foot shot through, holding it open. I pulled back my arm to throw the rest of the potion, but Trini grabbed my wrist and held tight. I thrashed around, trying to get free and ignoring the jolts of pain from my injured finger. "What about Wallace?" I panted.

"A regrettable…sacrifice." She oofed as I jabbed an elbow into her middle, but she didn't let go. "For the greater…good."

"Good, my patootie," I said. "You know perfectly well a thing is evil if it tells you to murder your friends."

I turned my attention back to the portal and began to chant a string of bright shining words to mitigate the chants of the Faithful. The portal shuddered, and a clawed hand hooked around the edge.

Trini seemed to be getting extra strength from somewhere, probably from the chants of her co-conspirators, while I felt more drained by the minute.

Then a little brown blur shot past me. It was Izzy, head down, wings back, the pupils of her eyes pinning. Like a chicken on a mission, she pecked at the foot, relentless as a feathered machine gun. The foot began to steam.

From within the portal came a howl of rage. The foot jerked back, and the gate snapped shut. The cultists collapsed like creatures made of straw and muslin. Trini stumbled backward, then sank onto a pew and covered her face with her hands.

It took Sheriff Tate almost twenty minutes to arrive, but when he did, he and his deputies loaded up Trini and the unconscious cultists and carted them away to jail. He couldn't charge them for the attempted apocalypse, of course, but there was plenty enough evidence of Wallace's murder.

Trini turned State's evidence and, according to her deal with the DA, will be out of prison in a few years. Once a month or so I visit her. Some folks ask why, considering she tried to destroy the world and all, but I refuse to give up on her. I still go to my classes, still line up a different bag full of supplies for each day of the week. It isn't as much fun without Trini, but sometimes Sheriff Tate comes over for dinner, and once I even managed to get him through the door of the ballroom dance studio.

"Maudie Lane Calloway," he says, "I must have been a black-hearted old bastard in a previous life, to have ended up with you in my town." He talks big, but he doesn't mean it. A girl can tell.

Most nights, Izzy and I sit on the couch, watch TV, and share a tub of popcorn. I do my crafts and work my small magics, weaving a silver web around our little village, a web of love and protection. Sometimes I catch a whiff of a woody, spicy cologne, and I wake in the morning to find my wood chopped or my leaky faucet fixed. Like Horton and me, Wallace knows what it means to be faithful.

THE END

Jaden Terrell is a Shamus Award finalist and the internationally published author of the Nashville-based Jared McKean private detective series. At the other end of the spectrum is *Trouble Most Faire,* a cozy black cat detective romantic mystery set at a Renaissance Faire. Terrell's short stories have appeared in several anthologies, and she is a contributor to International Thriller Writers' *Big Thrill* magazine and *Now Write! Mysteries*, a collection of exercises published by Tarcher/Penguin for writers of crime fiction. She is the recipient of the Killer Nashville Builder Award, as well as the Magnolia Award and the Silver Quill Award for service to the Southeast Mystery Writers of America. Terrell offers live and online workshops, coaching, and courses for writers. Website: http://www.jadenterrell.com

ROAD REPAIRS

Barry Lancet

What Ray Cooper finds most beguiling about the Samoan is his plum-colored eyes.

The two men sit on their kiteboards, floating in the water fronting the cliffs of Diamond Head. Their legs dangle in the cool evening Pacific current. The boards rise and fall with each languid, incoming swell. In front of them the ocean stretches out seemingly to the ends of the earth. The sky is high and calm. The sun is a red ball sinking toward the horizon, its dying rays brushing the blue canopy with streaks of orange and lavender.

The Samoan is known as Big Roi. He is actually only three-quarters Samoan, Cooper would learn later. The rest of the man's heritage comes from the Hawaiian side of the family, with a pinch of Portuguese. The Samoan genes are prominent. Big Roi has cocoa brown skin, a broad nose, and dark, purple-brown eyes. Unlike most of his family, he didn't skew large and chunky, he says. Cooper can see that. Big Roi went the other way. He is compact, muscled, and short. Carrying two hundred and twenty pounds of ripped bulk on a five-foot-six frame, he resembles nothing so much as an overfed pitbull in human form.

And that is before Cooper takes in the details of his tribal sleeve tattoo with its Tiki deity ringed in shark's teeth.

While the wind was up the two men rode hard, slashing back and forth across the water, waist harnesses taut, splayed strings shooting up to giant kites arched eighty feet overhead. Once the airstreams began to lose their punch, each man drifted toward the cliffs and settled in to watch the evening colors play out overhead.

They had nodded at each other as they shot across the ocean's rippling surface. Now they are taking in the kaleidoscopic sunset and comparing rides, their kites carefully gathered in and draped over the ends of their boards. They don't know each other and don't exchange names.

They do exchange compliments on the other's technique, however. Then they talk trade winds and currents and tomorrow's forecast. Their conversation drifts to favorite kiteboarding sites around the island, then on to headier subjects, which can happen when the scenery turns otherworldly. The Samoan does most of the talking. Ray Cooper does most of the listening. After some more rambling tales, Big Roi's wandering narrative returns to his inadvertent riding companion.

"Wyomin'? Das long way fo' here. Long long way."

"Yep."

Cooper is weathered, lanky, and thirty-one years old. He has blue-gray eyes and dusky brown hair streaked blond in places where the sun has touched it. At six-foot-four he is ten inches taller than Big Roi but out on the ocean the difference is slight.

"Not much water out dere."

Cooper chuckles. "Nope."

"But now ya ridin' here. Das cool."

Cooper nods agreeably, his eyes glued to the colors fanning out before them. Big Roi asks why a man from Wyoming would take up kiteboarding.

"My options dried up."

"Wot kinda options?"

"Horses. They're a little scarce around here." Cooper sweeps his arm over the water. "But wide-open plains, you got. Just needed a new ride."

Big Roi lets out an appreciative rumble of a laugh that reminds Cooper, a detective with the Honolulu police, of his Hawaiian-Samoan partner, Lou Palu. Physically, Roi is a compact version of Lou, who is a six-foot-one, two-hundred-and-eighty-pound fireplug.

"So ya choose kiteboardin'?"

"One road disappears best to look for another one."

Cooper began riding out into the Wyoming wilderness in his teens. First with friends and family, but gradually he preferred to go out alone. During his saddle time Cooper could settle into himself. Something would solidify inside of him. Then his backbone would firm and his chest expand. Over time, as he moved on from the family ranch near Jackson to take up the badge in Cheyenne, then Albuquerque, he would still ride. It gave him perspective. He came to understand that life was about options and the road you chose. If you chose the good side of the road and carried through, more of the good rolled in, with a few potholes along the way. There were always potholes. But you could navigate them. Choose the bad side and pretty soon you'd find more potholes than road. If you weren't careful, the path could disappear altogether. He never put his thoughts into words, but over the years the idea stayed with him.

Big Roi cocks his head at Cooper. "Sumtin' about ya famiyar, brah."

Cooper shrugs and turns back to the sunset.

Big Roi's dark eyes flare and he grunts. "Got ya. Ya one of da Inseprabuls."

Outed, Cooper simply nods, his face showing nothing.

Big Roi is talking about the local nickname for Cooper and his partner, Lou. The Inseparables. Coming from entirely different backgrounds but sharing the same outlook on the job, the two detectives became fast friends and a formidable team around the island. An odd couple. The cowboy and the Samoan. Even though Cooper didn't wear boots or a hat or belts with ridiculously large buckles, his birthplace and his mannerisms seemed to follow him around the island.

The locals noticed the pair *and* their aloha spirit, which when applied to the badge, translated as a firm manner coupled with a dose of understanding, Hawaiian style. Nothing slipped by the Inseparables but neither were they heavy handed.

"I hear ya *hapa*, too."

In Hawaii, the word originally meant anything half-Hawaiian combined with half of another element. It could refer to a song, a dance, a book, or a person. It is sometimes still used that way, but today it mostly describes a person who is half Asian, half Caucasian, with *Hawaiian* or *Polynesian* falling under the umbrella of *Asian*. In Cooper's case the word veers toward the classic meaning even if it isn't apparent from looking at him.

Cooper shoots the Samoan a squint-eyed look. "You hear a lot."

Big Roi lets out another rumble. "Dis small place, man."

In the deepening light of the evening, Cooper can't help but grin. There is no arguing with that. On Oahu everyone seems to know everyone else's business.

"Mother was Hawaiian from the Big Island," Cooper says.

Although he takes after his Wyoming-born-and-bred father, it is his mother Cooper misses. He lost her when he was fourteen, and when he'd looked in the mirror the day after the funeral he could find no sign of her. By the time he left the Cheyenne PD for the force in Albuquerque, he'd soaked up all he could of the Wyoming soul, and promised himself he would one day make it out to Hawaii, if only to recapture a part of what he'd lost.

Big Roi's violet-tinged eyes lock onto Cooper. "Das gud ting. Big Island gud place. Don't see much of her on da surface but maybe she deeper." He pounds his chest with the side of a fist. "Maybe dat why ya come Hawaii. Maybe dat why ya ridin'. Ya unnerstan wot we has here."

"Could be."

Big Roi starts in on a new narrative, this time about his reawakened love for his Hawaiian homeland. Cooper listens to the man's patter and watches the scenery evolve. Big Roi's low-pitched gurgle has a bouncing musical quality that lulls Cooper and blends well with the evening's final notes. Eventually there is this:

"Wen da world trow down on ya, gonna be like test, ya know?" Big Roi pokes his temple with a stubby index finger. "It all up here, brah. Ya choose how ya turn it ober in yor head. Ya unnerstand dat?"

"Believe I do."

Cooper has been on the island nine months and learned long ago that *brah* means *brother* and the guy is speaking Hawaiian pidgin, cleaned up for Cooper. Which is a good thing, because otherwise Big Roi might as well have been speaking Tahitian or Balinese or any other tropical language. Cooper is picking up pieces of the local creole as he goes along, but the pure form is a separate creature as far as he is concerned. What Cooper doesn't miss is that Big Roi continues to reach out with another *brah* even after he placed him with the police.

"I yusta fight a lot. Da feva get inside me like a virus an' take ovah."

Cooper has no trouble believing Big Roi has stirred up his share of trouble. Probably spent some time behind bars for his effort. By virtue of his size, Big Roi would have had to have been a natural-born rowdy to survive. The guy is a scaled down version of every other Samoan Cooper has run across, on island and off. He is a pint-size bottle to their gallon jug. From his earliest days, Big Roi would have been overshadowed and outmatched. He would have had to prove himself again and again. And clearly he did. Because regardless of size the man is no pushover.

Cooper also sees a stormy determination in Big Roi's curiously colored eyes. Which is echoed in the swirls of blue ink of his sleeve tattoo. It sweeps across the left side of the Samoan's bulked-up chest, crawls over his shoulder, then encircles the whole of his left arm to his wrist. The Tiki god inside the ring of shark's teeth glares with the same fixed determination. Big Roi's stunted size in youth forged the man before Cooper now.

But what kind of man? Cooper wonders. Big Roi is coming up on thirty, but the light in his eyes has run on ahead another decade or two.

"Dat da trooth, brah. I big fighta befo'. Den I cum back to aloha and *shaka*. Back to da old way. Wen I's youngah, I yus tink island way fo' fools. Now I see aloha hav big *pono*. Dat how we survive wot you guys done."

Pono is a Hawaiian concept of moral goodness. Cooper knows this and nods cryptically as he watches the last fiery sliver of the sun break into red-hot bars and sink from sight. He likes the bit about aloha and shaka. Unless you have been hibernating, you couldn't live on the island for longer than half a day before someone threw a shaka your way.

Shaka is the Hawaiian gesture with the three middle fingers folded over into a fist, leaving the thumb and pinky sticking out the sides. What kids visiting the island sometimes call "Mickey Mouse ears." Adults say something like "that wiggle-waggle thing they all do." California surfers hijacked it years ago for themselves to mean *hang loose* or *cool* or more recently, *awesome.*

Some of that has rubbed off on locals, but the gesture also carries cultural baggage, with layers of meaning.

For one, the aloha spirit is imbedded in a shaka. For another, the meaning depends on what is going on at the time. It could mean something as simple as *hello* or *thank you* or *have a good one*, or it might be a nod toward friendship or a shared understanding. At other times, it could signal a profound sense of gratitude or appreciation.

Cooper wants to accept Big Roi's story about dropping his hostile attitudes and embracing the traditional Hawaiian way. However, the sentiment about what Cooper and his "guys" are supposed to have done clashes with the Samoan's proclaimed conversion.

So Cooper pushes back with casual disregard, saying, "Us guys?"

"One way or anuddah I talking yor ancestor or long-ago relative, brah. All dat connected. Dot-dot-dot. Ya lucky we hav aloha spirit in our kingdom, udderwize *haole* bodies gonna be washin' up on da beach ebry time sun go up."

The corners of Cooper's mouth flicker with cold amusement at the mention of *kingdom* and *haole.* The first is about the American and European businessmen who wrestled the island from the Hawaiian monarchy in the 1890s. For that, Hawaiian's have his sympathy. The second is an *us* or *them* thing. Originally a neutral term, *haole* now means *outsider* at the best of times, or *white outsider* at the worst. Cooper has less patience for this.

"Good thing we're lucky, then," he says.

The luster in the Samoan's eyes seems to deepen. "Maybe I no say dat gud. It all okay now, brah. I find aloha again. No mo bad blood. I tink big pictha."

"That so?"

"Yeah. Big pictha mean makin' da *big* choice. Ya choose da light or ya choose da dark. Da dark gonna get ya nowhere but trouble."

Cooper sits up a little straighter on his board. He turns Big Roi's words over in his head. What he hears is an echo of his own clean-road-or-potholes mantra played back to him through a cultural filter.

Cooper says, "I got no argument with that. Ended up in the same place myself, only by a different route. Don't talk about it much, but I'd say you put words to the whole idea better than I ever could."

It's the most Cooper has said all night and the Samoan notices. His chest expands in the wake of Cooper's compliment. "I tink we sharin' da wavelength."

"Seems like it."

Big Roi nods, and without another word, the two men turn their full attention to the drama playing out in front of them. They look out across the water and take in the last of the twilight colors on the horizon. The light show dims and dies away. The sky shifts gradually from sapphire to navy to midnight blue. The stars sharpen to bright pinpoints.

This is the Hawaii Cooper has come for, although he hadn't known it until he'd found it during his first ride on the water.

He has a single question for Big Roi, and after the stars have established themselves he asks it: where'd Big Roi pick up his idea of dark and light? The Samoan mentions a local legend whose name Cooper has run across a half a dozen times in passing since his arrival in Honolulu.

"Really? Her?" Cooper's eyebrows underscore his skepticism.

Roi's nod is at once solemn and eager. "She got soul smarts like I nevah seen, brah. We all got our knowing, ya know? I got street smarts, fightin' smarts. Da woman, she whole uder smarts."

"She the reason you stopped fighting?"

"She *only* reason." Big Roi's gaze drifts toward the horizon. "I talk wid her straight up, man. One, two hour ebry day fo' five day. My talk-story strong, hard. Her talk-story deep an' soft like a pillow. Wot she sed break da feva in my head. Powerful mana. I get new unnerstandin an' come home. Ya know?"

Cooper thinks about the Samoan's walk from the fever to the light, then about his own road, which has had its share of twists and turns as well.

And he smiles.

Because he does know.

THE END

Barry Lancet's latest mystery-thriller is *The Spy Across the Table* (Simon & Schuster), the current installment of the award-winning Jim Brodie series. Lancet's first book is *Japantown*, which won the Barry Award for Best First Novel. The follow-up, *Tokyo Kill*, was a finalist for the Shamus Award. He has also been short-listed for the Macavity and the Derringer. Lancet is currently working on the next Brodie adventure as well as a standalone novel, and continues to split his time between Tokyo and California, travel conditions permitting. Website: https://barrylancet.com. Follow Barry on Facebook, Twitter, and Instagram.

THE 'R' WORD

Frank Zafiro

I'm going to use an 'R' word in this piece, but not the one you think. My mother teaches people with special needs, and my wife is also a teacher with her Special Education endorsement, so I'm very woke when it comes to *that* 'R' word.

It's not the other 'R' word, either—racism—which is a word we can say in this world but seem unable to eradicate.

No, this 'R' word is one that every human encounters. Each journey is unique, but the experience is, in some ways, universal. This is my journey. You tell me how universal it is.

A quick note for background. I was a cop for twenty years in a mid-sized city in the Pacific Northwest. I worked in patrol, investigations, and eventually leadership. That means I experienced the street, as well as internal *and* external politics. Was it the hardest job in the world? I can't say. I don't have the comparative experiences to truly judge, and there are a lot of hard jobs out there.

But I will say that law enforcement is a job with some significant, evolving challenges. I don't know many professions that require a skill-set of the same breadth and depth. A good cop has to be able to talk to a scared five year old, an adult caught in a cycle of violence, a senior citizen with dementia, a distraught victim, an angry citizen, a traffic violator who is experiencing their only interaction ever with the police, and, of course, a violent criminal—all with equal aplomb. She has to be able to successfully handle a domestic violence call, a school or community group talk, and a foot pursuit. Add to that having the ability to drive an emergency vehicle, write an effective report, know and apply the law, de-escalate physical confrontation, and handle it when it can't be de-escalated (and by that I mean successfully apply the correct amount of force that the situation requires, but without going over—the blue version of *The Price is Right*).

Many of these decisions have to be made in an instant, but will be second-guessed by people who have hours and days and years to examine them.

Throw in the resentment that police encounter in many quarters, and the resultant tribal closing of the ranks that occurs in response, and you get a career that is difficult, to say the least. I didn't even mention the frustration of seeing the same criminals get away with their crimes despite your best efforts, the kids you encounter who you can't do enough for to help them avoid their seeming fate, or the politicians who are more concerned with optics than true results.

Is it any wonder burnout is a very real thing?

It was for me. I did twenty years…and a day. For a variety of reasons, I pulled the pin after that day. Some of the reasons were immediate. I had a tyrant chief who was doing things I disagreed with, and once it was clear I wasn't on board as an axe-man for him, I got shuttled off to an admin position where I no longer had any opportunity to do good for the officers I led. But some of it was cumulative, too. When you work that many years, there are ghosts on every block, and around every corner.

It was time to go.

I only made it that far because of the 'R' word, anyway.

Can you empathize? Maybe your career or job was more demanding than mine, maybe less so, but everyone has dealt with something. Whether it was the work itself or a jerk co-worker/boss/client, you've had a tough go of it at some time in your life. You know.

All right, flash forward seven years to now (and stick with me—the dots will connect, I promise you).

Like many in this anthology, I've been writing for a long time. My first short story was published in 1990 in *Wide Open Magazine*. My first novel was published in 2006. That was my first River City novel, *Under a Raging Moon*. I drew on a lot of my own experiences for the color and flavor of that book and its sequels. Maybe even occasionally took a sliver from a real person or event. By the time I retired, I had written four books in the series, with number four published in 2011. That's four books in five years. And yet, despite prodding from readers, I didn't write another entry in the series for seven years.

Some of it had to do with the circumstances of leaving the job. River City was a thinly veiled version of where I worked. I had some emotional wounds when it came to how my career ended, and I already told you about the ghosts. So I didn't write River City for a long time. It was too much like the real thing, and I just couldn't be there. Some readers speculated that I'd quit on the series entirely.

When I finally picked up the fifth book again, I realized it wasn't the fifth book after all. There was a different story that had to happen first. So I set it aside and wrote that story instead. In 2018, I published that fifth book, *The Menace of the Years*. I meant to return to number-six-was-number-five pretty fast, but I ran into other issues.

Many of you out there may empathize with what those issue were. They don't apply just to writers.

I spent a large part of 2018 quietly and privately lamenting my writing career. It wasn't where I wanted it to be. I wasn't being widely read enough. The progression seemed incremental, if it was there at all. Worse yet, I saw certain others enjoy success whose work I thought was objectively no better or worse than my own. I wondered why luck hit for them and not me. I mean, I was prolific. I had good reviews. I made sure I had an author "presence" online. But the needle was barely moving.

I know I'm not the only one who experienced this. I had conversations with other writers that I'm close enough to have that kind of conversation with, and they shared my sentiment. They struggled with the same issues. The entire endeavor became a bit of a cost-benefit conundrum. Time and effort versus reward. The value of art for art's sake. All of that.

And so I almost quit.

I went as far as putting a sunset clause in place. I decided that I'd push hard until the end of 2020, and if I didn't like where I was at that point, I gave myself permission to step away.

Maybe for a while.

Maybe for good.

I wrote through all of 2019 with that mindset. I published books, hosted a podcast, went to conferences, blogged. I did everything I could think of to move the needle. No one was going to say that I sat around waiting for it to happen, that's for sure.

Along the way, I picked up the now-sixth River City novel— *Place of Wrath and Tears*—and got back to work. It was a struggle for a lot of reasons. The vestiges of those emotions that kept me away from River City for so long were still present, albeit less so. The book itself was sprawling, with so many characters and story threads that it became a beast to try to wrap my arms around. The premise itself was dark—a school shooting and its troubled aftermath. And as I was plinking away at this book, trying to overcome these technical and psychological obstacles, we got the beauty that is COVID-19.

I was at Left Coast Crime in San Diego when the enormity of the situation started to sink in. The cancellation of the conference after a single day, coupled with the scramble to get back home, was followed by the beginning of the still ongoing (as of this writing, at least) quarantine.

I didn't write at all for the first week of the quarantine. I did what a lot of you did—watched Netflix, played games, read, ate too much. But eventually I returned to the work-in-progress. And to my surprise, the words came. First in trickles, then in a flood. I kept at it. Even though I thought every word sucked (and there are those of you out there who know that feeling exactly), I kept at it. Then, sometime before tax day in the U.S., I finished the first draft.

I told no one, except my wife.

In the couple of days after finishing the draft, I was struck by this immense sadness. That's not my usual response to finishing a book. At worst, I might feel a little bittersweet. Usually I feel relief and excitement in equal measures. But this one made me feel sad.

I let it kick around in my head for a few days, unsure what to make of it. I knew some of it was a by-product of world events. This goddamn pandemic. My disgust at the politicization of it. A little anxiety concerning when or if things would ever return to normal.

Worrying about my parents, my kids, my grandkids. But some of it was the book, too.

Because I didn't know what it was about.

Oh, I knew the plot. That had been in place for a decade. A school shooting involving students. Misunderstandings and mistakes compound the tragedy. The police response comes under fire from the community afterward. Unfortunately not at all an unrealistic scenario.

Although River City features an ensemble cast of characters, one has emerged as the core of the series, at least for me. Officer Katie MacLeod is the tough but vulnerable patrol officer who started the series as "young" and is now a ten-year veteran. She's been through a lot in her career (or five books, however you want to see it). Spoiler alert, but she was unable to save an infant from a horrible death, got attacked in her own home by a sexual predator who she shot, and was in a massive gun fight and vehicle pursuit that resulted in multiple deaths. That doesn't count the other instances of fights, foot pursuits, or exchange of gunfire, getting sued for excessive force, nor that daily cumulative grind I described earlier when talking about my own career. A lifelong alcoholic of a mother is her only family, so there's little help there.

Thus, when she walks into that school on the day of the shooting, she's carrying baggage. And the events that play out in that school only add to that. Her actions are second-guessed, criticized, and pored over, all by people who weren't there. Of course, that's the job, and it needs to be that way, but it doesn't make it any easier.

She's not the only one carrying burdens in this book. Several characters have journeys that mirror Katie's but let's be clear—hers is probably the toughest.

It wears on her.

But she doesn't quit.

She struggles, she adapts, but she doesn't quit.

It was Katie who told me what this book was about. I should have seen it a mile away, but every writer out there knows the blindness that comes with being too close to your own work to see it clearly in the moment. A little distance usually helps, and it did in this case, but I'm giving Katie a lion's share of the credit.

The book is about the 'R' word.

Resilience.

Resilience is what they preach in law enforcement to try to save members from burnout, or at least delay and mitigate its impact. It's what I drew on to make it to my twenty. It's also what was flagging for me more recently with regard to my writing career.

I think it is what all of us are in need of in the face of this once-a-century pandemic.

It is said that we are all unique. Okay, I'll buy that. But our commonalities run just as deeply as our individuality. And every one of us has felt anxious, perhaps even hopeless at times in our life. Maybe you've had some kind of artistic or creative angst along the lines of what I've described, for example.

Most often, we experience this alone or in small groups. Think of someone getting cancer, for instance. It affects the patient, and those close to him, but the circle is limited, at least compared to what we're faced with now. Literally *everyone* is impacted by COVID-19.

This bastard is worldwide.

And so we find our collective selves all in need of resilience in the same moment.

I found mine thanks to a fictional character that has been in my life since 1995. She's tougher than I am. She's been through far worse than me, and she hasn't quit yet. Some of the people around her have, but she hasn't. And she won't.

So you know what? I won't, either. The self-indulgent despair that led me to put an expiration date on my writing career is gone. I'll be writing and working and struggling in 2021, believe me. I can't give up—there are too many stories still to discover.

I drew on Katie for resilience. It's weird, yeah, but it's true. But along with her example, I'm reminded of the Rocky movies (the first and last, anyway) when it comes to never quitting. It's about getting hit and keeping on. Or like the tattoo a fellow cop I met had stamped on his forearm in bold lettering—*Get knocked down seven times, get up eight*.

The point is, there's inspiration everywhere. I've pulled it from different places at different times in my life. Most recently, from the book I struggled with far more than every other book I've written put together.

That's my journey. In the midst of personal struggle and being part of our collective struggle at the same time, I found my resilience.

You'll find yours.

I know you will.

THE END

Frank Zafiro was a police officer from 1993 to 2013, holding many different positions and ranks. He retired as a captain. Frank is the author of over thirty novels, most of them crime fiction, including the River City series (procedurals), Stefan Kopriva mysteries (private eye), SpoCompton novels (anti-hero), the Charlie-316 series with Colin Conway (procedurals), the Ania series with Jim Wilsky (hard boiled), and the Bricks and Cam Job series with Eric Beetner (hard boiled/dark humor). He has also collaborated with Lawrence Kelter (*The Last Collar, Fallen City*) and Bonnie Paulson (*The Trade Off*). In addition to writing, Frank hosts the crime fiction podcast *Wrong Place, Write Crime*. He is an avid hockey fan and a tortured guitarist. He currently lives in Redmond, Oregon. <u>Sign up for my newsletter</u>! For more information on Frank Zafiro, visit his website: http://www.frankzafiro.com

SAINT NICHOLAS

Bruce Robert Coffin

Author's Note: *Several years ago I penned a short story titled Saint Nicholas to remind us all what is truly important, and to provide an emotional lift to those in need. Given the current state of the world, I can't imagine a time when the need for positivity could be greater. If I've done my job well, my story will put a smile on your face and some warmth in your hearts.*

I've always believed that it's part of the human condition to focus on the negative. Maybe it has something to do with our upbringing, although upon reflection we are all raised very differently, so perhaps not. Whatever it is, it definitely exists in each of us. How else can we explain the age-old news reporting axiom "if it bleeds it leads?" Police officers are even more inclined to focus on the negative. Being exposed to it day in and day out tends to make one jaded. But, I'm getting ahead of myself. I should probably begin by telling you a little bit about me before I tell you my story.

My name is Crispin Mallory and, if you haven't guessed already, I am a police officer. I've been with the same department for three decades, pushing a cruiser around, investigating motor vehicle accidents, breaking up domestics, chasing down criminals, and writing the occasional traffic citation.

One day, several years back, I was working a double shift. Cops aren't paid that well so when an overtime opportunity presents itself most of us are quick to say yes. It was December twenty-fourth and I had just finished my first tour. I'd returned to the station to attend roll call before heading back out for another eight hours. I was tired and not in a particularly festive mood, mostly due to the fact that I had to work on Christmas, which meant my wife and two children would be celebrating without me. Another holiday missed. Such is the life of a cop. Anyway, the sergeant held me back after the briefing, said he had a task for me. I was instructed to return some valuables to a local home for the aged. Apparently one of the nursing staff had confessed to stealing jewelry from some of the residents at the home, to support her drug habit. See what I mean? All negative. The sergeant provided me with the name of the medical administrator and asked me to deliver the items to him.

After checking out a squad car and loading my gear, I got on the radio and requested that the dispatcher show me 10-6 (busy) on assignment. I drove toward the nursing home, stopping long enough to grab a drive-thru coffee along the way.

I parked in the lot and made my way inside. The receptionist was speaking with one of the orderlies and they both turned as I entered.

"Hello, officer," the receptionist said. "Merry Christmas."

I returned the greeting.

"What can I do for you?" she asked.

"I'm looking for Mr. Ashby," I said. "I'm supposed to deliver something to him."

"I'll try his extension."

I wandered around the lobby as she attempted to locate Ashby. Everything was brightly colored and decorated for the season. In one corner stood a small, lit Christmas tree from which emanated the pleasing scent of balsam. I wondered if the employees were still allowed to call it a Christmas tree.

"Officer," the receptionist called out.

"Yes."

"Mr. Ashby will be right out."

I thanked her and continued to look around. Ashby walked up to me and introduced himself as the facility's head administrator. I explained my purpose for being there, and he led me back to his office so we could talk in private.

Once we were seated, I handed him the package and an evidence slip explaining that he needed to sign for the items.

"I am so pleased that your detectives were able to recover so many of the things that our former employee took. I'm sure you can imagine how much these items mean to the residents here. Some of these pieces of jewelry aren't all that valuable, but they represent gifts from and memories of loved ones. As I'm sure you know, some things are worth far more than money."

I agreed. After going through each of the items he signed for them and returned the evidence sheet to me. As I stood, preparing to leave, he stopped me.

"I don't suppose you'd be willing to do me one small favor, would you, officer?"

I wondered why I would need to do another favor. After all, I'd just returned a number of stolen items. Shouldn't that have been sufficient?

"I really do need to get back on the road, Mr. Ashby," I said.

"You're right. I shouldn't impose. You've got places to go I imagine."

Now verbally he was letting me off the hook, but his tone and facial expression told another story. I knew he was attempting reverse psychology on me. Something my wife and I did to our kids daily.

"What do you need?" I asked.

"It'll only take a second. I promise. But it will mean so much to her."

Ashby proceeded to tell me about an eighty-one-year-old patient named Ruth Perkins. Mrs. Perkins was suffering from Alzheimer's.

"She's all alone now," Ashby said. "Her husband passed last year. They had one son, Nicholas, and he was a police officer. Nicholas was killed during a shootout many years ago. Apparently, he would visit her every Christmas, whether he was working or not, and it meant the world to her. Her Alzheimer's is advanced but she still manages to put several good days together each month. I have no idea how she does it, but she does."

I sat down again as he continued.

"Every month since the death of her husband, just prior to the twenty-fifth, she gets it into her head that Christmas is approaching. She gets so excited and makes a point to tell all of the staff that her son is coming to visit. She even has a lighted ceramic tree that she makes us put up in her room. Of course when the twenty-fifth passes and Nicholas doesn't show up her condition quickly worsens and she reverts back to her former state. It really is quite sad."

"What do you want me to do?" I asked. "I'm not her son."

"I know that, but I thought it might cheer her up to get a visit from an officer in uniform. If you could just stop by and wish her a merry Christmas."

I only wanted to get back to my comfort zone. Back to my cruiser.

I really wasn't enjoying the idea of popping in on an already confused old woman, possibly making her situation worse. But Ashby's attempt at manipulation must have worked because I found myself saying okay.

He said he'd introduce me, then led me down the hall to her room. I followed, amid the stares and whispers of the other residents. Each of them probably wondering what the cop was doing there. At last he stopped and entered a room. The sign on the door said R. Perkins. A white ceramic tree with lit colored bulbs stood on a table beneath a window. As I rounded the corner I saw her sitting up in bed, wearing a festive green robe over a red sweater. She wore makeup and it looked like she had even paid a visit to the hairdresser. She looked dignified and radiant, like someone waiting to be called upon, not at all what I had expected.

"Mrs. Perkins," Ashby said. "I've brought you a visitor."

She turned toward me and her blue eyes lit up. "Nicholas," she cried out. "My Saint Nicholas, I knew you'd come. Didn't I say he would come? Oh, this is the best Christmas ever."

She held her arms out to me as I approached the bed. Awkwardly, I bent down toward her. She hugged me tightly, even kissed me on the cheek.

"Merry Christmas," I said, feeling myself blush.

"I should leave the two of you alone now," Ashby said, as he left.

I sat down in the chair beside the bed and she began asking me all sorts of questions. I was afraid that I might say the wrong thing, but as time passed it became obvious that nothing I said would lessen her faith that I was her son. We talked for close to an hour. I told her all about my family and about my work. She asked if I remembered this thing or that and of course I told her I did. The smile never left her face.

I stayed with her until she began to tire. The excitement had worn her out. She hugged me again and made me promise to return the following day. Christmas Day. I promised that I would and kissed her on the cheek. I returned to my cruiser and radioed that I was back in service. My heart was full and I was happier than I'd been in a long while. It was clear that my visit to Ruth Perkins had had a positive effect on both of us. I no longer cared that I'd be missing this Christmas with my own family. Don't get me wrong, I still wanted to be with them, but after visiting a lonely old woman I realized I had no right to complain. There would be other Christmases to spend with my family. Mrs. Perkins' family was gone, leaving her with only memories.

I returned to work the following day. Christmas turned out to be busier than any of us had imagined. A light snowfall had left the roads slick, resulting in many accidents. The calls for service were already piling up by the time I hit the street.

It was nearly one o'clock in the afternoon before I was finally able to take a lunch break. I grabbed a sandwich and a couple of eggnogs at the local market before heading over to see Mrs. Perkins. I was excited about being able to keep my promise and looking forward to seeing her face light up at the sight of me.

I parked in the nearly vacant lot and headed inside. The receptionist was a different girl than the one I'd spoken to the previous day. Holiday help I assumed. She asked if she could help me and I politely declined. "Thank you but I'm all set. Just visiting someone."

I walked down the corridor to her room, stopping as I reached her door. The room was empty. Her personal belongings were gone and the nameplate was missing from the door. I felt like someone had knocked the wind out of me.

"Can I help you, officer?" a soft feminine voice asked from behind me.

I turned and saw a young orderly. "I'm looking for Mrs. Perkins. Ruth Perkins. Has she been moved?"

"Are you a relative?"

I pondered her question before answering. "Sort of. I just visited her yesterday."

"I'm sorry to have to tell you this. Mrs. Perkins passed away last night."

✳✳✳

Many years have passed since that Christmas. I'm still a police officer with the same department. I've been a cop so long now that I get every holiday off. But I've never forgotten Ruth Perkins or her gift to me. Oh, I know what you're thinking. That it was I who gave her one last visit with her son. But I think of it a little differently. I believe Mrs. Perkins is the one who bestowed upon me a great gift. She restored my faith in humanity, helped me appreciate what I have. Her belief that I was her son was so strong and so real that I couldn't help but feel the same love for her in return. Her faith changed me forever. And isn't that what Christmas is all about?

THE END

Bruce Robert Coffin is the award-winning author of the Detective Byron mystery series and former detective sergeant with more than twenty-seven years in law enforcement. At the time of his retirement, from the Portland, Maine police department, he supervised all homicide and violent crime investigations for Maine's largest city. Following the terror attacks of September 11th, Bruce spent four years working counter-terrorism with the FBI, earning the Director's Award, the highest honor a non-agent can receive. Winner of Killer Nashville's Silver Falchion Award for Best Procedural, Bruce's novel, *Beyond the Truth*, was also a finalist for the Agatha Award for Best Contemporary Novel, and a finalist for the Maine Literary Award for Best Crime Fiction Novel. Learn more about Bruce on his website http://www.brucerobertcoffin.com

Where Blue Birds Fly

Julie Bates

Blinking lights from the ambulance illuminated the dark street. Dark clouds rumbled overhead, warning of an ugly night. Normally, this side of town glowed from the neon of the neighborhood bars and late night restaurants: COVID-19 ended that. Everything had shut down. Nothing slowed the calls that Garland and his partner Sally went on. Ballooning requests for help left them exhausted. He stared out at the foreboding clouds. "No rainbows there," he muttered. Rapping on the window jolted Garland out of his reverie.

"Wake up sunshine, there's no one here." Sally went around and climbed back in the passenger seat. They were about the same age, but she had been an EMT far longer than he had. She looked over at him, her eyes shrewd beneath her sturdy black glasses. She glanced over at him. "Tough time for you to come on board."

Garland shrugged. He didn't need sympathy. An injury ended his college football dreams and his scholarship—all he had left was the grind of the real world. Garland knew that some people had it worse. But it was hard to find much to look forward to. Once he had dreamed of a pro career, but now he struggled to help his mom with bills. There was just him, his mom, and his little brother Calvin—and not nearly enough money. A pro career would have changed everything.

As he stared at the dark exterior of the Pot O' Gold tavern, the neon rainbow glittered before dissipating into the night. "What the hell?"

"What's up with you?" Sally asked. She laughed when he told her. "It's probably a trick of the light, but if you want to check for a pot of gold, be my guest. This was a speakeasy back in the day. The owner was an Irishman named Lucky O'Dool. He died during a raid. He swore only a deserving soul would find his gold. Maybe you will find it." She snickered.

"Just forget it," Garland snapped as he put the ambulance in gear, backing up to pull out of the narrow parking space. A brilliant flash lit up the sky as the deep bass of thunder reverberated off the old bricks of the bar.

Something darted out behind the ambulance. Garland slammed on the brakes, his heart pounding as he heard a telltale thud. Putting the vehicle in park, Garland and Sally leapt out, each pulling up their masks in what had become a habit since the pandemic had taken hold.

An enormous blue parrot lay halfway under the back bumper. Sally set her medical kit down beside her and took out a slender flashlight she always kept nearby. "Is it dead?"

The bird started moving its wings and legs like an upended insect. Garland didn't see blood, but it was hard to tell given the poor lighting. "Who do you think it belongs to?"

"Who knows," Sally said. "The animal shelter is closed this late."

"Curses," the bird muttered. "Find the gold, find the gold."

Garland's eyes met Sally's. They had dealt with all kinds of situation in their three weeks together. This was their first bird. She shook her head and turned to the bird. She gently rolled him over and started checking for injuries. An impressive beak nipped her gloved hand. "Geez!" she recoiled shaking her had. "That hurts!"

"Not for you, not for you." The bird rose into the air and circled

Garland. "Pretty boy, pretty boy, there's no place like home." He rose and flew into the night, a bright blue blur that disappeared into the darkness.

He looked over at Sally. "You okay?"

"I think so. It was a nip. Stupid bird. It will probably get hit by a car."

"Should we report it?'

"Leave a message for animal control. Let them try to catch it." She hopped back into the passenger seat, digging out the first aid kit they kept up front.

Garland paused before joining her; the air felt charged as if lightning were about to strike. Hair rose on his neck as an unexplained shiver went down his back. He paused to look around sensing danger. The sky rumbled moodily off in the distance sending a restless wind that scattered trash and leaves over the road. He jumped as a noise like the rustle of wings sounded overhead.

"Dang it!" Something smacked him on the head before falling to the ground. Looking down, he spotted three large coins. "What the . . .?" Garland muttered as he reached over to scoop them up. All he wanted was to finish his shift, grab a cold beer, and watch the next episode of *Tiger King*. He didn't need anything else on his plate.

Sally was amused. "They look like casino tokens. Planning a trip to Vegas?"

"Hell, no," he snapped as he got in, shutting the door behind. "Only fools believe they're going to strike it rich. There's no gold at the end of the rainbow, just another mud hole to fall into."

She eyed him thoughtfully. "Just a touch cynical, don't you think?"

He shrugged. "I'm done dreaming. That leads to disappointment." Garland started the motor and moved back onto the road.

Sally stared at him. "Well Bud, sometimes that yellow brick road really does go somewhere."

"If you say so." He focused on the road as the rain came pelting down.

They finished their shift with little incident. They suited up in hazmat suits when they faced coronavirus patients, swaddling in protective gear that was hot but helped kept them safe. He eyed his partner as they got ready to go home for twelve hours sleep before coming back for another twelve-hour shift. Sally looked worn out.

"Everything okay?"

She shrugged. "Headache. It's probably all the pollen in the air. I'll be fine after I get a shower and some sleep." She picked up her purse. "See you in 12 hours."

Dawn streaked the sky with rosy pink fingers. He watched as Sally got into her bulky minivan, racing home to her husband and their 8-year-old twins. No one waited up for Garland. His mom and little brother were long since in bed. He stopped at the washing machine, stripped down to his boxers, dropped everything else inside, added soap, and started the load. Ebony the cat greeted him at the garage door with a twitch of her elegant tail.

"What are you looking at?" He said as he passed her on his way to the shower. Twenty minutes later, soaped, rinsed and repeated, he stepped out, dried off and threw on an old t-shirt and boxers. After sliding a frozen pizza into the oven, he went to change his uniform over to the dryer. Something clinked as he shoved his damp clothes over to tumble dry. As he leaned over to look in the washer, he spotted three large gold coins. He placed them on the table, using the dining room light to examine them. His grandad loved old coins and Garland had helped the old man sort them, so he recognized the design.

"Double eagles," He breathed. "Where did these come from?" Garland stared at them until the timer on his pizza went off. Exhausted from the night, he downed his food while his mind swirled with possibilities. They had to belong to someone. Maybe there would be a reward. Garland stacked his plate and dragged himself to bed. His dreams featured the harsh cawing of a parrot as its claws dropped handfuls of gold coins down on him. Each one streaked with blood. He awoke before dawn drowned in sweat. Giving up, he rose, put his uniform back on, and went downstairs. His mom was up early and in the kitchen. Her hours had been cut in half a month ago.

"Here," she said. "I made waffles, eat up."

Garland carefully took two. With one and a half incomes, they had to watch the groceries.

Sally met him at the ambulance. She didn't look like she had slept well either. Dark shadows wreathed her eyes and her skin looked paler than usual. "He died." Her voice was flat.

"Who died?" Garland asked.

"The guy we hauled in late last night. He didn't last the night. Nobody even knows his name. All they found in his pockets was a pack of nabs."

"What did he die of?" From the look on her face, he knew he didn't want the answer.

"Complications from COVID-19. We're both going home to quarantine for fourteen days." Sally moaned. "I don't have time for this. We're needed here."

"Not if we caught it," Garland looked at her. "Didn't you just refinish your basement? Now you can hang out there for the next fourteen days." He wasn't sure what he was going to do. He hoped his sick leave would cover the bills.

The house looked quiet as he pulled in. He saw his mom's SUV on one side of the carport. There was just enough room for his compact to slide in beside it. She should be at work right now. He hoped Cal wasn't sick. He was just barely old enough to be home alone for any length of time. A chill went down his back when he considered all a 13-year-old could get into. He walked in a little more quickly than usual.

His mom was on the couch. He could hear the sound of a video game in Cal's room. "Hey," he said as he entered the living room. "You're home early."

She straightened at the sound of his voice, wiping at her eyes. "I lost my job."

"But they were supposed to bring you back up to full time when things got better," Garland started.

She shook her head. "It doesn't matter. There's no money coming in, so they're closing for good." She looked at Garland, realization hitting her. "Why are you home?"

"Quarantine. I'll go back in fourteen days. Until then, I will live in the basement. No worries." He went to grab a soda from the fridge. "How's Cal?"

"Fine," she said. "He's playing video games in his room. He finished his online school a few minutes ago."

"Okay," Garland said. "I'm going to pack up some stuff and move down in the basement for the next two weeks."

She nodded. "Good idea."

The basement wasn't too bad. It had been his dad's retreat. No one had really used it much since he died in a traffic accident five years ago. It would work as a separate living space just fine. Garland changed into his favorite sweats and red high tops before settling on the couch with his laptop. Beside him was a duffle full of his clothes and toiletries. With nothing better to do, he decided to investigate the history of the old speakeasy downtown.

Knowledge was scanty at best. The Pot O'Gold had been a speakeasy during prohibition and a bar afterwards. It's owner, one Lawrence "Lucky" O'Dool, had owned it from whenever it had opened in the 1920's until his death during a raid in 1932, after which the tavern had been sold to various parties through the years. No mention of a hidden fortune, so he was sure Sally had been having fun at his expense.

He clicked on a series of photos of the bar. His heart stopped at a large portrait of O'Dool with a gigantic blue parrot on his shoulder. According to the caption, it was O'Dool's. The macaw was named Jolly Roger. Garland took a deep breath. It was a coincidence. It had to be. Nonetheless, his hands shook a little as he clicked down to the paragraph below.

"O'Dool's will stated that his fortune would belong to his avian companion to do with as he willed. The bird and the fortune were never found after O'Dool's unfortunate demise at the hand of federal agents.

Garland sat back on the couch. Carefully, he took out the coins. They were the right age for a depression era stash. It couldn't be the same bird, could it? He didn't believe in ghosts—much less ghost birds—and there hadn't been anything ethereal about its bite. Still, there had to be some explanation for why three rare valuable coins had rained down on him.

It was driving him crazy. With nothing but time on his hands, Garland found himself obsessing. Finally, he shoved the coins into the pocket of his jeans, grabbed a flashlight, his newly emptied duffle, and his pocketknife. As a final measure, he grabbed a bandana and a set of nitrile gloves before heading upstairs. Thankfully, both his mom and his brother were in the backyard. He got in his car and headed for the old bar before his common sense took over.

The Pot O'Gold was deserted as he pulled into the alley behind it. Garland paused as he got out and looked around. No more gold coins littered the ground. He shook his head. "This is nuts," he muttered to himself as he pulled the bandana over the lower part of his face. No matter what else he did, he was not risking getting anyone else sick.

"'Bout time," a voice said as something pinged off his head.

Garland ducked as another object struck his ear before tumbling to the ground. Two more coins lay by his shoe. He looked up to see a bright blue bird perched on the gutter.

"Jolly Roger?" He whispered. His day couldn't get any crazier, could it?

"Follow, follow, follow," the bird squawked before taking off behind the building and into the weedy lot.

"You devil, get back here!" Garland yelled as he leapt in a vain attempt to capture the parrot. His bad knee folded as he came down, leaving him on all fours in gravel. He looked up frantically. A flash of cerulean led him down the steps to the basement of the old building.

The large macaw flew through an opening in the broken door and into the darkness. It took a minute to pull enough broken boards aside to get in. Outside, Garland heard the muted sounds of a siren and hoped the cops hadn't been called. The sound faded and he signed with relief. Another coin hit his nose.

"Ouch. Take it easy bird. I'm coming." He stumbled through the derelict underbelly of the bar. Faint light glimmered in from a cracked window, which was good since his flashlight was still in the car. The bird led him on a noisy chase dodging in and out with the skill of an acrobat. Garland was about to give up when the bird paused by another open window. The bird squawked in malicious triumph before barreling outside. It took Garland a few minutes to find his way out, as he considered how to kill a certain obnoxious macaw. The sky was misting rain, leaving the ground treacherously slippery, and the sky gray. Garland raced out the door only to hydroplane over the grass and into a bush. Swearing, he rolled over on all fours before hauling himself upright. The bird was nowhere in sight.

It would be full dark soon. Garland looked around, trying to gain his bearings. Just then, a narrow finger of light split through the clouds illuminating the shadowed yard and revealing a small mass of bright blue in the limbs of a sapling that had fallen over and was almost entirely uprooted from the ground. As Garland ran forward, the bright lines of a rainbow shimmered into view ending at the base of the tree.

An old root caught his foot, heaving him to the base of the tree. As he lifted himself up, a gold coin slid down the trunk and bounded off his nose before continuing its journey. Garland's eyes followed it down into the ground.

"No way," Garland breathed. In the hole left by the tree, gold coins cascaded down into a black pot at this feet. As the last one dropped, he looked at the macaw. "Who are you?" he asked.

"Lucky's boy, Lucky's boy. To the victor goes the spoils," the bird replied before taking off into the mist. It may have been a trick of the light, but the bird seemed to fade away rather than vanish in the distance.

Garland reached down and gently pulled up the old black pot. It was in good shape for being buried under a tree. The rainbow slowly faded from sight. His gaze returned to the pot of gold. "Thank you," he called as he unlocked his car. It could have been a trick of the light, but Garland swore the rainbow glimmered one more time as he left for home.

THE END

Julie Bates grew up reading a little bit of everything, but when she discovered Agatha Christie, she knew she what she wanted to write. Along the way, she has written a weekly column for the *Asheboro Courier Tribune* and published several articles in magazines such as *Spin Off* and *Carolina Country*. She has blogged for Killer Nashville and the educational website Read.Learn.Write. She currently works as a public school teacher for special needs students. She is a member of Mystery Writers of America, Southeastern Writers of America (SEMWA) and her local writing group, Piedmont Authors Network (PAN). When not busy plotting her next story, she enjoys doing crafts and spending time with her husband and son, as well as a number of dogs and cats who have shown up on her doorstep and never left. *Writers Crushing Covid-19* is her anthology debut. https://juliebates.weebly.com/

A World Gone Mad

Introducing
Vice Booji – The Bengal Tiger

Lawrence Kelter

The new Superheroes Building rose toward the heavens, a glistening testament to truth, justice, and futuristic architecture. It was constructed entirely of an immutable vibranium-adamantium alloy with transparent Inertron one-way windows capable of withstanding impact from a supersonic missile traveling at over twenty-three hundred miles per hour. From the ground up to the tip of the two hundred story bullet, the skin was unvarying, a coating of super ceramic material impervious to all forms of technological intrusion.

Superman and Thor shared the highest floor. Captain America and Batman occupied the floor below. Hulk and Aquaman, Scarlet Witch and Wonder Woman, Spider-Man and Black Panther, and so on, floor-by-floor, superheroes from every galaxy working and living together, united in the commitment to protect the inhabitants of the universe.

The subbasement, however, that was another story entirely. One story below Deadpool's basement studio resided the least known of all the superheroes, a man who wore his anonymity as if it were a second skin. There amongst the mole rats and hagfish was the refuge of Vice Booji, the bravest superhero of them all.

Water dripping from his hair, Vice Booji stepped from his third shower of the day and toweled off. He was in slacks and a clean shirt when he walked into his office and sat down to put on his socks.

"Another huge hole in my sock, Ma." He balled up the black Ban-Lon sock and tossed it into a hamper already overflowing with laundry."

"What do you expect, Viceroy, four, five showers a day—they're not made out of iron, you know."

"Don't remind me, Ma. This is the bane of my existence. Captain America gets super strength, Flash is superfast, and me . . . my most notable superpower is excessive sweating."

"Nothing to be ashamed of, Viceroy. Hyperhidrosis is a common medical condition—millions have it."

"Is that so? Can you name another superhero in the building with the same issue?

"No, and that's part of what makes you so unique." She walked over and pulled the sock off the pile of dirty laundry. "I'll mend it for you while you eat your lunch. We can't keep buying new ones, you know. We're not minting rupees down here."

"I knew I smelled something delicious." He sniffed the air and his cheekbones rose dramatically. "What did you make, ilish macher jhol? I love the tingly flavor it leaves in my mouth."

"No such luck, Viceroy, our groceries budget is almost gone."

"So, what then did you make?"

"Doi fulkopi."

He wrinkled his nose. "The cauliflower gives me gas. Can you imagine the look on a victim's face? A villain is about to bludgeon them to death when I burst in to save the day, sweaty and farting like a pig. 'No thanks, I'll take my chances with the hooligan.' It's very embarrassing, I tell you. Very, very embarrassing."

"What can I tell you, fish is expensive—cauliflower is cheap."

"Fish is brain food."

"Hasn't helped you so far." She blew him a kiss. "Just having some fun with you, Viceroy. The oil is hot. I'll fry some fresh luchi to go with it."

He smiled and moved to the mirror to comb his wet hair. "There's nothing like fresh bread." He turned toward the door as Tony Boba narrowly squeezed through it.

Boba closed the door and cringed. "Come on, Vice. Man, go take a shower."

"He just did," Krisha Booji said.

"He's sweating like a pig."

"He's still wet from the shower."

"Then what stinks?"

"You're just in time for lunch," Vice said.

Boba pinched his nostrils. "Pass."

"Who are you kidding? When was the last time you passed up a free meal? Or any meal for that matter?"

Boba let the question hang in the air alongside the aroma. "Wh-what are you having?"

"Doi fulkopi," she said with a singsong lilt in her voice. "An old family recipe." She used a soupspoon to scoop some of the stew from the kettle and approached Boba holding the spoon at full arm extension to reach his mouth.

He recoiled. "But the *smell*."

"You'll get used to it. To Viceroy and me . . . the aroma is sheer heaven. Now open your mouth you sissy superhero sidekick."

"I'm not a sidekick. I'm a full-fledged superhero."

"Of course you are, and Thor has trouble meeting women. Now, open your mouth."

His eyes were closed as he savored the exotic concoction.

"Good, isn't it?"

He nodded, acquiescing reluctantly.

"But the smell."

"Nonsense. It will put hair on your chest."

"Heaven forbid," Vice said. "Have you seen Boba without his shirt? He needs more wool like I need heavyweight long johns."

The two superheroes sat down over large bowls of stew while bread sizzled on the stovetop.

"This is frustrating. I can't mend this sock. The hole is too big," Krisha said. "Boba, how often do you change your socks?"

He held up his pointer finger.

"Once? There, you see, Viceroy, once a day is all you should be changing them."

Boba cleared his throat. "That's . . . once per week."

Her eyes opened wide. "Really, you change your socks just once a week?"

Vice snickered. "Don't ask about his Calvin Kleins."

"Never mind. He makes my point for me, Viceroy. At this rate we simply can't afford to keep you in hosiery."

"I wish you wouldn't bug me about this, Ma. You know, Jerry Lewis used to throw away a pair of socks every day."

"No, I didn't know that but what I *do* know is that Jerry Lewis was a multimillionaire when gas was thirty-cents a gallon and you could buy two houses for the price of a current model Honda. The hero business is all very well and good, my son, but it pays *shit*."

Vice studied his mother with a solemn face. "You know I don't do this for the money."

"This you have proven beyond a shadow of doubt."

"Mother!"

"I understand this is your calling, but if you want to save lives, you have to do it on a shoestring budget or get a medical degree like your nine brothers."

"Please, don't throw that in my face. They're all podiatrists. Anyone can do that."

"It's true, Mrs. Booji," Boba said. "All you need is a nail clipper and a jug of lotion."

"Not Viceroy with all the holes in his socks. What patient in their right mind would have confidence in a doctor like that? And those bunions . . ." She touched the statuette of Vishnu that sat on the table, then her heart, and finally her head. "Where did you get such terrible feet? Your father, bless his soul, had such beautiful feet. Like doves, they were so soft and smooth."

"Dad's feet didn't resemble doves in any way, shape, or form, and certainly not in color. Now, if you had said crows . . ."

"Any chance you got a frozen pizza in the fridge? I don't think this here cauliflower is gonna sit right."

She waved her hand dismissively and stood to fetch the hot breads. "You'll love it, Boba. Trust me."

The Tiger Phone flashed once. Vice grabbed the receiver. "Yes?"

"It's Commissioner Gordon. Where's Batman?"

"Oh, hi, Commissioner. It's Vice Booji. You must've reversed the last two numbers again. He's three-seven. I'm seven-three. Happens all the time."

"Guess I'm getting old. It didn't sound like the Caped Crusader, but I thought I recognized that Bengali dialect. How are you, Vice?"

"COVID-19 or not, crime never takes a holiday. Tony and I are busier than one-armed paperhangers. Something going down?"

"Just got word there's a human trafficking auction taking place and half my department is home sick or in quarantine. Think you can handle it?"

"Oh, that is *so* up my alley. That is if you don't think Batman would feel slighted."

"Don't sweat it . . . I mean he's not the sensitive type. I'll shoot you the address."

"I'm on it. Thanks!"

Krisha glared at him. "Viceroy Booji, why must you always overdo? Superhero HQ is on lockdown. The COVID-19 virus is everywhere. Even Hulk is practicing social distancing."

"Mother, did you hear Commissioner Gordon? A human trafficking auction is under way. How can I sit still while that's going on?"

Vice had been embroiled in several trafficking crimes before. *And now*, he thought, *when average citizens are afraid to have contact with their dear friends and family. . .* He found the very nature of the crime abhorrent.

"True, this trafficking business is disgusting. The very thought of forced physical contact under any circumstance . . . but Gordon was looking for the Batman. Let him take the call. He's covered head to toe in Kevlar and aramid fiber. He's better protected than a little Indian boy in a trench coat and wingtips."

"No."

"Then wear a mask. You too, Tony—better safe than sorry."

"Of course we'll wear masks," Tony said. "Think I got a death wish or something?"

"Gloves too."

"Yes, *Ma*, don't worry."

"Then go, before I lose my mind from worry. I'll keep lunch warm for the two of you."

"Can I grab some of those hot breads for the road?" Tony asked.

She used a round mesh skimmer to fish the fried luchi out of the bubbling oil and dumped them into a brown paper bag. "Now, *go*. And mind your Ps and Qs."

✳✳✳

They bumped into Thor just outside Superhero Headquarters. He was casually whipping his hammer, clearing the sky of clouds. "Vice, Boba, where are you lads off to? This isn't the first time I caught you breaking quarantine."

"Crosstown," Vice began, "Human trafficking auction going down."

"Need some help? It'll take more than a pair of compromised lungs to keep the son of Odin out of a fracas. I'd *love* in on a good melee."

"I think we can handle it," Vice said, "but time is of the essence and we could use a lift."

Thor sized up the bulky Italian superhero. "One hand for the hammer and one for Vice—Boba, my friend, I'm afraid you'll have to bring up the rear."

"No problem," he said as he popped a bun in his mouth as if it were a Tic Tac. "I'll hustle down to the garage and grab the car." He hurried off, the thuds of his heavy footsteps echoing in the distance.

"Then we're off," Thor said as he grabbed Vice and whipped Mjölnir faster and faster until the velocity of the magical hammer yanked them skyward.

***

Thor set Vice down on the pavement. "Sure you don't need help? I've always got time to crack a few heads."

"I'll take it from here, Thunder God."

"Probably best—we treat enslavers harshly in Asgard. We banish them to the troll wilderness."

"Aren't those adorable little creatures with fuzzy hair?"

"You speak of toys, Vice. No, trolls are colossal man-eating ogres, great big vile-looking things capable of stripping a fully grown man to the bone in one disgusting gulp."

"Magic hammers *and* trolls—man, you deities really have it all, don't you? Though the punishment seems commensurate with the crime I think I'll turn these slave traders over to Commissioner Gordon . . . *after* I lay a little Bengali hurt on them. Know what I mean?"

"Very well. Then I'm off on a beer run. Can I bring anything back for you?"

"No thanks."

Are you sure? The bakery next door to the minimart makes killer chomchom." He waved his hand. "Never mind. I'll get enough for everyone." With an abrupt whirl of the hammer he flew off skyward.

As the Thunder God vanished from view a bloodcurdling shriek filled Vice's ears. He turned and saw a small child clinging to a sixth-floor balcony railing for dear life, just beyond his mother's reach. With a running start Vice leaped and seized the lowest balcony railing and pulled himself up using only his arms, then once again and again and again. His arms were weary as he reached for the highest strut. His arms burned as he pulled himself up alongside the dangling boy and pulled him to safety. She began to cry with her child now safe in her arms.

"Thank you. Thank you with all my heart."

"Keep an eye on this little one and make sure he stays out of harm's way," he said, noticing how frightfully thin she was. He crouched down and looked the little boy in the eye. "What's your name, little man?"

"Leo," he answered in a tiny voice. "It's short for Leopold."

"That's a very strong name. Can I trust you to be a good boy and look after your mom?"

The boy nodded convincingly.

"Don't forget your promise. I'll be back to check in on you later."

Vice stood, snared a laundry line, and used it to repel down to the ground, then ran across the intersection to the location Commissioner Gordon had provided, a high-rise building with security gates and bars over the windows. The auction was supposed to take place in the basement. He checked for access and found the exterior staircase protected by a gate with razor-tipped spires. He grabbed the bars and pulled with all his strength, but they held fast. "I wish I had a damn magic hammer." He calculated how high he'd have to leap to clear the top of gate when the blare of a horn startled him.

Boba was behind the wheel of his car, closing in fast. The impact of the high-speed vehicle into the gate tore the steel bars from where they were moored in the concrete. Vice leaped them and was hustling down the stairs to the basement before Boba could get out of the car. Confronted with a metal fire door, Vice took to the air and landed boots-first against it, ripping it off the frame. Boba grabbed the fallen door with one hand and tossed it aside.

The basement was dark, not a light bulb illuminated anywhere. Vice and Boba split up and made their way through the underground lair, going room to room.

"Vice, the place is empty," Boba said. "I think Gordon gave you some bad intel."

"The auction must've been rescheduled. There's a case of champagne in the refrigerator and flutes in the cabinet. The pantry is filled with Russian caviar and boxes of crackers—food enough to feed a hundred."

"There's enough TP in the toilet to wipe every butt in the Seventh Fleet."

"Come on, let's—"

They were headed for the door when they heard a car screech to a stop outside. "Two large men were emerging from an old sedan when Vice and Boba hit the sidewalk. They drew guns immediately.

"Who the hell are you?" the bald one asked in a heavy Russian accent.

Vice was always happy about not being recognized. He was the least known of the superheroes and was intent on keeping it that way. "We're here for the auction," he said. "Are we too late or too early?"

Baldy eyed his associate with lamb chop sideburns uneasily, who turned to Vice. "I don't know what you're talking about. It looks like you trashed our place."

Boba looked over his shoulder at the security fence crumpled around the bumper of his car and the steel door lying on its side. He pushed up his sleeves revealing forearms the width of steam pipes. Veins like jumper cables ran from the pits of his elbows to his wrists. "Looks okay to me, Lamb Chop."

"No need to be a rude, American," the man with the fat sideburns said.

"I'm not American," Boba said. "*I'm* Italian."

"Makes no difference, those big forearms don't make you bulletproof," the bald man said. "Maybe you want to take a hike, *da*?"

Vice picked up on the faint sound of muffled voices. Like the other senses he had inherited from his spirit animal the Bengal tiger, his hearing was especially acute. "Open the trunk," he said, his tone both cold and demanding.

"No," the bald man said as he looked around in all directions. "Wuhan virus has advantages, *da*?" He wiped the safety on his gun. "No witnesses."

Boba cracked his neck and pounded his fist. "That works two ways, Numb Nuts."

Vice took off like a shot—airborne, his feet out in front of him, fists ready to strike. He craned his head to avoid the bullet that whistled by. He landed squarely in the center of Lamb Chop's chest, cracking ribs and disarming him.

The ground thundered as Boba stormed toward the bald man. He leaped and body-slammed the bulky Russian against the trunk of the old sedan. As he rolled off the pummeled trunk onto the street it popped open. Within, three young women were bound and gagged, lying side-by-side, squeezed in like sardines. Boba took one look at the hostages and stomped down on the bald man's wrist with his jackboot as he made a move to retrieve his gun.

They zip tied the two Russians to the door handles of the car, then released the women. They looked to be teenagers—frightened and malnourished, crying, dirty, and unsure if they were safe or not.

"You can wait in here," Boba said offering to accompany them into the basement, but they refused to budge. "There's food and drink in here," he said, but they stood fast.

"I don't think they understand you, Boba. They probably think you're a rival slave trader."

"Yeah, I can' see that."

Vice thought for a moment. He pulled out his smartphone and dictated. A digital voice translated into a foreign language.

One of the girls nodded and the other two followed her inside.

Boba seemed impressed. "Google translate?"

Vice nodded.

"What did you say?"

"You're safe. There's food and water inside. The police are on the way."

"I should've thought of that. Anyway, what are we going to do with these two animals? Personally—"

He was cut off by a screaming noise that grew louder and louder each second. It sounded as if a supersonic missile was headed for them. Vice picked up on a spec descending from the heavens, growing larger and larger against the backdrop of the sky.

"The hell is that?" Boba asked.

For all his strength, Boba didn't possess the enhanced senses that Vice did.

"It's Thor and . . ."

It wasn't until Thor was almost upon them that they were able to comprehend the scope and vile nature of the massive savage Thor was pulling at the end of a thick chain. Thor landed with a thud and pulled the chain taut until the beast was at arm's length, flailing desperately to get at the Thunder God and free itself.

Boba cringed. "Thor, that's not a—"

"I couldn't resist," Thor said. He wrestled to keep the savage under control. "Is that them?" he asked gazing at the two shackled men.

"Yes," Vice said.

"Then it was worth the trip. These beasts are all over Midgard. You just have to know where they hide."

"Where's Midgard?" Boba asked.

"Earth is Midgard," Thor said. "I found this one stalking a polar bear in the Nordic tundra. He must be ravenous to venture out during the day."

"Thor, you're not going to . . . are you?" Vice asked.

A massive construction crane stood nearby anchored by a twenty-ton counterweight. Thor wrapped the chain around the chassis and pinned it with his immovable hammer, leaving just enough slack so that the vile troll could reach its prey.

Thor ushered Vice and Boba inside. "You don't' want to see this," he said. "Trolls are disgusting slobbering creatures."

"Will they suffer?" Vice asked.

"Only from fright. The troll will be quick—like stripping two chicken legs.

***

Thor had already ferried the sated Troll back to the wilderness and returned by the time Commissioner Gordon and his crew arrived. He explained that Vice Booji and Tony Boba had rescued the women but that the slavers were nowhere to be found when they arrived.

"The word of the Thunder God is good enough for me," Gordon said as his men escorted the freed women to the special services van. "So where are our heroes?"

"They had other work, Commissioner. I was on a nearby beer run and offered to babysit until you arrived."

"I see. No story?"

"None that I'm aware of, Commissioner. Now if you don't mind there's a case of lager waiting for me with my name on it." He took off skyward and disappeared in an instant.

***

Just a block away and around the corner, Vice and Boba climbed an apartment stairwell, each toting fifty-five gallon garbage bags filled with the provisions they'd found in the Russian's basement lair.

"Where we going with all this stuff, Vice? You know, your place isn't exactly flush with groceries."

Vice came off the stairs and rang a doorbell. "Where it will do the most good, my friend. Where it will do the most good."

He heard the click of the peephole swing open and closed. The door flew open and a woman stepped into the hallway, her clothes hanging from her body, tears in her eyes. Leo rushed past her and hugged Vice around the leg.

"Thank you, Mister."

"Yes," his mother said. "It's the nice man who saved you." She pressed her hand to her chest, beaming thanks while she wept.

What's in all the bags?" Leo asked. "Toys?"

"It's not Christmas and I'm not Santa Claus," Vice said.

The little boy motioned for Vice to kneel, then whispered in his ear. "I know who you are. You're—"

Vice shushed him. "That must remain our secret."

The boy nodded, his eyes wide, registering the importance of their pact.

"Now, be a good boy," Vice said. "Help your mother put these things away."

The child nodded again. "Okay," he said as he formed claws with his fingers and growled like a tiger.

THE END

Lawrence Kelter never expected to be a writer. In fact, he was voted the student least likely to visit a library. Well, times change I suppose, and he has now authored several novels including the internationally best-selling *Stephanie Chalice Mystery Series*. Early in his writing career, he received support from best-selling novelist, Nelson DeMille, who reviewed his work and actually assisted in the editing of the first book. DeMille has been a true inspiration and has also given him some tough love. Way before he ever said, "Lawrence Kelter is an exciting new novelist, who reminds me of an early Robert Ludlum," he told him, "Kid, your work needs editing, but that's a hell of a lot better than not having talent. Keep it up!" Lawrence is excited to announce that he's been working on something completely new: books based on the film "My Cousin Vinny." A sequel entitled *Back To Brooklyn* is the first in a modern day Nick and Nora-type series with Vinny handling the litigation and Lisa in charge of investigation. He guarantees these stories to be laugh-out-loud funny! He now resides in North Carolina but lived in the Metro New York area most of his life and relies primarily on locales in Manhattan and Long Island for story settings. He does his very best to make each novel quickly paced and crammed full of twists, turns, and laughs. Look for him at lawrencekelter.com and my-cousin-vinny.com.

THE BICYCLE

Marvin J. Wolf

When I was almost ten, I needed to earn money, so I asked Mr. Miceli, the *Herald-American*'s man in my Chicago neighborhood, about an after-school paper route. He was old, about 30, but he spoke to me as though I was a grownup, and I liked that. After we'd spoken for a while, he said that if I would show him my bicycle, he'd give me a route.

My dad worked four jobs: He built neon signs in a sheet metal shop during the day, delivered flowers until 8:00 in the evening, drove a cab till midnight, and on weekends sold life insurance door-to-door in a poor neighborhood. He bought me a used bike—but both my parents had been orphans, and neither knew how to ride a bike, much less teach me to do so. Dad promised to find someone to teach me.

But before that happened, he was hospitalized with double pneumonia. His recovery was slow and painful; after a month he was allowed to return to the sheet metal shop on condition that he pulled no overtime and gave up all his other jobs.

That was why I needed to make money.

Fortunately, Mr. Miceli hadn't asked to see me ride; he just wanted to see my bike. I pushed it to his garage, showed it to him, and I had a job.

I watched the other boys take a few running steps down the alley with one hand on the handlebars and one on the seat. Then they raised their seat hand and swung their left leg over the seat to mount the bike.

The first time I tried it, I wound up in a tangle of spokes and newspapers while catcalls issued from the garage. Same thing the second time.

So I slung my delivery sack, stuffed with rolled papers over the handlebars, and walked my bike down the sidewalks. But pushing a bike with a load of papers is hard work, slow and very awkward; after a few days, I borrowed Mom's two-wheeled shopping cart, a folding, steel-mesh device.

Delivering papers from a bike is a little tricky. You get one chance to throw each paper, and if it misses a porch or a stoop, too bad. Delivering from Mom's cart was different. I left it on the sidewalk and carried each paper to its destination. If that was a second or third-floor porch, and I missed the first throw, I retrieved the paper and threw it again. Sundays, when the paper was so heavy that I couldn't heave it above the first floor, I carried each up the stairs. When it rained or snowed, I put Dad's old raincoat over the canvas bag to keep everything dry and left papers inside screen doors or apartment entrance halls.

All that took me much longer to deliver my route than if I was on a bike, but I didn't mind. I got to meet everyone in the neighborhood. These were working-class people, many of Italian, German, or Polish descent, and they were invariably kind to me. If I saw something interesting on my route, such as a cat with kittens or a rainbow of oil on wet asphalt, I could stop to watch for as long as I wanted.

Eventually, Dad resumed his place in the sign shop. But he'd given up his other jobs and bills began to pile up. To raise money, he sold several items that we could get along without, including my bike. I still didn't know how to ride, so I didn't object much.

Mr. Miceli must have known that I wasn't using a bike, but he said nothing about it to me. In fact, he rarely spoke to any of the boys, unless it was to give him hell for missing a customer or leaving a paper in a puddle.

Eight months after I started work, I'd built my route from 36 subscribers to 59, mostly because customers referred me to neighbors who wanted to take the paper. Sometimes, people stopped me on the street to tell me to add them.

I earned a penny a paper, Monday through Saturday, and a nickel for each big Sunday paper. I collected every Thursday evening, and since most customers gave me a nickel or a dime extra, soon I was making almost as much in tips as delivery fees. That was good because Dad still couldn't work as much as before. I gave most of my wages to Mom. She usually let me keep a dollar if I shared it with my younger brother.

Out collecting on the Thursday evening before Christmas, 1951, I rang my first customer's doorbell. Nobody answered so I went to the next house. No answer. Nor did anyone respond at the next door on my route, or the one after that. I visited every subscriber on the first of my two blocks—but no one was home. Not one person answered the door.

I had to pay for a week's papers every Friday; unless I collected enough to do so, I'd be out of a job. I knew it was almost Christmas, but I couldn't believe *everyone* was out shopping. *Something bad must have happened*, I thought, fighting panic. Maybe a gas leak. But as I hurried down the sidewalk to my next customer's house, I saw people coming from or going to other houses. I saw people through their windows.

But no one answered the door at my next address. Or the next. Or any of them.

Where were *my* customers?

Almost overcome with dread, I approached the last house on my route, the home of my favorite customers, the Gordons. I had an adolescent crush on Mrs. Gordon, who was much younger than my mother and very beautiful; tall and shapely, she had flawless olive skin and long, thick dark hair, and smelled faintly of violets. Throughout the hot summer, she had often invited me into her kitchen for a cookie and cold lemonade. When cold weather came, she had hot cocoa waiting when I knocked on her door to collect.

Moving up the Gordons' driveway, I was thrilled to hear music and voices. I rang the bell. Instantly the door was flung open, and Mr. Gordon, a burly man with huge hands, all but dragged me inside.

Jammed into the parlor was almost every one of my subscribers! In the middle of the room sat a brand new Schwinn bicycle—candy-apple red with a generator-powered headlamp and a bell. A shopping bag bulging with colorful envelopes hung from the handlebars.

"This is for you," Mrs. Gordon said. "We all chipped in." Then everyone applauded.

Dumbstruck, I didn't know what to say.

Finally, Mrs. Gordon called for quiet, took my shoulder and gently led me to the bicycle. "You are the best paperboy we've ever had," she said. "There's never been a day when a paper was missing or late, never a day when it was wet. We've all seen you out there in the rain and snow with that shopping cart. We thought you should have a bicycle."

When I found my voice all I could manage was "Thank you." I said it over and over.

When I got home that night I pushed the bicycle up two flights of stairs and into the kitchen. At first, my mother was sure that I had stolen it. But when together we opened all the envelopes in the shopping bag, we found a Christmas card from each subscriber, along with their weekly fee and altogether over $100 in tips—much more than my father took home for a week's pay with overtime. Dad's eyes grew moist. He didn't say why, but he asked to borrow eighty dollars. What would a kid need with that much money? Of course, I said yes.

The Gordons must have called Miceli, because the next morning when I picked up my papers, he was waiting outside. "Bring your new bike tomorrow at ten, and I'll teach you how to ride," he said.

When I was comfortable on a bike, Miceli offered me a second route. Delivering both from my new bike went faster than delivering just one from the shopping cart.

But when it rained, I dismounted to carry every paper to a dry place. If I missed a throw to a high porch, I circled back, stopped, put down the kickstand and threw again. I knew my subscribers expected nothing less.

After high school, I joined the Army and gave my bike to my brother Ted; I can't recall what became of it.

Many years later, just before he died, my father told me that my arrival that night with a hundred dollars was a full-fledged miracle. Our rent was forty dollars a month and we were two months behind and about to be evicted. We would have lost most of our belongings and been forced to beg friends and relatives for shelter until my father could save enough for another apartment.

So my kind and generous customers saved my family. Along with the bicycle and cash, however, came an even more valuable present, a shining life lesson about taking pride in even the humblest work. It's a gift I try to use as often as I remember those wonderful Chicagoans.

THE END

Marvin J. Wolf learned the basics of journalism as an Army combat correspondent in Vietnam.

He served thirteen years on active duty in the Infantry and the Signal Corps and afterward worked in corporate communications for four years. He has been a self-employed writer and photographer since 1978. He lives in Asheville, NC with an adult daughter and two spoiled dogs. Web site: Marvinjwolf.com.

THE QUILT

J.L. Delozier

Lilith hunched over the antique quilting frame and cursed the darkness. Outside, the February wind, icier than the devil's lips, gusted through cracks in the home's two-hundred-year-old foundation and kissed the windows with frost. The sun had set six hours ago—too early, it seemed—but she labored on. She had to finish this tonight.

Her eyes, milky with age, strained to follow the black cotton thread as she sewed the final row of fabric squares around the border of her newest creation. The stitches paid testament to her years of hard work and practice. They were perfect—evenly spaced, tiny, and uniform in size despite the gnarling of her arthritic hands. Lilith practiced a lost art.

She paused to massage her cold fingers. The gooseneck lamp, copper with the green patina of age, sputtered in protest against the hours of relentless use. She focused its dim light on the hem and struggled to stretch the blanket taut over the rigid frame. Even before the COVID-19 pandemic had begun to rage, this queen-sized monstrosity was destined to be her final project. Ring quilts, subscription quilts—Lilith's artistry had run the gamut throughout her many years, yet she had nothing to show for it save the simple, threadbare blanket covering her twin bed. Her handiwork went to her neighbors—peace offerings for her frequent indiscretions.

A woman of strong faith, she prayed over these gifts, imbuing each quilt with a spirit of its own. Her blood, harvested from the prick of a callused finger, lay hidden in the batting. After a gentle pressing, she'd fold the blanket into a tidy square, bind it with ribbon, and drop it on a neighbor's front porch or doorstep. But this latest quilt was destined for a different fate and a greater purpose. A triumph of design and ambition, it represented the grand finale to her life's work, her *pièce de résistance*. A special kind of gift.

Her daughter Lucy watched her mother's progress from the portrait on the wall, staring down her airbrushed nose at the mounds of fabric and piles of tangled thread on the floor. Her daughter wanted the house but not the quilt frame. Ten generations of daughters had toiled over its sturdy oak legs, but Lucy planned to lay it to rest. She'd never bothered to learn the craft.

Lilith rubbed her tired eyes and returned her daughter's condescending gaze with a glower of her own. Leave it to Lucy to reappear at the dawn of the Apocalypse, when plague and pestilence would soon rule the land. Her daughter always had a flair for the dramatic.

Lucy had fled New England for the City of Angels as soon as she was old enough to run, and that was that. Until a week ago when she'd called. Said she'd heard about the goings-on in the neighborhood, the rumors, and the escalating accusations. She'd heard from the young couple down the road who, a few days after their newborn died, returned Lilith's gift, a handmade baby quilt. Cursed, they'd called it. Offended, Lilith had disagreed. Imbued, cursed … semantics. It's all about what you believe.

Lucy believed the neighbors. She'd flown in from California and found her mother a nice room at Heavenly Acres in Salem, where someone could watch over her at all times—keep her out of trouble. Refusal was not an option. If Lilith didn't go voluntarily, Lucy threatened to petition the court and have her mother declared incompetent by way of dementia. The hearing was yesterday. Lilith didn't go.

Lucy called again today and told Lilith to pack her bags. They were coming for her in the morning. Who "they" were remained unclear but Lilith didn't care. She'd heard nothing but silence from Lucy for forty-five years. Now, two terse phone calls later, and her daughter conspired to evict her.

The agenda behind the timing was obvious, and it had nothing to do with cursed quilts, uneasy neighbors, or embarrassing indiscretions. Lilith heard demons whisper and angels sing. They told her the truth. And the truth was, now was the perfect time for her daughter to lock her away. The virus had already spread like hellfire through a nursing home in Seattle. It targeted the fragile elderly. Soon it would march east, and long-term care facilities coast-to-coast would lock their doors. The window of opportunity would pass. Being committed wasn't enough. Lucy wanted her dead.

Lilith threw the final stitch in place and jabbed the needle into its cushion, knocking her sewing kit to the ground with a clatter. She flinched at the unaccustomed noise. A spool of pure white thread rolled to rest on the floor beneath her daughter's portrait. Lilith turned her back, and let it be. Lucy's behavior wasn't a surprise. It's all in how you raise them.

The grandfather clock dolefully tolled the quarter-hour, reminding her she had only fifteen minutes to spare. Lilith stood and stretched her back, waiting for her creaky knees to unlock. She kicked the scattered thimbles and spools aside and shuffled to the kitchen where she pulled a monogrammed silver platter out of the cupboard. The tray had been special once, used for Thanksgiving dinners and other holidays long since passed, before her family had unraveled like a torn hem. She rubbed her thumb over its tarnished surface and grimaced at her distorted reflection. The poor thing hadn't seen the light of day in decades. But for tonight, it would do.

She rooted through her freezer with both hands. Buried in the back corner under an expired bag of frozen peas, Lilith found a small plastic container. She dumped its contents onto the butcher block for closer inspection and flashed a toothless grin. The frosty black paw was still in pristine condition. The neighbor's cat had been far too trusting.

The cookie jar came next. She rummaged around its ceramic interior until her fingers brushed something soft taped to the bottom. She released the tape and pinched a thin lock of hair between her thumb and index finger, inching it out so as not to lose a single strand. She held it to her nose and inhaled, sighing with pleasure at the familiar scent. Old Spice. Her husband had been far too trusting, too.

Lilith loaded the silver salver with her treasures and added five pillar candles from the pantry. Her gaunt shoulders quivered under the weight as she doddered to the living room. The massive frame, said to be hewn from timbers of the Mayflower itself, impeded her progress. As she slid past, she allowed herself a moment to pause and appreciate the artistry of her work. The blanket's star pattern was a traditional one, pieced together from leftover fabric in various shades of black and red, all sewn at perfect angles. She hoped its new owner would be pleased.

She rested the platter on the cushion of her favorite high-back armchair. With a crank of a lever, the quilting frame's stiff wooden gears turned, releasing the hefty quilt from the frame's tight grip. It dropped to the floor with a dull thud. Panting, Lilith dragged the blanket around the sofa and spread it over the floor's wide oak planks, centering the black-and-red star under the chandelier and smoothing away any wrinkles with a loving hand. One by one, she fussed over the placement of the pillar candles, positioning them exactly at each of the star's five points. With a strike of a match, her husband's hair smoldered and smoked. Shielding the flame with her palm, she paced counterclockwise along the quilt's border, using the flaming lock to light each candle in turn.

Satisfied with her efforts, Lilith retrieved the tray of offerings from where it listed precariously on the lumpy cushion and walked to the center of the quilt. She lowered herself to the floor and sat as cross-legged as her stiff joints would allow, displaying the tray before her. The clock chimed twelve, and she sighed. A new day. The day of her eviction. But if she was going to hell, it would be on her own terms.

In the hearth, the evening's fire, long since reduced to glowing embers, burst into flame, the sudden warmth a welcome embrace. She rocked back and forth, chanting in a low voice, gaining speed and volume as she went. The candles crackled in response, sparking a line of fire that followed the stitches on her quilt to the fabric's hemmed edge. A fiery arc jumped through the air to the wall below Lucy's portrait, darkening the surrounding wallpaper until the damask curled and dripped like molten black wax to the floor below. Lucy's chin and cheeks bubbled and blistered before melting in a final burst of flame.

Only her eyes remained, gaping, bearing witness once again to her mother's heinous crimes.

The old woman bowed her head in thanks—and relief. Master had heard her prayers, and he'd found her offerings acceptable. She would not succumb to COVID-19, would not rot away, struggling to gasp her final breaths, in a nursing home like the others her age. Her transformation was nigh, and her daughter's punishment guaranteed. Lucy should've known better than to return, to leave her City of Angels. She certainly should've known better than to interfere. Whether via the virus or by his own devilish hand, Master would make her pay.

The fire spread along the razor-straight lines of Lilith's handiwork, highlighting the pentagonal pattern until it glowed in the darkness. With her living room walls ablaze, the windows shattered one by one, choking the neighborhood with thick, black smoke. In the distance, Lilith heard a siren, but she did not move. Let the Apocalpyse rage. Let the locusts and earthquakes and pestilence come. It didn't matter anymore. Master was calling her home.

THE END

As a physician, J.L. Delozier draws inspiration from science that exists on the edge of reality—bizarre medical anomalies, new genetic discoveries, and anything that seems too weird to be true. The first of her four thrillers was nominated for a "Best First Novel" award by the International Thriller Writers organization. Her short fiction has appeared in the British crime anthology, *Noirville: Tales from the Dark Side,* NoirCon's e-journal, *Retreats from Oblivion,* and *Thriller Magazine.* Her first sci-fi short story won a Roswell Award and appeared in *Artemis Journal.* She lives in Pennsylvania with her husband and three cats.

THE PARTICULAR TALENTS OF LENNY BRIGHT

Zoë Sharp

Lenny Bright sat opposite the Holland and Seagrave Building Society in a gunmetal Honda Accord with the engine running. He hadn't taken his eyes off the front door for twenty minutes, and right at that moment he would have sold his soul for a cigarette.

Lenny's cigarettes were in the inside pocket of his bomber jacket, but it was more than his life was worth to reach for them. He couldn't even chew his fingernails, on account of the string-back driving gloves he'd been told to wear.

"Come on," he muttered, flexing his skinny fingers around the rim of the steering wheel. "What's taking you so long? Just get the money and get out of there!"

As if on cue, the building society's door was thrust open. A figure emerged, carrying a large bag, and hurried across the road towards him.

"At last!" Lenny said under his breath. The rear passenger door opened and the bag landed heavy on the cloth upholstery, followed by its owner. By the time the door slammed shut again Lenny was already moving out into traffic.

"Not too quickly, Lenny dear," Mrs. Esmé Wendover said from the back seat. "I should hate you to get a speeding ticket. My poor Harold never got one, you know, not in forty years."

"You'll miss your train if we don't hurry, Mrs. Wendover," Lenny said. He flashed a cheeky grin in the rear-view mirror. "'Sides, it's your car, so you'd be the one getting the ticket."

"Quite so," she murmured, dragging her voluminous handbag towards her and burrowing through the contents. She paused long enough to favor him with a regal smile over her half-moon glasses. "All the more reason to go steady, then."

"Yes ma'am," Lenny said smartly, not altering his pace.

After nineteen years under the thumb of his domineering mother, Lenny was used to pretending to toe the line. Old Mrs. Bright had a lightning tongue and the uncanny ability to hear the ring-pull being snapped open on an illicit can of lager through two floors and a soap opera.

An academic make-weight, Lenny left school unscathed by the knowledge his teachers tried to impart. Then a despairing career officer dumped him into a youth training scheme at a local garage. There it was discovered, much to everyone's amazement, that when it came to anything mechanical, Lenny Bright was close to a genius.

Of course, that didn't mean his new employers were prepared to pay more than minimum wage. Nowhere near enough for him to move out and get a place of his own.

His mother viewed his oil-stained profession with disgust. On his daily return, she made him strip and scrub down by the cold tap in the outhouse, in all weather.

That winter was bitter, and Lenny grew desperate. He was caught copying the keys to a customer's car and although the garage didn't press charges, they gave Lenny his marching orders and put the word out. He couldn't get another mechanic job for fifty miles in any direction.

Lenny told his mother he'd been made redundant. She berated him for his incompetence, kicking him out of the house during the day to wander the town center. He spent his time daydreaming of his own space.

***

Two months later, Lenny trudged home to find the elderly Mrs. Esmé Wendover sitting on his mother's sofa, drinking tea from their best china. He was horrified. Mrs. Wendover owned the car whose keys he'd copied.

"Since you stopped working on my Honda, it's just not the same," she'd said, making him sweat. "My Harold kept it running sweet as a nut." She'd sighed and fixed him with a fiercely intelligent eye. "All his tools are still in the garage. I'd like you to carry on servicing my car for me at home. I'm prepared to pay."

Lenny had gaped, right up to the point his mother stepped in and grimly assured Mrs. Wendover that her boy would do the work for nothing. Mrs. Wendover must have seen the urgent desperation in his eyes because she held up a peremptory hand.

"My Harold left me comfortable and I won't have charity," she said with a sweet smile. "Saturday at nine, Lenny? You know the address."

So Lenny began looking after Mrs. Wendover's Honda, driving her when she needed to go anywhere, like the garden center, where his eye was caught by one of the assistants, Julie, who smiled at him with particular brightness.

That smile kept him warm when his mother sent him back, shivering, to the tap in the outhouse.

And then two things happened. By chance he bumped into one of his old classmates, Daz, fresh out of prison for turning over a Post Office. Daz had seen Lenny running an errand in the Honda and had casually buttonholed him.

"Nice motor," Daz had said. "Fancy using it to earn yourself something extra? Decent bit of cash, no questions asked?"

"Doing what?" Lenny had said and then, before he had the chance to be tempted, admitted quickly, "Only, the car's not mine, see."

"Oh." He'd watched the respect die out of Daz's eyes. "Never mind, then, eh? See you around." And Lenny had watched him saunter away in an agony of indecision.

At the garden center, he'd seen Julie poring over the classifieds. "They've done a conversion down near the canal," she told him. "Lovely places, but they want two months rent up front." She'd eyed him with a certain gleam. "I've been thinking of taking in a lodger."

"I'll do it," Lenny blurted, and went home dazed.

And the next time he saw Daz, Lenny listened.

***

They reached the station five minutes before the Southampton train. Lenny saw Mrs. Wendover safely to her carriage, trying not to let his agitation show.

Half an hour later he picked up Daz and two heavyset mates outside a boarded-up pub on one of the sink estates. Daz handed him a pair of fake license plates and a black balaclava.

"All right, Lenny mate?" he said. "Remember, you just sit outside with the motor running like a good lad, and the money's yours."

"All right," Lenny had said gruffly, trying to swallow down the sudden lump in his throat.

He was already scared witless, even more so when they seemed to be heading for exactly the same branch of the Holland and Seagrave where he'd waited for Mrs. Wendover that morning. He eyed the two heavies in his rear-view mirror and desperately searched for a way to tell Daz, but when they pulled up outside, he still hadn't found one.

Besides, Daz and his companions were already out of the car and charging across the pavement. Lenny debated on driving off, but the robbers were almost certain to get caught and he knew Daz wouldn't hesitate to name him if he betrayed them.

Instead, he waited, his nerves in tatters and dying for a cigarette, until the doors burst open and the three men emerged. Daz threw himself into the front seat.

"Go, go, go!" he yelled.

Lenny smoked the tires halfway along the High Street, driving like a man possessed, drifting through corners and making wild turns to throw off any chance of pursuit. Eventually, he took them back to the pub by a very circuitous route, changing the license plates back while Daz split the haul.

"There you go, Lenny," Daz said, putting a fat brown envelope into his hands. "You ever want more work, I can find you plenty."

"No thanks," Lenny said dazedly, staring at the crumpled edges of more money than he'd ever seen in his life before. There must have been hundreds! "I've got what I need."

Daz eyed him with speculation. "So, what're you doing with it, then?"

Lenny looked up and smiled. "My getaway," he said.

Daz clapped him on the shoulder and laughed. "About time you moved out from under," he said. "You let me know if you change your mind, though. You're a natural."

"Not me," said Lenny, shaking his head. *Never again*, he thought.

****

Several days later, Lenny was washing Mrs. Wendover's car when the police turned up. Two large uniforms, reminding Lenny of the bank robbers and just as threatening. He thought of the money, still hidden under the mattress of the narrow bed he'd slept in from childhood, and almost made a run for it there and then.

"Can you tell us your whereabouts on Thursday morning, sir?" one of the policemen demanded, pen poised over the page of his notebook.

Lenny's mouth dried.

"I, er—"

"What seems to be the trouble, officers?" inquired a voice behind them. All three turned to see Mrs. Wendover had emerged from the house carrying a tray with two cups of tea and a plate of biscuits. "I do hope this isn't because Lenny was driving too quickly?" the old lady said anxiously. "We were rather late, you see."

"Er, no, ma'am," said one of the policemen through a mouthful of Garibaldi. He straightened importantly. "Actually, we're investigating a robbery—the Holland and Seagrave Building Society."

"Oh yes, I saw something about it on the news," Mrs. Wendover said. "Dreadful business. And we were there only that morning, weren't we, Lenny dear?"

The policemen eyed Lenny with great suspicion. "Were you?"

He cleared his throat. "Er, yes," he said.

"I imagine that's what all this is about, isn't it?" Mrs. Wendover said calmly. "Somebody saw my car and heard about the robbery and put two and two together and came up with five, hmm?"

One of the policeman shuffled his feet and mumbled an agreement. "A car matching the description of—"

"Lovely cars, Hondas, but there are *lots* of them about," Mrs. Wendover interrupted. "Lenny's a good boy. He wouldn't get involved in something like that. And besides," she added to Lenny's astonishment, "by the time I'd finished conducting my business we discovered that I'd missed my train, and he very kindly drove me all the way down to Southampton." She beamed at the policemen and held the tray out to take their empty cups. "So, you see, officers, it couldn't possibly have been him."

✳✳✳

As they watched the police car disappearing down the drive, Mrs. Wendover said breezily, "The first thing you should learn if you're going to break the law, Lenny dear, is to have a good alibi."

Lenny could only stammer, "How…how did you know?"

She smiled. "Because that particular branch of the Holland and Seagrave has the worst security in the area. It was only a matter of time before they got turned over," she said. "You've been looking incredibly guilty since last Thursday, dear. We'll have to do something about that conscience of yours."

"W…wh—?" Lenny stopped and started again. "Why?"

"Because you won't last very long as a getaway driver if you're going to stutter every time you're brought in for questioning. Those CID boys will make mincemeat out of you."

"There's not going to be a next time," Lenny said quickly. "I'm not doing it again."

"Don't be silly, Lenny dear," Mrs. Wendover said. "I didn't stick my neck out for you, only for you to get cold feet now. As Daz no doubt told you, you're a natural. And I should know—my Harold was the best wheelman in the business. Forty years and never got caught. I knew if I offered you a big enough carrot you couldn't resist it. Why stop now?"

"Because…" Lenny began, then his voice trailed off. He'd already counted out the money Julie needed for the deposit on the flat and there wasn't much left over. But supposing that wasn't the last of it? Lenny's mind was suddenly filled with thoughts of being able to take Julie out, buy her presents, of her clinging to his arm and laughing as they walked home by the canal. Maybe he could even buy a car!

"Of course," Mrs. Wendover went on, "we can't afford for you to attract attention to yourself—no sudden changes in lifestyle, dear." She smiled at him, like butter wouldn't melt in her mouth. "So maybe it would be best if you stayed living at home with your mother."

THE END

Zoë Sharp's award-winning crime thrillers, featuring ex-Special Forces trainee turned close-protection officer Charlotte 'Charlie' Fox, have been used in school textbooks, inspired an original song and music video, and been optioned for TV and film. "If Jack Reacher were a woman, he'd be Charlie Fox."—Lee Child. Sharp's latest book, BONES IN THE RIVER, is No2 in the Lakes crime thriller series with CSI Grace McColl and Detective Nick Weston—a story of old scores and new lies set against the backdrop of Appleby Gypsy Horse Fair.

Website: www.zoesharp.com
Facebook: www.facebook.com/ZoeSharpAuthor
Twitter: twitter.com/authorzoesharp
Instagram: www.instagram.com/authorzoesharp/

THE HUNT FOR JACK REACHER

Diane Capri

Were you wondering where I got the idea for ***Don't Know Jack*** and my whole ***Hunt for Jack Reacher Series***? Well, here's the true story.

"Where is Reacher hiding?" I asked my friend, Lee Child, at a writers' event in New York City.

"Reacher doesn't hide," Lee said. Maybe a little huffily?

Lee's a lot bigger than me. And he writes violence like a man with experience. I've always thought him a gentle giant, but.... I backpedaled a bit.

"Right. But where does Reacher live?"

"Wherever he wants," the tall guy said.

I thought I detected a slight challenge in his tone. I backed out of arms' reach before I pressed on.

Like my characters, I don't know when to quit sometimes. We call it tenacity, but maybe it's plain old stubbornness.

"Okay, well, Reacher waits until trouble finds him and then he wipes the floor with the bad guys. Perfect. But what's he doing between books?"

Lee shrugged, said nothing.

I took a deep breath and tried again. "Reacher's killed a lot of people by now. A lot of books. A lot of bodies. Surely someone wants payback, don't you think?"

Lee leveled the patented Reacher stare at me. His tone was faintly menacing now. "Who in his right mind would go looking for Reacher? You?"

Good question.

Only an idiot with a death wish -- or an FBI agent who knows nothing about Reacher's, er, talents -- would undertake such a foolhardy quest.

Even then, she wouldn't do it if she had a choice. She's not an idiot.

But matching wits with Jack Reacher, now that would be interesting, I thought, even though it could very well be deadly.

Then again, the bigger they are the harder they fall.

Whoever tames Reacher will become a legend in some circles.

What if a determined, ambitious woman...?

Not long afterward, with Lee's full support and encouragement, I began writing what became the first book in my ***Hunt for Jack Reacher series***.

Lee loves what I've done with it. In fact, here's what he said, "Kim Otto is a great, great character. I love her."

To date, more than three million readers have joined the hunt and read my books. ***Don't Know Jack*** and the other books in my series have made every bestseller list out there, several times. How cool is that?

I'm hoping you'll love FBI Special Agent Kim Otto, too. She's a tiny stick of dynamite with a deadly aim. And her partner, Agent Carlos Gaspar, is a devoted family man who might have turned out to be a loner like Reacher, in an alternate universe. Two FBI Special Agents on the hunt for Reacher who never, ever give up.

Join the hunt to find out what happens in ***Don't Know Jack***. And work your way through the whole series as Otto and Gaspar discover that what they don't know can be more deadly than Reacher. Oh, you might want to read Lee Child's **Killing Floor** either before or after **Don't Know Jack**. Many readers tell me that these books are even better together.

But beware. The **Hunt for Jack Reacher** is dangerous business.

THE END

Diane Capri is an award-winning *New York Times*, *USA Today*, and worldwide bestselling author. She's a recovering lawyer and snowbird who divides her time between Florida and Michigan. An active member of Mystery Writers of America, Author's Guild, International Thriller Writers, Alliance of Independent Authors, and Sisters in Crime, she loves to hear from readers and is hard at work on her next novel. Please connect with her online: http://www.DianeCapri.com.

Twitter: https://twitter.com/DianeCapri.
Facebook: http://www.facebook.com/Diane.Capri1.
              http://www.facebook.com/DianeCapriBooks.

Join Diane Capri's Mailing List at: http://dianecapri.com/get-involved/get-my-newsletter/ For a complete list of Diane Capri Books visit http://dianecapri.com/books/ or Diane's Amazon Author Page.

Unmasked

Debra H. Goldstein

Gabriel bent forward; hands pressed against his head. Without thinking, he ran his fingers through his dark hair. The soft curling of its ends reminded him that he was at least two weeks overdue for a haircut. He laughed. Who cared?

The length of his hair was the least of his concerns. Until the past few days, other than himself, no one had seen his hair, face, hands, or anything else that might identify him for weeks. Perhaps, at some point in time, in his cap, mask, gloves, and gown, he should have tried walking in and robbing the bank on the corner. He probably would have had a better chance of getting away with it than he had of surviving this beast.

Exhausted from sitting up, all Gabriel wanted to do was lie back and rest, but he knew he shouldn't. Upright, the pain of his chest tightening as he struggled to catch his breath, despite the oxygen pumping through the prongs in his nose, frightened him. It was a sign his oxygen levels were dropping. If he didn't act now, some helpless sap, desperate to do something in the face of Gabriel's deterioration, would intubate him. That was the last thing Gabriel wanted.

Giving himself permission, he slid back on the bed, but onto his side. Slowly, he twisted, careful not to disturb the oxygen monitor on his finger or any of the other tubes being used to give him air and fluids, until he lay on his stomach. It was so uncomfortable. He wasn't sure how long he could stay in this position.

He reminded himself of what he'd told patients. "Proning works. It's a sure way to bring up your oxygen level. Everyone dislikes it, but the longer you can prone, the better it will be." Of course, he hadn't said aloud, "that no matter how much you dislike being on your stomach, you're going to hate having a tube stuck down your airway so a ventilator can breathe for you."

Now, as sweat drenched his bedsheets, Gabriel repeated "proning works" over and over as his mantra of life.

Dosing, Gabriel's mind wandered. He saw the face of the elderly woman who he'd sat with, thinking she wouldn't make it through the night. She'd surprised him by rallying and eventually going home. And then, he had an image of the young runner. Fine on Monday, except for a bit of exercise induced asthma, but gone on Thursday.

That was one of the curses of providing care for this virus. Despite trending inflammatory markers, oxygen saturations, and days since symptom onset, it remained almost impossible to predict which direction patients would take.

For a moment, Gabriel thought about praying, even though that wasn't something he'd done for a long time. Maybe he could strike a bargain—heal me to be a healer. But then he realized he was no angel. There was no bargain to be struck. It was only going to be a matter of making it to morning. He held on to his mantra.

When the sun came up, Gabriel took a breath. There would be a day to get that haircut. He'd had confirmation that life happens between an exhale and an inhale.

THE END

Judge Debra H. Goldstein writes Kensington's Sarah Blair mystery series (One Taste Too Many, Two Bites Too Many, Three Treats Too Many). She also wrote Should Have Played Poker and IPPY winning Maze in Blue. Her short stories, including Anthony and Agatha nominated *The Night They Burned Ms. Dixie's Place* and Derringer Finalist *Pig Lickin' Good*, have appeared in numerous publications. Debra serves on the national boards of SinC and MWA and is president of SEMWA.

HALLOWED GROUND

Cheryl Bradshaw

I was new in town and looking to start up a home remodeling business. I figured the best way to attract clients was to purchase a fixer-upper, fix it up, and then use it as an office to woo potential clients. I met with a real estate agent, and we viewed all the homes in my price range, but nothing seemed to resonate.

A few days later I decided to explore the area, and I ventured out on my own. I drove around for a while and then spotted an old, rundown, wooden house on a sizeable piece of land just outside of town on County Road 305. It was a two-story home and looked a bit more like a barn than a house. There was no For Sale sign out front, but from the looks of things, no one lived there, and it might have been abandoned for several decades. The home needed a lot of work, but it had good bones. I figured if I could talk the owner into selling the place to me, the asking price would be low enough for me to afford a generous remodel.

I called the realtor and explained where I was and what I'd found.

"I know the place well," she said. "You're at the old Sampson house."

"Will you contact them and see if they are interested in selling it?"

"Tom and Mary Sampson both passed away, but I think one of their kids is still around. I'm sure he'd be keen to get rid of the place, but even if he is, you don't want to buy it."

"Why not?"

"It's haunted."

I paused a moment, taking in what I thought she'd just said.

"What do you mean by *haunted*?" I asked.

"Tom and Mary died in that house. They were—"

I didn't want to know.

"It might be best if you didn't give me the details," I said. "I don't believe in ghosts or spirits or haunted houses."

"Even if you don't, you should look up the home's history before you consider buying it."

She struck me as a Nervous Nellie type, and I figured she was making a big deal about nothing. People died at home sometimes. It didn't mean the place was haunted.

"I'll take my chances," I said. "Will you find out if the family would be willing to sell it to me?"

She was reluctant, but she agreed. She called me a few days later to say Tom's son, Howard, had no interest in the home after his parents died, and he had deeded it to the state. The state had no plans for it and was more than willing to sell it to me. We settled on a price, and I moved in.

The first couple weeks in the house were ordinary. I assessed the work to be done, drew up renovation plans, bought supplies, and hired a few guys to assist me on the projects that required a bit more muscle.

On my twenty-third day in the house, the nightmares began.

I woke one night to the sound of a woman's sobs. They were loud and foreboding, echoing through the halls like the whine of a siren. I wasn't alone. Someone was there with me.

I sat straight up in bed, staring into the darkness.

"Hello?" I said. "Is anyone there?"

The sound of her cries became louder, and I decided to take action. I ran to the kitchen, grabbed a knife out of the drawer, and tiptoed to the door leading to the living room. Before I entered, I leaned against it and listened. The cries I'd heard were coming from the other side.

I thrust the door open, flipped on the light, and held the knife straight out in front of me. I surveyed the room. It was empty. I was alone. It didn't make sense. I knew what I'd heard, and yet no one was there.

It took a few hours for my mind to settle enough for the rational side to kick in, and I convinced myself what I'd heard had been nothing more than the whistling of trees outside. The next night it happened again, and the night after that, and the night after that. Each night was the same. I'd turn on the light, the crying ceased, and I was all alone.

I wasn't sleeping.

Something needed to change.

The following night I didn't go to bed. I lit a fire in the living room, sat on a chair, and waited. For the first couple of hours, nothing happened. Aside from the creak of my rocking chair along the wood floor, all was silent. The hours ticked by, and my lack of sleep kicked in. My eyelids were hot and weighted, and the fire had burned down to a pile of ash.

I was just about to nod off when the embers in the fireplace ignited on their own. My eyes flashed opened, and I was stunned. Kneeling on the ground in front of me was a woman dressed in a simple, brown, full-length dress and moccasins. Her arms were crisscrossed in front of her, and as she sobbed, she rocked her body back and forth chanting the same two words over and over again: *mitawa wakanheja*.

I called out to her, trying to get her attention, but she seemed unaware of my presence. I walked over and reached for her shoulder. My fingers passed through her body like she was nothing more than a hologram. Then she evaporated and disappeared into the air.

For a time, I sat it the room in silence and tried to make sense of it all, but there was no sense to make. I wanted to know who she was and why she kept returning to my house each night. I wanted to know why she never stopped crying.

I grabbed the poker from the metal can on the side of the fireplace and pressed it into what remained of the fire. A heavy gust of wind shot out, the force of it hurling me against the opposite wall. The fireplace filled with the smoldering face of a man wearing an Indian headdress. He didn't speak, but no words were needed. I could read his expression easily enough. He was angry, filled with rage.

I snatched my keys off the kitchen counter, ran out of the house, and tore down the road. I drove to the nearest hotel, checked in, and then found the hotel's business center. I got on the internet, typed in the address of my home, and clicked the search key. The first page of results showed a photo of woman. I clicked on the photo to enlarge it. The woman was the same one I'd seen in my living room. Standing next to her was a man I assumed to be the chief of her tribe and sitting on the ground in front of them were three young children.

I investigated further and learned the property my home had been built on had once belonged to them, the Lakota tribe. It had been their land and their home. In 1878, after a fierce battle to protect their tribe from those who sought to take it from them, the entire tribe was annihilated. Men, women, and children. The bodies of the dead were buried in the same location my home now stood. I also learned the words the woman had chanted, *mitawa wakanheja,* meant *my children.*

I had been living over an Indian burial ground.

In 1939, Tom and Mary Sampson had purchased the property and built a family home. Less than a month after they moved in, Howard went into his parents' room one morning and found them both dead. They appeared to have been strangled. No one knew how or why, and the culprit was never found. Howard was sent to live with his aunt, and the house had been vacant ever since.

I now understood why the real estate agent had tried to warn me. The house didn't belong on the property, and the property had no right being owned by anyone. I couldn't undo the purchase, but there was something I could do to pay my respect. I could return the land to its rightful owner, and tomorrow I would, right after I set the house on fire.

THE END

Cheryl Bradshaw is a New York Times & USA Today Bestselling Author writing in the genres of mystery, thriller, romantic suspense, women's fiction, poetry, paranormal suspense, and all things that go bump in the night. Raised in California, she now lives in Cairns, Australia and spends her free time traveling the world. Website: http://cherylbradshaw.com/

Sheltering in Place

Charles Salzberg

Sometime in mid-March, after a week or two of rumors, the call came in from Governor Andrew Cuomo: New Yorkers were going to have to shelter in place.

As the epi-center of the Coronavirus or COVID-19—take your pick of names for the virus evidently started in a province in China most of us had never heard of, I prefer COVID-19 since the idea of a deadly virus being named after a beer doesn't sit that well with me—New Yorkers were in particular danger.

We had all the makings of a pandemic times one hundred. In the city alone, there are somewhere around eight million of us and in many cases sardines have more room between each other than we do. Add to that the fact that we're a tourist magnet, meaning we could be importing the deadly disease from anywhere around the world, it was a foregone conclusion that in order to stop the spread we'd have to contract rather than expand.

The rules were simple. Unless you had a damn good reason to be out on the streets, like if you were in an essential industry or need to shop for medications or food, you were to stay the hell home. And now, several weeks later, we're instructed that we must wear some kind of face covering, not so much to protect ourselves, which it will to some extent, but to protect others in case we have the virus, active or with no symptoms.

Since no one's ever considered writing an essential industry, though I certainly do since it's one of the few things I can do and have done for almost all my working life, that meant me.

But unlike most New Yorkers, this wasn't a sentence as much as it was a gift. I say this with more than a little guilt, because I know how serious this is and I know to most others it's more than an inconvenience; it's playing havoc with feeding families and keeping roofs over heads.

The stay-at-home edict has been in place for almost four weeks now, but unlike most New Yorkers, especially those brave, wonderful souls who are on the front lines, which means not only the medical folks but everyone who has an essential job, including people like grocery clerks, the building staff where I live, as well as those who deliver essential items to us while we stay home doing our part to stop the virus dead in its tracks, I embrace this edict.

Let's face it. If I'm to be honest, and I promise at least in this case, even though I am a writer of fiction, to stick to the facts, I have to admit, I am thriving.

Now, before you pull out your pen or sit down at your computer to write me a nasty note — "How dare you! People are dying! People are losing their loved ones!" or shake your head and say to yourself (or anyone within earshot) "what a despicable person he is," or, "true New Yorker, just thinking about himself," — here's what I mean.

As a writer and a former introvert (I lost a lot of that through necessity when I had to make my living as a magazine journalist) I love staying home. And I even like being alone (perhaps this comes from having to share a bedroom growing up with an annoying younger brother who did his best to get on and then stay on my nerves). In fact, one of the perks of being a magazine journalist was that I didn't have to go to an office. I didn't have to leave my apartment at all, especially in bad weather, if I didn't have an interview to do or an errand to run.

Bottom-line: I've been rehearsing for this self-isolation gig my entire life.

In case you're interested, this is pretty much how I spend my day. Netflix, Prime, HBO, binging like never before. I'm amazed at how much good stuff one can find, and even "bad" stuff like Tiger King, which rivets me to the screen. I'm catching up on movies and shows, and it seems that these premium channels never run out of addictive programming like Babylon Berlin, Ozark, Bosch, Deep Water, and documentaries like The Keepers, Evil Genius, The Staircase. (Notice a heavy dose of crime? My excuse is that's what I do for a living now, writing crime novels, though given the pay for doing this job, living is not actually an appropriate word.)

I've also been hooked once again by reading. In the past three weeks I've started and finished at least four books: John LeCarre's *Agent Running in the Field,* Casey Cep's *Furious Hours, The Third Rainbow Girl,* by Emma Copley Eisenberg, and an as yet unpublished manuscript by my old friend, Roy Hoffman. I'm now reading the new Mel Brooks biography as well as a manuscript I've been asked to blurb. And that stack of *New Yorkers* and *Vanity Fairs* piling up on my table are beginning to be whittled down.

I've discovered true crime podcasts, and how addictive they can be. *Crimetown, Up and Vanished, Teacher's Pet, Crime Junkie*—and that's just the beginning of the list.

I've rediscovered the art of the nap, which, I'm afraid, seems to be more prevalent and for longer periods of time than I'd like.

Eating. Yes. I do have to eat. But also, I have to plan for what to eat and how to get it. And how to shop for food and for how much. As an aside, I just don't get this run on toilet paper, and perhaps I'm going for some kind of record, but not only have I purchased no new toilet paper since this pandemic began, but I am not even down to my last roll. All I can do when I do make it to the supermarket and see people with carts loaded with maybe half a dozen multi-packs of toilet paper is ask myself, how much damn toilet paper can someone go through in a week? And perhaps they have more serious problems than just preparing for the end of times. But at least if that comes, they will have a very clean (you can add your favorite word for that part of the anatomy here, but I'll resort to the word "bum.")

Have I mentioned writing? Yeah, well, probably not enough of that is taking place but yes, I am using the time to write. I've written a couple short stories and I'm a quarter of a way into a new novel, *Man on the Run,* which is kind of a spin-off for *Second Story Man* which (self-promotion alert) won the Beverly Hills Book Award and was nominated for a Shamus Award and a David Award, after having finished a novel, *Canary in the Coal Mine,* just weeks before the pandemic hit.

Zooming. I have, like most of us, discovered Zoom, where you can meet without really meeting in the usual sense of the word, friends and colleagues. I'm on the Board of New York Writers Workshop, PrisonWrites, and Mystery Writers of America-NY, and we've had several meetings online. I'm not sure, when this is over, how I'm going to adjust to actually appearing somewhere at an appointed time for one of these meetings. Do I dare suggest that all of them occur online? We'll see. I also had my first Zoom lunch with one of my best friends, Ross Klavan. We've done a weekly lunch now for over twenty years and I do miss those in person meetups, and yet the Zoom lunch was oddly satisfying. The only drawback was I had to clear away my own dishes and then wash them. I also belong to a small writers' group and now we're meeting every other Sunday afternoon. Surprisingly, it really is like having those six people in my living room only I don't have to rearrange furniture nor do I have to clean up after it's over.

Eating. I'll let this speak for itself.

And here's the most amazing part. Because I'm doing my civic duty by not leaving the apartment, it's all guilt-free!

Oh, I guess I should mention the occasional long walk by the river (I live right next to the Hudson River, on Manhattan's Upper West Side) with one of my writer friends. We keep a safe distance apart and wear masks when appropriate. This, I tell myself, counts as "exercise." Though in all honesty, I also tell myself that searching for the remote every so often also counts as physical activity. (Who knew remotes can actually move around on their own power?)

Of course, I know that all over the world people are truly suffering, not only from the rampant and unrelenting march of the virus, but also because their livelihoods have been snatched out from under them. And I don't make light of that. In fact, I'm worried. Very worried. I'm pretty sure after this is over, and it will be over, though who knows when, life will have been forever altered. But for now, I can't possibly pat myself on the back for sheltering in place, thereby helping my fellow man and woman by not spreading the virus, but I can actually imagine a time in the future when I'll be waxing poetic about the good, old days when I didn't have to leave my apartment. At least not until they work out the kinks in that teleportation thing.

THE END

Charles Salzberg is a novelist, a journalist, and an acclaimed writing instructor. His new novel, Devil in the Hole, a gripping work of literary crime fiction based on the notorious John List murders, is on shelves now. He is the author of the Henry Swann detective series: Swann Dives In; Swann's Last Song, which was nominated for a Shamus Award for Best First PI Novel; and the upcoming Swann's Lake of Despair. His non-fiction books include: On A Clear Day They Could See Seventh Place: Baseball's 10 Worst Teams of the Century; From Set Shot to Slam Dunk, An Oral History of the NBA; and co-author of My Zany Life and Times, by Soupy Sales; Catch Them Being Good; and The Mad Fisherman. He has been a Visiting Professor at the S.I. Newhouse School of Public Communications at Syracuse University, and has taught writing at Sarah Lawrence College, Hunter College, the Writer's Voice, and the New York Writers Workshop, where he is a Founding Member.

He is a consulting editor at the webzine Ducts.org and co-host, with Jonathan Kravetz, of the reading series, Trumpet Fiction, at KGB in New York City. His freelance work has appeared in such publications as Esquire, New York Magazine, GQ, Elle, Redbook, Ladies Home Journal, The New York Times Arts and Leisure section, The New York Times Book Review, and the Los Angeles Times Book Review. Learn more about Charles on his website http://www.charlessalzberg.com

STAR OF THE SEA

Gabriel Valjan

About fifty yards out in front of them were two objects bobbing in the drink. Visibility was poor because of the fog after the recent Nor'easter, though the ocean was as calm as the water in Saturday's bathtub. Captain Barksdale shined a light from his Coleman into the blackness. He fanned the light over one of the inflatables and then over the other.

"Empty lifeboats?" he said, amazed, to his first mate at his side.

The captain aimed the lamp's beam over the surrounding water. There was no sign of life in the water. Nothing. They traced the line that connected the two dinghies to something else and discovered the lettering of a ship in the distance.

They recognized the name.

The ship, built to withstand ice, had become a legendary derelict, a rejected mistress, a ship with no home and lost at sea for three years. A ghost ship. Reported sightings had conveyed every flavor of the paranormal, from phantom figures at the helm to a spectral lady on the deck. Ships sent after her like bounty hunters would fail to catch and return her to port.

The vessel had been sighted over the years; it had been seen and then lost by sailors and satellite alike. Here, her course suggested that she was wending her way towards the Harbor Islands, down a dangerous chute of currents, rocks, and other obstructions in the treacherous alleyway into Boston.

"What do we do, Cap? Call the Coast Guard?"

"And admit to illegal lobstering?"

The ship's side loomed into view, her name in white. STELLA MARIS.

They heard the metallic frenzy of chains, followed by a splash of water, despite not one sound of an engine. "She's dropped anchor."

"Something stinks about this, Cap, and it's not Boston Harbor."

"We're anchored," Barksdale said. "Let's man those two boats and bring them back to mother and board her. It'll be something to walk around her. Along with the Bermuda Triangle, the Stella Maris remains one of the great unsolved mysteries."

"Aye, Captain."

"And bring security."

Barksdale heard the squish of muck boots. When his chief mate reappeared, two life vests hung from his left shoulder. He held a pole in his left hand, and a Smith & Wesson in his right hand. The boat hook did double-duty, first to lure the lifeboats to them, and then as a hook to board the ship.

"You really think we're gonna need the .38?"

"I hate rats."

"You really think there are rats, Cap?"

"Why take chances? I'm sure they're gone by now, after they ate everything on board and then turned on each other."

They had noticed the unused oars, tucked in nice and neat, when they had settled into one of the lifeboats. The mate fixed the oars into the eyelets.

"Cannibal rats, huh. Did you know a lobster's blood is white, and it'll turn blue as a penny when it is oxidized? It's the copper in their blood."

"Just row, please."

Transit required a few strokes to manage their egress. They both admired the dark hull. She was a bruiser, capable of smashing through ice in the Antarctic and the Arctic. The captain had read that she could break through 14 inches of ice at a speed of 10 knots. They climbed their rope like spiders and stepped onto the deck.

"I don't see any rats, Captain."

"They'd be down below. Never forget, there are always rats on a ship. Always. Now, let's check how she steers."

"Aye."

Once they'd entered the bridge, they threw a switch. The lights revealed piles of dead paper on the workspace, squared off and stacked neatly. The bridge was pristine. Barksdale could see his reflection in the glass. He ran a forefinger on it, then along the counter. Both times, it squeaked and he said, "A dust mite would starve to death here. How is it that this place is so clean?"

They searched for the log, any sign of documentation. It didn't take them long to locate the captain's logbook. Pages and pages spoke of an accountant's love of details for daily events, facts, and navigational coordinates, in neat handwriting and black ink.

"Says here she was last headed for Ireland," Barksdale said. He looked up for the radio and telecommunications instruments. Turned off. Dead. "Let's look below. Lead the way, First Officer."

"Aye."

The lights yawned on and illuminated walkways so immaculate that they'd be the envy of any hospital. They snooped like burglars in a house. Doors opened. No signs of life. All the bunks were made, sheets tight and tucked into corners. They found the Engine Room splendid.

The hallway to the galley, however, revealed a different story. There were four-toed front and five-toed back footprints. Rodents. This made sense since the galley was a food-source. There were gnaw-marks everywhere, and yet there were no droppings, stains, or odors anywhere. Nothing. They were both sweating in their lifejackets.

"Rats are nocturnal," Barksdale said.

"So are vampires."

The captain flicked one of the stainless-steel skillets, hung above the stove. He opened the oven and peered inside. They heard nothing except the periodic drip, drip of water at a sink.

"Her crew had water," Barksdale said. "You can live without food, but not water."

The first mate turned the door handle to the hold and confirmed that there was a generous supply of food inside. There was a rumble and then a grinding noise, like the crushing thrum of cicadas.

"Rats?" the mate asked, his voice raspy and throat dry. He scratched his shirt several times. The idea of rodents, their dark eyes in the night, their tails and whiskers twitching, unnerved him.

"You've got nothing to worry about, Mate."

"Why is that?"

Barksdale looked about to indicate the sudden silence. "Rats only make noises when they're happy. Let's return to the bridge."

They walked fast down the leeward side towards the bow. Barksdale said he had an idea and dipped into the First Mate's quarters, where he found a journal on the man's desk. As they moved to the bridge, he reminded his mate that the ship's second-in-command almost always kept journals, filled with details not found in the captain's log or supplemental.

"In other words, the truth," the mate said.

Back up on the bridge, they set the two books next to each other, the Captain's Log and First's Mate Journal, and opened to pages with identical dates. Barksdale would read from the First Mate's notes. They'd each read entries, like they were playing a tennis match.

"The Stella's captain says nothing out of the ordinary here. He made some bland comments about the weather and he recorded the coordinates they used."

Barksdale found his entry and said, "For the same date, the First Mates wrote, 'The captain blames the Norwegians.' He underlined Norwegians twice."

"Norwegians? Do you think he's talking about pirates?"

Barksdale answered, "The last time Norwegians were pirates was when the Vikings prowled the North Atlantic. No, here the man was talking about the Brown Norway rat, known for being a carrier of bubonic plague. Next, please."

"Captain mentions a storm, a report from the Medical Officer. Anything on that report?"

"Yes," Barksdale had his finger on it. "Medical Officer reported a case of a sailor complaining of a fever and a sore groin. Recommendation was to 'quarantine the man.' Let's jump to the next week. I have a suspicion."

The second man turned a page. "All I've got is a list of comms to vessels, the time for communication, and a number with an acronym."

"Read me the acronym."

"56. SIQ.

"56 sailors. Sick in Quarters." He turned to his ledger and saw the same lingo, but nothing from the Medical Officer. "Screw the Captain's Log. Let's read the First Mate's account."

The captain ran his finger down the page. 'Original sailor pronounced dead at zero five hundred. Of the 56 quarantined, 45 died within five days, as expected."

The first mate grabbed the ledger. "As expected? What the hell does that mean?"

"Three to five days for incubation and illness, and another three to five for…eighty-percent fatality, as expected for bubonic plague."

The first mate read the next entry.

"'The men disobey orders, perform minimal duties to keep ship running, and they drink heavily at night. Some sailors are convinced that they are doomed and abandoned by all.'" The first mate looked around. "Cap, this is a cargo icebreaker. A ship this size had to have a crew of a 130 sailors. Where did they all go?"

"Overboard when they died, and the rest went to the rats," Barksdale said.

"Bones included?"

"Rats eat everything, if they're hungry enough." Barksdale took back the journal. "Communications. There's got to be some record of them in the man's notes."

While the captain riffled through the pages, his first mate asked, "Isn't bubonic plague ancient history, and caused by rats, those Norwegians you mentioned, right?"

"Bubonic plague was never eradicated, and it's not ancient history. The last outbreak back home occurred in Los Angeles in 1924. Thirty dead in less than two weeks. Rats are the carrier, but the real culprit is the flea." His finger tapped the page. "I found something."

"Not for nothing, Captain, but how did you know all that?"

"My old man was a public health official. He used to scare the bejesus out of my mother and us kids with horror stories. Now about those comms. First mate says here, the captain had first contacted other vessels around the Stella. He must have told them what'd happened on board, and they must've relayed the situation to the mainland."

"How do you figure?"

"The First Mate detailed it here. Every European country with a port city denied the Stella entry, which might explain why they set course for Ireland. The way I see it, Ireland was their last chance before they returned to the United States."

"With 45 dead within two weeks and a crew of 130, I doubt they—"

"They were left to die at sea. Politicians on both sides of the Atlantic couldn't give a damn. What were a hundred or so lives to them. Nothing. People are numbers to them, until they need your vote. A ship lost at sea is an item for the media, and then it's nothing."

"The news did say the ship was lost at sea."

"A half-truth, Mate, and it plays well for the cover-up."

"Cover-up?"

"To avoid widespread panic. What else?"

The sound of chains told them that the anchor was being pulled up. The ship then lurched and started moving. They ran to the door, but found it stuck. They looked through the clean glass all around the bridge and saw that their lobster boat had started to recede in the distance. Even if they could've jumped overboard, hypothermia would've killed them before they reached the lifeboats or their beloved Lucky Claw.

The captain crossed the bridge and verified that the door to the leeside opened, and they could access quarters and the mess hall. Now that the boat was moving, he could work the steering gap and set course for Boston.

"We can do this, Mate. It'll be a challenge, but it's doable."

"We've got no radio or telecommunications. Use the stars for navigation?"

"The ship was named the Stella Maris for a reason. Consider it our good fortune."

"Captain."

"What?"

"There's a bottle here under the counter, Master of Malt Speyside. Thirty-year old, and there are two glasses."

"There's a proper omen. Our luck is improving already. I checked. The autopilot is set for Boston. We'll be dockside in less than three hours. Imagine the fanfare there'll be when everyone sees us in the morning."

"Captain."

"What?"

The mate walked over. He had placed one of the small glasses on top of the First Mate's journal. "I've trapped something under the drinking glass here. I'd like for you to take a look." He raised the book and glass together so the captain could see what he had trapped. "What the hell is that thing?" he asked.

"A flea. A fucking flea!"

THE END

Gabriel Valjan lives in Boston's South End where he enjoys the local restaurants. His short stories have appeared online, in journals, and in several anthologies. He has been a finalist for the Fish Prize, shortlisted for the Bridport Prize, and received an Honorable Mention for the Nero Wolfe Black Orchid Novella Contest in 2018. Gabriel is the author of two series, *Roma* and *Company Files*, with Winter Goose Publishing. His second Company File, *The Naming Game* was nominated for an Agatha Award for Best Historical Mystery in 2020. *Dirty Old Town* is the first in the Shane Cleary series for Level Best Books. You can find him on Twitter (@GValjan). Gabriel attends crime fiction conferences, such as Bouchercon, Malice Domestic, and New England Crime Bake. He is a member of International Thriller Writers (ITW) and the Historical Novel Society (HNS). Gabriel is a lifetime member of Sisters in Crime.

CHALK IT UP!

Jill Fletcher

I live on Main Street, U.S.A. These days, the sidewalk warriors are out in full. Masked dog walkers. A woman with a cat in her bicycle basket. Teddy bears placed in windows for children to spot on a "bear hunt". The Pokémon go-ers.

Back and forth and back and forth we tread.

Colorful crumbs of chalk dust stuck to our shoes.

Spaced along split-rail and picket fences we see easy-to-grow and easy-to-draw flowers. The daffodils are out! Now the tulips! Iris on the way. Magnolia, crabapples, dogwood, lilac in that order. Planting moonflowers while waiting for the daylilies to bloom. It is as if the chalk from the sidewalk is flowering the trees. Pinks, whites and yellows dot bright green leaves. One pastel palette. One sun. Spring conquering winter. Warmer air moved by a slight breeze is the ghost of a former embrace. We can't hug each other, anymore. Even air kisses are no longer allowed.

Pent up energy needs an outlet. Ideas are kicked around. Can we start a drive-in theater in that parking lot? How about putting outside seating in the one over there? Which cross streets can we make one-way? Turn the car show and graduation into parades. Curbside veterinary care and curbside take out. Drop off your cat, pick up Chipotle.

****

The ice cream shop has circles drawn six feet apart to help families keep their distance. Their chalkboard sign reads, "Why not eat your ice cream in your car? Pretend it's the 1950s." It features a cheerful group of stick figures in what looks like a vintage Thunderbird holding their cones out the car windows.

Hopscotch is back. Chalk drawings have become driveway art galleries. Inspirational messages are everywhere. We can't speak to you face-to-face, but we can send you a message from our heart through our hands to your eyes. Thank you, nurses! Hearts for essential workers. We love teachers. This, too, shall pass.

Strolling is the new scrolling, each square with a message to keep us going.

Don't worry, be happy.

Bee Positive.

Let's not go back to what was, let's build something better.

Smile! We'll get through this.

And the big one—"# We're all in this together." Together, but six feet apart.

Back when we had festivals, I'd see sidewalk art where clever artists created three-dimensional effects that look like a canyon or a rope bridge or some other precarious setting. This is not the art we are seeing today. Ours is simple. Rainbows. Smiley faces. Flowers. Hearts. Back to the first forms of creativity we remember making ourselves and enjoying from our children. Scrape, scribble, rub. Coloring.

I record these steps on my Fitbit. Fourteen thousand today, thirteen thousand yesterday. I've added a tracking app to my cellphone where I voluntarily report my outside-the-home activities and any COVID-19 symptoms. Luckily, none for me, yet. Others are not doing as well. Of 8,264 checking in, 285 in my town report feeling ill. When I woke up this morning, there were 608 new cases in my county, over 8,000 total cases in the Hartford area, 36,000 in Connecticut and 1,467,065 in the U.S., where 88,709 have died nationwide. 1,044 of those lived in Connecticut.

I knew three of them. A talented and warm-hearted fifty-five-year-old chef who celebrated life through food and drink and family gatherings. We lost Matteo, and his parents. Luciana passed away on April 22nd, Matteo on April 23rd, and Angelo on May 7th.

Chalk tallies.

Life has never felt more intense while this shadow hangs over our heads.

Chalk is washable, and it keeps little fingers busy.

The children of late-night TV host Jimmy Fallon and actor John Krasinski now draw the formerly sophisticated graphics for their television and online shows. Millions of viewers stuck home are seeing this form of child art. Rainbow colors. Their Magic Marker letters just beginning to be well formed and proportioned, spelling out the URLs of the various charities celebrities encourage us to support. Why does this bring us comfort? Is it that we can relate to working at home with kids banned from school? There is no cure or even a treatment, but their innocence has become our balm.

Chalk is impermanent.

Did we choose this medium because we want to believe it is all temporary?

Let the rain wash away the virus, and then doses of our

encouragement won't be needed anymore.

Yet chalk leaves indelible lessons. Most of us learned sentence structure, history, multiplication tables, chemistry, biology, and statistics taught with white chalk on blackboards. The knowledge now being used to document and fight this thing.

Thank you, teachers!

June will bring roses. And their thorns. Today, Connecticut reopens for business.

THE END

Jill is a freelance editor and frequent contributor of essays, short stories and flash fiction. She lives on Main Street, in Wethersfield, Connecticut, one of the state's oldest towns and largest historic districts where she is currently co-editing a book on the town's unique architecture and historic preservation efforts. As a member of Mystery Writers of America, New York Chapter, she develops marketing promotions and programming for the writing community, including the annual crime writer's conference, CrimeCONN, held each year except 2020, because of the COVID-19 virus.

https://www.facebook.com/AvidReaderjvf/

MISTER SAD

Phil Bowie

The girl looked at his right hand and said, "What is?"

Absently, Frank Dove said, "It's a gun."

"I hold?"

"What? No. It's . . . not a toy." He felt numb. Surreal. Disconnected.

She was four feet tall. Chunky. Round-faced. Half-lidded brown eyes with a slight upward slant. She wore a green knitted ear-flapped cap with a cartoon character on it and a tasseled top. Jeans and a quilted winter coat. Vaguely, he remembered Joan had said the new neighbor couple had a Down syndrome child.

The girl had found him here at the end of the path that ran downhill a short way into the woods behind his house, staring into the cold brook. It was a late fall day. A low billowing gray overcast banded with deeper grays. The trees were naked and brittle. He wore a light inadequate jacket. Chilled inside and out, but he hardly felt any of it.

His throat was dry.

He swallowed and said, "You need to get on back home, kid."

"I not kid. I Bianca."

"How . . . how old are you?"

She fanned all ten small fingers.

The clear brook was filled with its own distorted writhing shadows. He said, "I had a boy your age." And he thought, *He and I used to fish right here.*

"You sick?"

It took him dim seconds to answer. "I'm . . . sad."

She thought, scowling. Made a decision. "You hungry, Sad." A statement. She grabbed two fingers of his free hand and pulled. "I feed."

"No. Not hungry. You go on now."

"You hungry. You sit. I feed. Den go." She tugged him to a large rock and he sat. She pointed at the gun. "You put away. I *not* hab at table. Put away. *Ri now.* Hear, Sad?"

He looked at his hand. The pistol was a cold precise thing. A perfectly machined instrument that could bring, if not peace, then instant oblivion.

He took his cramped index finger off the serrated trigger and slipped the revolver into his jacket pocket.

"Kay. Oh, wait. Got call. I take." She pulled a red plastic toy phone out of her coat pocket. The face of it was printed with childish nonsensical icons. She held it against a green earflap. Nodded. "No. Mom take nap. Ri. I tell Mom. Bye." She poked it and put it away.

"Kay. I Bianca." She pointed a stubby finger at an imaginary name tag. "Bee . . . ahn . . . ka. I take care." She mimed holding a waitress's pad and pen. "What you want, Sad?"

"Kid—"

"You hungry. What you want?"

He wiped the back of a bluish hand across his mouth. "Alright, a big steak."

"Big take." Writing motions. "More?"

He shook his head. "Baked potato. Iced tea."

"Tado. I-tee." Writing. "Got good cake."

"Cake, then."

"Kay. I cook." She made cooking gestures and sounds. Set a pretend plate on his knees. "Be care, Sad. It hot." Handed him an invisible glass.

She squatted, chin on her fists. Brown eyes serious. "Eee. *Eee, now, Sad.*"

He made a few half-hearted eating motions and she smiled.

A voice behind him said, "Oh, thank God. *There* you are."

He stood.

The woman, her hair a mess, a raincoat hastily clutched around her, said, "Oh, you must be Frank Dove. I am *so*, so sorry about your wife and son."

He could only nod because suddenly everything was melting, and his throat ached. He wiped his eyes with clumsy thumb and fingers. They hadn't let him near the wreck site, but he'd overheard one state trooper tell another, "Worst I've ever seen."

The woman said, "Bianca, you come along now. I'm sure Mister Dove wants to be alone."

"He not Dub. He Sad." She looked up at him with pure innocent concern. "I go, you call me?"

"Go with your mother, kid."

She was becoming agitated. "You call?"

"Kid, you have to go." The pistol was heavy in his pocket. Waiting with infinite patience.

She scowled but let herself be guided away along the path, looking down at her pink sneakers.

Frank watched her leaving. A shiver seemed to bring an

awareness. He felt the cold breeze that he realized had been making the trees whisper and sigh. He heard the familiar brook clearly.

In a few seconds she would be gone around a bend in the path.

He heard himself say, "Kid? Bianca?"

She pulled her mother to a halt and looked back, frowning.

He cleared his throat and said, "Hey, I . . . I'll call you, okay? I'll call."

"Kay." The frown dissolved into a full-faced smile and she waved a small hand.

THE END

The story behind the story:

One Thanksgiving my daughter Lisa rented a condo on Kiawah Island, South Carolina, for a long holiday weekend and she asked me to join her for a day. My grandson Michael was there. She'd also invited a close girlfriend of hers, a single mom, and her ten-year-old Down syndrome daughter Bianca, who turned out to be an absolute delight. I had sprained an ankle days earlier so I hobbled in with a cane. Lisa hugged me and said, "Glad you could make it, Dad." Her mother tried to introduce me to Bianca as Mister Phil, but because she'd heard Lisa's welcome the girl insisted, "No. He Dad," and that's what she called me throughout my visit.

Bianca knew something was bothering me, so she cooked me an imaginary meal because she'd seen her mother, an excellent cook, put smiles on people's faces with her culinary creations and she decided maybe a good meal would fix me, too.

It worked. I couldn't help but smile as she tugged me to a chair and made cooking sounds and serving gestures. She had a toy phone, which she pretended to be engrossed in occasionally. Later, as I was limping out to leave, she was ensconced on a breakfast stool with her knees up on the bar, long black hair hanging down, poking at her phone and mumbling.

I said, "Bye, Bianca. It was good to meet you."

Without looking up, she said, "Call me."

Bianca lingered in a corner of my mind for almost a year before I concocted "Mister Sad," starring her as an unlikely heroine. The story took second place in the UK Flash Fiction Contest.

Phil Bowie is a lifelong freelancer with 300 magazine articles and short stories published. He has four-novel suspense series in print and Kindle, set in North Carolina and endorsed by top gun authors Lee Child, Ridley Pearson, and Stephen Coonts. His stand-alone novel *Killing Ground* is about African elephant poaching. His short story collection includes an award-winner begun by Stephen King. Visit him at www.philbowie.com or see his blog about life and writing at philbowie.blogspot.com

Mattie's Brother

Cathy Cobb

A flat. At midnight. In the middle of Bumfuck, Indiana.

Of course.

Mattie's car limped to the shoulder and died. She dropped her head and closed her eyes.

Wasn't the funeral enough?

His she-devil wife swooning like Magdalene under the cross? His cold face pillowed in more luxury than he'd allowed in life? All those people droning, "We know you're going to miss him!"

Miss what? His stonewall isolation? His holier-than-God granite stare? His absolute knowledge of absolute right gained from—what? Hog farming?

It sure hadn't shown him how to raise the orphaned mistake of aging parents.

And now her brother was dead. Wasn't that enough?

Nope. She had to get a flat, too.

So get out and fix it.

Mattie snorted. That's what her brother would have said. But big brother was dead. So frig off.

Mattie inhaled and blew out. She turned on her flashers. At least they still worked on this rusted hunk of junk. She creaked open the door and pulled herself out.

No niceties like streetlights on these dark county roads. The moon was out but cast weak shadows through the feral trees. A faint forward glow promised gas stations, coffee, and car repair. But that was there, and she was here.

She reached in and grabbed her keys from the ignition. She had a spare but wasn't sure about a wrench. Or a jack. She walked to the back of the car. Her taillights blinked sadly, like beacons on a sinking ship.

She opened the trunk and bent in to unload her portable life. She found the spare, but a one-finger probe told her the wrench and jack didn't matter. There was more air in the trunk than there was in the spare.

Okay, what now?

She sensed a lessening in the shadows. She straightened and saw headlights moving down the road. A good Samaritan coming to save her?

She waved her arms, but the car blew by. So much for saviors.

She gazed at the retreating taillights.

Don't just stand there. Do something.

Yep. That's what brother would have said. Mattie sighed, walked back to the driver's seat, and picked up her phone. She sat and studied the screen.

Call someone to come get her? Anyone who wouldn't hang up on her lived in another state. Her only local lifeline was her brother. And he was dead.

Call the cops? And go to jail for unpaid parking tickets? A warm cell didn't sound that bad right now, but she'd lose her job if she were derailed for more than a couple days, let alone a month.

How many times had she gotten offers to sign up for roadside assistance? Every time she applied for new insurance after she lost her old. Every time she added minutes to her pay-as-you-go phone. Every time she signed up for a new credit card in her perpetual credit-card kiting scheme. But people who resort to credit-card kiting seldom have mad money lying around for roadside assistance.

So she didn't have roadside assistance—but who knew she didn't?

She searched a number on her phone.

A woman's voice came on the line. "Are you in a safe location?"

"Not really. I'm on County Road 1010 with a flat."

"I'm sorry to hear that. We'll get help to you right away. What's your membership number?"

Mattie bit her lip. "That's the thing. I don't seem to have it on me."

"Don't worry. We can look it up under your name. What's your name?"

"Mattie Yoder."

There was a pause.

"Ah! Here it is!"

Mattie smiled. Not much of a long shot. Plenty of Mattie Yoders in this part of the world.

The operator came back. "Could you verify your street address, please?"

Mattie's smile faded. "Uh…" She gave the woman her brother's address.

There was a longer pause.

"I'm not finding you. Could it be under another name or address?"

Mattie ended the call.

She sat and weighed her options. She could limp forward on the rim, but then she'd need a new wheel, and she could barely afford air for the tire. She could hunker down in the car until morning. She'd done it before. Or she could start walking. She might get to the distant settlement by the time the repair shops opened.

She got out, went to the back of the car, and slammed the trunk shut. Walk it would be.

She turned back, grabbed her bag, and shoved her phone in her pocket. She looped the bag over her shoulder and looked down the road.

She saw a headlight moving toward her.

Just one. One single light.

Mattie considered. This could be good news. The code of bikers she'd known in the past covered people stranded on the road. But when the light came closer she saw it was a car. With one functioning headlight. Which meant the car was in bad shape—like hers—which meant the driver was in bad shape—like she was—and that wasn't good.

Watch your back.

Mattie quick stepped to the driver's side and let herself in. She locked the doors as the car pulled in behind.

In her rearview mirror, Mattie watched a man emerge and sway on the shoulder. He approached her window, leaned down, and peered in.

"Hey, little lady. Got trouble?"

"Sure do," Mattie said through the glass.

The man turned his ear toward her.

"Can't hear you. Roll down the window."

"That's okay. I'll yell louder."

He frowned at her through hooded eyes.

"I see."

He straightened and turned to the flat. "You got a spare?"

"I do, but checked, and it's as flat as the tire on the car."

The man raised his eyebrows. "That so? Well that's a problem. 'Cause I don't have one either."

He leaned down and put his face close to hers. He propped his arms on the ledge of the window.

"But if you need a ride little lady, my chariot awaits." He leered unsteadily through the glass.

At five foot two, Mattie acknowledged the "little" part of "little lady." But he was wrong about the "lady" part. She let loose a monosyllabic string of words that clarified her lack of intention to ride with him in this life or the next.

He jerked back from the window. Then spit on it. He kicked her rear panel as he stumbled back to his car. He tore up turf as he peeled away.

Mattie mentally thanked him for reminding her what might happen if she walked down the road.

So walking was out. Which left camping in the car.

She punched the armrest like she could make it softer. She grabbed a hoodie from the back and zipped it on. She drew up her knees and wriggled to settle.

She lay still—and felt her bladder tighten. Of course.

She sighed. Sleep wasn't going to come as long as she had to pee, so she unwound, checked outside, and pushed the door open.

She looked for a discrete location and then heard a faint rumbling. She turned to see headlights again, but this time higher up.

Over car height. Like a truck. Like a big truck.

Mattie straightened. She knew her share of trucker's, too, and knew they had more rules than Fort Knox. So if this person stopped, it would be to help her. With grinding gears and exhaling brakes, the tractor truck pulled onto the shoulder at her front.

But it wasn't pulling a trailer. It pulled a flatbed. With a winch. A towing winch.

No! This wasn't her kind of luck. Yet, there it was. Why?

Mattie noted the religious symbols on the cab's rear windows. She ventured a guess. The driver was doing a good deed. Well, if anyone needed a good deed, she did. She just hoped the impulse extended to waiving the fee. She watched the driver swing down from the cab. He pulled off his gloves as he approached.

"Looks like you got a flat."

Mattie laughed. "You got a good eye."

The man smiled. "Got a spare?"

"Not one with air in it."

The man nodded. "I'll see what I can do."

"Great!" Mattie's smile could have graced a billboard. "I'm sure lucky you came along!"

"No luck. My neighbor drove by and saw you in trouble. She didn't want to stop this late at night, so she called me from her cellphone."

Mattie remembered the car that blew by. Seemed like a long time ago. Had there been others?

"I need to send your neighbor a parcel of petunias!"

The driver chuckled. "Just pass it on the next time you see someone in trouble." He squatted down to look at the tire.

"Looks like I'll have to tow you."

Mattie glanced at the small compressor under the cab's rear

window. "I think my spare would hold air. At least long enough."

The man looked up and followed her gaze. "And if that compressor were working, that's exactly what I'd do."

Mattie nodded. "Then I'm glad you've got a hoist."

The man straightened. "That's what I call my trolling hook!"

Mattie frowned, but gave a weak laugh.

Watch your back.

Mattie shook her head. Too bad big brother never figured out the difference between caution and paranoia. Right now she needed a tow. She wasn't turning up her nose at a man with a truck.

The man walked to the rig, picked up a military-style flashlight, and started unhooking some chains. Mattie's bladder reasserted itself. Damn. After a bumpy ride in a truck, she might owe the man a new set of seat covers along with a towing fee. She crossed and uncrossed her legs.

The man knelt by the wheel. The flashlight lit up the underside of the car.

Mattie paced. What the heck. He was occupied. It was dark. She'd be quick. She spotted the perfect tree.

She called to the driver. "I'm going to go look for my hubcap!" He didn't need to know the car was missing the hubcap the day she bought it.

She trotted to a tree, shoved down her jeans, and squatted. She felt her bladder ease—

As the flashlight smashed into her head.

The pain waited—then roared. She saw stars. She clutched her head and fought the blackness. She forced her eyes to open.

The man stood with the flashlight in his hands. He took a step toward her.

Mattie scooted back. "I got herpes!"

The man's face curled. "I don't want to touch your filth."

Stupidly, Mattie struggled to her feet and pulled up her jeans. Her hand touched her phone. She froze.

Reality surfaced. She had her phone.

But to use it, she'd have to light it up. And he wouldn't stand still while she swiped two screens and tapped three numbers.

"Harlot." He took a step forward. "Prepare to meet your Maker."

Harlot? She knew this one. She fell to her knees.

"Please, sir, please. I know I must be punished. But before you do, please let me pray."

The man stopped.

She shuffled around on her knees until her back was turned. She curled in an attitude of supplication. She began to rock.

"O, Lord, forgive your poor sinner!" She worked the phone from her pocket. The pace of her rocking increased.

"O, Lord, your will be done!" She eased down her zipper and slipped the phone inside her hoodie. She pulled the thick fleece around it and cupped her hands over it. She punched it on.

"Dear, God, please help me!"

She swiped. She hit 911.

But forgot to hit mute.

"911. What is your emergency?"

Big mistake. The man jerked her up by her jacket. The flashlight smashed the phone from her hands. He kicked it into the trees.

Mattie twisted from the jacket and dove after her phone.

She found it—a handful of splintered plastic.

Find your strength.

Strength? What strength?

She scrambled through the trees and heard the man fighting the brush behind her. She dodged under limbs and heard crashes—but coming from farther behind.

She clawed through branches and heard curses—

But sounding still farther behind.

Why?

The big man couldn't breach the trees as fast as the little lady.

This was her strength? Being smaller than spit? Not much of a superpower, but right now she'd take it.

She cut through more trees, and then more—and then realized her problem. The farther she went into the brush, the farther she got from him—but the farther from the road too—and safety.

She calmed her mind. She knew what happened to little girls when they got lost on a hog farm. And how not to do it again. She drew a bead on the moon and the North Star and noted the direction of the denser trees.

She circled. The man went straight.

Mattie found the truck, the cab door ajar. She took a running leap—and missed the cab floor by two feet. Apparently being small is a superpower when you're getting out of something—not when you're getting in.

She backed off six feet. She ran and jumped at the opening. Her feet hit the running board, but her hand missed the wheel. She fell back on the ground. She heard crashes in the brush behind her.

She backed off eight feet. She dug her feet in the ground, she locked her eyes on the cab, and cut herself loose. She hit the running board at a crouch and propelled into the cab. She swung behind the wheel. She slammed the door and locked it. She jumped over to the passenger side and locked that door.

As the flashlight smashed into the driver's side window.

The glass spider webbed, but held.

Mattie pushed against the passenger door. A fist hit the glass. The driver's door shook.

Then the shaking stopped.

And the door handle began to twitch. Twitch up and down.

He was using something. A screwdriver? A knife? To jimmy the driver's door.

Which meant he didn't have the key.

She shot a look to the steering column and saw a flash of brass. The keys were in the ignition.

Then the door handle twitched again and the steering wheel tunneled away.

"No!"

Her hands found a tobacco tin. She threw it at the window. It fell short. Her hands found a mug and threw it at the window. It bounced off.

You fight like a girl.

A girl? Yes! A girl! Tip to tail. Through and through. She pressed hard against the passenger door and coiled into a knot. This was a man! What was she supposed to do? Ask him to leave? Push him away with a wave of her hand?

Don't push – Punch!

The door cracked open.

She launched like a steel spring and slammed into the door.

The impact flicked him like a fly off a hog.

Mattie grabbed the handle as she fell and swung back into the cab. She yanked the door shut, felt for the key, and turned.

Nothing.

Ever hear of a clutch?

Her feet found the clutch.

She twisted the key again. The motor growled. She heard a thud on the window.

The man's face reappeared.

She got it in gear, stepped on the gas, let go the clutch, and the truck lurched forward. The man's face disappeared.

How the hell do you steer a tractor?

You did it before. Do it again.

The truck swerved madly. She waited to run off the road and die.

But she didn't.

****

When sirens finally sounded, she breathed a sigh of relief. Then smiled. Smiling at a cop? That had to be a first.

She had no idea where the shoulder was, so she stopped in the middle of the road.

In the mirror she could see two officers circling the cab on the passenger side, guns drawn. Two others came up on the driver's side and stopped short of the cab. A spear of light stabbed her eyes.

"Put your hands up where we can see them!"

Mattie obliged.

The driver's door yanked opened and hands flipped her to the ground. She felt cuffs on her wrists. They hauled her to her feet.

She smiled weakly. "Mister, am I glad to see you!"

They stared at her like they were the ones in the headlights, not her.

"What were you doing in that truck?"

Mattie shrugged as well as the cuffs would allow.

"I had a flat."

***

Mattie sat in the back of the cruiser as an officer radioed dispatch. His partner, a female, turned around toward her.

"Okay. Tell me what happened again."

"I had a flat. My car's back there somewhere on the road. I turned on my flashers but no one stopped. Some drunk pulled over but took off. I didn't know what to do."

The woman frowned. "You must have tried a roadside service. An operator called and said someone was in trouble out here."

"Oh. Yeah. That too."

"We came out to check but saw the truck with the towing gear and figured everything was under control. We were going to stop and make sure, but we got another call."

Mattie grunted. "I got a call, too—a call to glory."

"You say the driver of the truck attacked you?"

"Tried to kill me. Almost did."

"Did you call 911?"

"Yeah," said Mattie, automatically feeling for a long dead phone.

"Thought so," the woman continued. "A 911 operator got a call from a tower near here, so that's when we came back and found you driving down the middle of the road."

The officer looked into Mattie's eyes. "What were you doing out here all by yourself so late at night?"

"I was coming from my brother's funeral."

"Oh!" The woman inhaled. "You poor thing. I know you're going to miss him."

Mattie snorted.

Then felt her throat tighten.

"Yeah," she said. "Maybe I will."

Then the tears came.

And she cried.

And cried.

And cried like a little girl.

THE END

Greetings! My name is Cathy Cobb and I am the author of Crime Scene Chemistry for the Armchair Sleuth; Joy of Chemistry (which has been translated into Japanese, Chinese, and Arabic); Magick, Mayhem, and Mavericks; Creations of Fire; and my latest effort The Chemistry of Alchemy and perhaps my favorite so far. But I haven't always been a chemist (or alchemist for that matter) I was seventeen in '67, the Summer of Love, and I've been a waitress, a secretary, cook, clerk, hippie, hitchhiker, bartender, dancer, teacher, truck farmer, and mom. And through it all, I've been a writer because I love telling stories. As a kid, I told stories to teachers, neighbors, strangers--anybody who would listen. I started sending stories to magazines--and collecting rejection slips--when I was twelve, and finally, in my thirties, I sold my first story to Easyriders—and now I've sold nearly 30 short stories to outlets as diverse as Woman's World, Mystery Weekly, and Outlaw Biker. So there you have it, my life, and it's time for me to get back to writing stories! https://cobbfetterolf.wordpress.com

REMEMBRANCES

Tom Wood

Author Note*: Dipping into the fountain of youthful memories, I realize how many of my favorite ones involved water. Like listening to the roaring waves and praying for an ocean breeze to flow through the open windows of our un-air-conditioned beach cottage on hot summer nights during our family's annual trip to Myrtle Beach. Or learning to bait a fishhook on the rod and reel Dad got me one Christmas. Or 'moonfish' jumping out of the water as we camped for days on an Intracoastal Waterway beach near Cape Kennedy to watch the Moon launch of Apollo 11 in 1969. Experiencing the eerie calm of the hurricane eye passing over our home in Largo, Florida. Getting soaked on the Log Jamboree flume ride at Six Flags Over Georgia and later on the Grizzly River Rampage at Opryland USA. Watching the fun of my little sisters' first trip to the wave pool after we moved to Nashville. Or like the first time Dad let me steer the new speedboat on Percy Priest Lake, wind whipping my already receding hairline.*

Here's another memory about Dad—this one from my Uncle Bill, whose heartfelt tribute flows in the accompanying poem. In April of 1986, my dad, Tom Sr., was facing surgery—and his mortality—when his brother, Dr. William Wood, traveled from North Carolina to offer support and spend time with our family. It was the brothers' final visit together, a cherished week. Dad passed two weeks later.

Before leaving Nashville, my uncle penned a poem for Dad, an insightful childhood reflection from a simpler time with his brothers at the family farm (about 1938 or '39, my uncle recalled). I get choked up every time I reread it. Thank you, Bill, for allowing me to share your words in this anthology. And as you lovingly told Dad before departing, "Thumbs up, Podner!"

A Summer Walk in the Pasture

We walked along, Pete, Tom and I, without
purpose, beside the pasture creek that day.
Willow poles, tobacco twine, and hook in hand,
and Tom said, "Billy, did you ever wonder
what makes it this way?"

Green grass, lush and soft in the meadow with
wild grape hyacinth growing there, the
brook's fresh water over smooth stone,
and blue endless sky with sweet clean air.

Pete had stopped to tease a crawfish
only to be diverted by a trout near a stone.
Tom and I, with attention to other things
as I puzzled over his words, continued walking on.

"Yeah," I finally replied, "…I guess sometimes I might."
But underneath, deep down so this older, wiser
brother wouldn't see my doubt, I was not
sure the answer I had given was right.

As if sensing my uncertain ease, read
from apparent confusion on my face,
Tom looked all about and with no further
word drew closer as he slowed our pace.

"I mean…" he then began, "how it all fits together;

we are all a part of God's plan to be kept."

And we talked as friends and brothers can.

That night, with a sense of belonging, I slept.

William Wood

April, 1986

THE END

Retired *Tennessean* sports writer and copy editor Tom Wood is the author of *Vendetta Stone*, a fictional true-crime novel set in Nashville. He has freelanced for the *Nashville Ledger, Knoxville News Sentinel, Country Family News*, the *Naples News* and *Ft. Myers News-Press* among others. His most recent works are the ebook "A Night on the Town" (March 2020) co-authored with Michael J. Tucker and several stories in the *Words on Water* (Oct. 2019) anthology published by the Harpeth River Writers. Tom's other short stories "A Live Wire in Deadwood" and "Death Takes a Holliday" were published in Western anthologies, and another was published in a Civil War anthology. Tom also contributed to the 1989 anthology *Feast of Fear: Conversations With Stephen King*. Two of his screenplays have reached the semifinals of the Nashville Film Festival screenwriting competition.

NOW IS THE HOUR

Shawn Reilly Simmons

Cassie watched Mrs. Lynn's chest rise beneath her thin nightgown for the final time, then shudder back down. Her last breath wheezed from her clogged lungs, fogging the respirator vent over her mouth. Her lips settled into a frown beneath the plastic dome as she sank heavier onto the mattress. Cassie bit the inside of her lip to hold back tears as she watched her patient slip away. She rubbed the paper-thin skin on Mrs. Lynn's hand lightly through her glove, letting out an exhale that steamed the inside of her protective face shield.

Somewhere in the room a machine buzzed, but none of the nursing home's doctors came rushing through the door to help Mrs. Sylvia Lynn. After her most recent bout of pneumonia the Do Not Resuscitate order had been signed by Sylvia and her grandson, Damon. Cassie had been at that meeting both as the senior nurse on the wing and at Sylvia's request as her advocate. Cassie remembered how rushed he'd seemed, fumbling with his phone to answer calls and respond to texts. And how Sylvia had refused to let Damon into her private room after the meeting. She'd said she didn't want anything to do with him again, and that he was just waiting for her to die so he could pick through her things like a vulture after she was gone.

Cassie had heard that kind of family argument many times during her short career.

"Everyone I've ever really loved is already gone," Sylvia whispered to Cassie one night during her final rounds. Her eyes were glassy in the darkened room as she stared at one of the paintings on the wall across from her bed.

"That's not true," Cassie said gently. "You still have me." She lifted Sylvia's wrist gently and monitored her pulse for a few seconds, following her gaze. "I like the one of the woman in the field. I wonder who she's waiting for?"

Sylvia's lips writhed and her eyes grew wider as she took in the painting. "Someone special."

***

Cassie stood and noted the time, wondering how long her mind had been drifting, then jotted it on the sheet next to Sylvia's bed.

The door to the room eased open and Dr. Singh stuck his head through the gap, his dark brown eyes falling first on Cassie and then to the lifeless elderly woman in the bed. "Has she passed, then?"

"Yes, Doctor," Cassie murmured. "Just a few minutes ago."

"Very well. You can clock out. Go home and get some rest."

"But..."

Dr. Singh shook his head. "You were up all night with her. I'd rather, at this point, you get some rest at home. You're no good to us here as a walking zombie. And we've just diagnosed three more cases of the virus as of this morning so we need you fresh."

"I guess," Cassie said, relenting. The five rooms next to the one she was standing in all contained COVID patients, many of them critical. But she had been on shift for over twelve hours, refusing to leave Sylvia's side. The woman really hadn't cared for the other nurses that worked at Fairplay, and Cassie got the impression they didn't much like Sylvia either. But Sylvia had treated her kindly for the better part of a year.

Dr. Singh's eyes softened and he opened the door slightly wider. "I'm not asking. Okay?"

"Understood, Doctor," Cassie said. He'd already slipped his head back through the doorway before she'd finished talking.

***

Cassie tried to read a book as the mostly-empty subway car bumped along the tracks, but her concentration wouldn't hold. Her apartment was eight stops down the L line from work, and normally at this hour she would have to stand, wedged into a human jigsaw puzzle of strangers who were coughing, laughing, yelling, eating, and shedding germs, some out in public with fevers and viruses, pre-pandemic. The memory of how life had been a handful of weeks earlier pulsed coldly in her chest, and she shivered, pulling her pink fabric mask tighter over her nose and mouth and her knit hat further down her forehead. The spots where her fingers had touched her skin tingled and she imagined germs crawling across her face, even though she had scrubbed her hands raw before leaving work after dumping her scrubs into the bin outside of the staff showers. She was probably completely fine. But that's what everyone had thought not too long ago.

***

Cassie's tenth-floor Brooklyn apartment sat high above and three neighborhoods away from her patients at Fairplay. Immediately after entering her apartment, Cassie stripped off her coat and hat and hung them on the hook behind the door, then slid her feet out of her boots.

She went to the galley kitchenette that sat right inside her door and turned on the faucet with her elbow, scrubbing her hands with anti-bacterial soap under the cold water. It always took forever for hot water to climb to the tenth floor in her pre-war building, and in normal times she had no problem waiting, but the thought of germs contaminating her home was something she couldn't handle.

Drying her hands with a clean kitchen towel, she flipped on the light switch, illuminating the living room right past the kitchen and the floor-to-ceiling windows that looked out onto a small balcony. She pulled off her sweater and jeans and threw them into the stackable washing machine in the hallway and made her way to her bedroom to find clean clothes.

A few minutes later, wine glass in hand, Cassie stepped out onto her balcony and leaned against the railing. "Rest in peace, Sylvia," she said, then raised the glass to her lips.

The lights were on in most of the apartments of the building across the courtyard. On a normal evening it wouldn't even be half of them, but everyone in the city was under a Stay-at-Home order. Only essential workers like her were supposed to be out and about, and it was still too chilly most days for much social distancing outside. Cassie watched her neighbors go about their activities through their windows as she sipped her wine, as if twenty individual plays were simultaneously being acted out under glass. A woman in pajamas on the fourth floor was sprawled on her couch, flicking buttons on a remote control, the light from the TV casting her face in different shades of blue. A man and woman two stories up sat at their dinner table and ignored each other as they ate, a phone in her hand and a tablet in his. A young man in the top far window pumped furiously on a stationary bike, wiping his forehead with a towel every few minutes.

Cassie pulled her eyes to the eighth floor center window, saving it for last as had become her habit. She took another sip of wine as she waited for him to appear. She was about to give up but suddenly he was there, a beer bottle in hand, wearing a tight black t-shirt and jeans slung low on his narrow hips. He took a hard swig then sat down on the edge of his tattered couch. He was working on a new drawing, the charcoal pencil in his hand moving quickly over the sketchpad on the coffee table in front of him.

Cassie drank her wine and watched him work. After a while he placed his pencil down and held up the pad, angling it this way and that, then setting it down again. He got up from the couch, the light going off behind him. Cassie looked down at her empty wine glass, her eyelids heavy.

As she crawled into bed a few minutes later, she imagined him sketching her, and how it would feel to have him study her face and body as he drew.

***

The phone buzzing on her nightstand woke Cassie the next morning, a few hours before she'd intended to get out of bed. She opened her eyes and glanced at the screen. Not recognizing the number, she set it back on the nightstand. Dragging herself from the warm bed, Cassie went to the bathroom and opened the medicine cabinet, pulling out her digital thermometer and placing it on her forehead. Yawning, she glanced at the number after the beep, then crawled back into bed and pulled the covers over her head.

****

Cassie woke two hours later, feeling disoriented but rested. Placing the back of her hand against her forehead she got out of bed and headed to the kitchen to make coffee. Picking up her phone she remembered the phone call from earlier that morning, and saw that there were two more missed calls and a voicemail from the same number and half a dozen more from an unknown number.

"So much for a relaxing morning," Cassie sighed as she sat down with her coffee on her couch and began reviewing the messages.

The first call was from a law firm, informing her she had been named a beneficiary in Sylvia Lynn's final will. The next six calls were from Damon, Sylvia's grandson, asking her urgently to call him back.

Cassie set the phone down on the coffee table, a slight tremor in her hand, and stared at the blank wall in front of her.

****

"Sylvia left me her art collection?" Cassie asked the attorney on the other end of the line.

"Correct," he said. "Our office finalized the paperwork with Mrs. Lynn several weeks ago. I take it she didn't mention anything about this to you?"

"Um, no," Cassie said. "I mean, she was always nice to me, and we talked about the paintings in her room once in a while, but I never imagined she'd remember me in her will."

"Well, sometimes people like to thank those who care for them in some special way."

"I guess," Cassie said. "So should I just go to work and take

Sylvia's pictures from her wall?"

"We've already taken care of that," Sylvia's attorney said. "Mrs. Lynn was very detailed in her final wishes. The paintings at her residence have been secured and will be sent to you, and the others will be placed in your care."

"Others?" Cassie asked, looking around her small living room. "How many others?"

She heard the clicking of keys, then, "Sixty-two paintings, all told."

Cassie's mouth felt numb. Movement outside her window caught her attention. He was standing on his balcony, swiping on the screen of his phone, then typing something. Cassie pulled her phone away to look at the screen, but no message appeared. How could it? He didn't even know she existed.

"Which brings me to the next piece. Mrs. Lynn assumed you might not have a residence or storage space for a collection of that size, so she has transferred ownership of the space where the art collection is currently held. It's under a company name, and her wish is that you not share the name or location with anyone. Anyone at all."

"Okay," Cassie said.

"Right," the attorney said. "Once the world has come back to normal somewhat, we can meet to go over the details."

"But..." Cassie said. "What does the collection consist of? And why can't I tell anyone?"

He pulled the phone away but Cassie could still hear his sigh. "Look. The collection is quite valuable. I don't have time to go into particulars right now but it's mainly early twentieth century European paintings. I have another call to take, so...stay safe. We'll be in touch."

***

"How did you get my number?" Cassie asked.

"It's on your business card," Damon said. "And also Grandma Sylvia had you listed in her personal contacts."

Cassie winced. "What can I do for you?"

"I think you know," Damon said. "Look, I know you got close to Sylvia right at the end. But that art doesn't belong to you."

Cassie sat up straighter on her sofa and glanced out the window. He was back on the couch, but there was someone else too. She got up and slid open the glass door, stepping out onto her balcony and squinting in the late morning sun. A woman was next to him, her hand on his thigh as they kissed. Cassie's stomach did a flip and she almost dropped the phone.

"Hello?" Damon's voice in her hand.

Cassie brought him back up to her ear with a shaking hand and watched him slide his arm around the woman's waist. "Well, Sylvia thought I should have it. I don't know why you're contacting me." A heat began to burn in her chest. "Where do you get off calling my private number to...to what? Threaten me?" Cassie's voice was rising, her eyes burning.

He laid her down on the couch as they continued to kiss and grope, and she circled his neck with hungry arms. He'd never had anyone over before, at least not that she knew of. Who was she anyway? *Some stranger from a dating app*? Cassie closed her eyes and stepped back inside.

"But you don't understand," Damon said.

"Don't call me again," Cassie said and hung up.

The tears were hot on her cheeks as she headed to the shower, dropping her clothes across the floor.

****

Cassie sat on the edge of her bed rubbing her wet hair with a towel.

"You don't even know his name," she mumbled.

She glanced at the phone she'd tossed on the bed. There was a text from Damon: *Sorry. But the art isn't yours. Or mine*. And a link to an article. Cassie hesitated then clicked the link. A few minutes later she called Sylvia's attorney back.

"We need to talk. About the art."

****

Six weeks later, Cassie sat in her apartment, staring at the painting of the woman in the field from Sylvia's room. Cassie still wondered what she was waiting for, but thought that maybe she'd be rewarded if she waited a little while longer.

The painting was one of the half dozen pieces that hadn't been collected by the Art Recovery group she and Damon had contacted. This one had been legally obtained, not brought home by Sylvia's husband after the war. Damon had accidentally discovered the origins of the art while setting up Sylvia's estate, which had caused the family rift. Damon had insisted Cassie keep the reward offered by the recovery agency. He only wanted the right thing to be done in the end.

Cassie poured another glass of wine and stepped onto her balcony.

The plays were still showing across the courtyard, but some restrictions had been lifted, so not as many.

She had called the paramedics when it looked like he was having trouble breathing. He hadn't moved from his couch in days.

His apartment was empty now. Cassie had watched the movers in their safety gear take out the furniture.

He wouldn't be coming home anymore.

THE END

Shawn Reilly Simmons is the author of The Red Carpet Catering Mysteries and of over a dozen short stories appearing in anthologies including Malice Domestic, Best New England Crime Stories, Bouchercon, and the Crime Writers' Association. "The Last Word", which appears in Malice Domestic 14: Mystery Most Edible, won the Agatha Award for Best Short Story. Shawn is an editor at Level Best Books, a member of Sisters in Crime, Mystery Writers of America, the International Thriller Writers, and the Crime Writers' Association in the U.K. www.shawnreillysimmons.com. @ShawnRSimmons (TW and IG) @RedCarpetCateringMysteries (FB)

THE DARK HOUSE DOWN THE STREET

Richard Helms

I spent most of my twenties and thirties terrified I might die young. As the owner of every anxiety disorder in existence except for obsessive-compulsive disorder *(Is that spelled right? Is there a hyphen in it?)*, I passed many stressful hours in my youth waiting for some doctor or another to enter the room with a somber expression and utter the ponderous name of the dire affliction which would surely put me on the wrong side of the sod before the end of the year.

With the passage of years, and the impossibility anymore of dying young, I look back on those angsty decades with embarrassment. The rolling years and the occasional betrayal of my trust by the world has mellowed me somewhat. Dying sucks, for sure, but it seems the older I get, the less it sucks compared to continuing in a world I find increasingly befuddling.

Not that I'm in any hurry, you understand. No rush here. Happy to keep plugging along for a while yet, if it's the same to you. That's why my wife Catherine and I sheltered in place as this damned virus held the country hostage. We were early adopters. Had been in self-quarantine lockdown for almost seven weeks. Our groceries were delivered. We left the house only to walk to the mailbox and take out the trash. We were in a high risk group for serious complications—you know, old folks—so we took it seriously.

I didn't mind it so much. As I reached retirement age a few years back, I decided to give in to my inner J.D. Salinger. Four years into retirement, I was doing a bang-up job as a recluse even before the virus came along. Living on lockdown was barely an inconvenience for me.

My more socially competent wife, though, was a different story. No more evenings at wine tastings or trivia nights with pals. The Y was closed, so she couldn't work out. No shopping. No grandkids. Cath took her Zumba classes through the miracle of Zoom, but it's just not the same, is it?

So, like millions of other households across the country, we coped, as best we could. Some days were better than others. Some were even great. Others? Not so much.

We downsized several years back. We decided to move to a place with a higher population density and a lower mortgage. Nearby shopping, doctors, and dentists were an incentive as well. Priorities change as you age. We wound up in a neighborhood largely populated by other retirees, a fact we discovered only after moving in. For a while, I joked that we had landed in a Geezer Ghetto, which would be unfair because it's really a lovely place. Convenient, too. We weren't newcomers for long. Boomers stick together, having been hippies and communists half a century ago, so—despite my blissful introverted seclusion—over time we've gotten to know our neighbors. People on our street look after each other, in normal times. Under lockdown, we waved at each other from across the street and three doors down, because social distancing was a priority.

I went out to get the mail the other day, and found an envelope addressed to a house a couple hundred yards away, on a dark cul-de-sac at the end of our street. It's happened before. Our house number and their house number can transpose easily. Mistakes happen. The envelope was from a lawyer's office. Looked official and was fully stuffed. Probably important.

The sidewalk was empty. I strolled to the cul-de-sac and opened the mailbox at the address on the envelope. Noticed it was addressed to someone named Earl Crosland. I couldn't recall hearing that name, but Cath was on the social committee for the homeowners' association, so maybe she'd recognize it. I shrugged, slid the envelope into the mailbox, and closed the door.

"Hey!" someone called out. Startled, I turned so quickly I got a stinger in my neck. A man stood in the front doorway of the house. He wore dark trousers and scuffed loafers, with a white shirt and suspenders. His collar was open. His tie hung partly loosened. His head was bald. "What are you doing?"

"Mr. Crosland?"

"What?" the man said. He had a low, gravelly voice.

"I'm from up the street. A letter from the bank addressed to you wound up in my mailbox. I just put it where it belonged. You're…you are Earl Crosland?"

"Thank you for bringing the letter. I'll get it in a bit."

"Sure," I said. Something about the man was curious, and I hesitated before leaving. He watched me from his front stoop until I reached my front door.

Cath was wrapping up her Zumba session as I walked in. She shut down her computer.

"Damnedest thing," I said. Cath sipped ice water as I told her about my encounter with the strange man down the street. "The letter was addressed to someone named Earl Crosland. Ring any bells?"

"Nope," she said. I followed her back to the bedroom as she

peeled off the sweaty Zumba outfit. "But my social committee duties mostly involve incomers and outgoers."

"Outgoers?"

"Those who leave. You know. Feet first."

"Oh," I nodded. "I see."

"So, if this Crosland fella has been here for a while, and nothing bad's happened to him, I might not be aware of him. Maybe he's a hermit like you."

"Hope I don't put out his kind of vibes," I said, as she stepped into the shower.

"Oh, I'm sure you don't, dear."

***

The name on the envelope was Earl Crosland, but that didn't mean the house belonged to him. That whetted my curiosity. I wondered who exactly *did* own the house.

While Cath showered, I phoned our neighbor Jean, three doors up. Jean's a hoot. Transplanted Long Island triple widow. Just turned eighty, but still a force of nature. Bought the first house built in the neighborhood, seventeen years ago. Knows all, tells all. Holds nothing back.

"What's up?" she asked. Her accent could etch glass.

"Wondering whether you know anything about the house at the end of the cul-de-sac. The one with the faux stone exterior on the front porch."

"Earl Crosland's house," she said. "He bought it about a year after I moved in. Nice fella. Widower. We went around the park a while, but it was just for laughs. Why do you ask?"

"Seen him lately?"

"Not in ten years, sweetie. Not since we buried him."

"Wait. He's dead?"

"Keeled over on his back porch. Heart attack."

"So, who owns that house now?" I asked.

"Beats me. It was empty for a couple of years. I heard there were estate issues. Then, it wasn't empty anymore, almost overnight. Strange thing, though."

"What's that?"

"You ever walk down that way after sunset?"

"Not lately."

"Well, sure. But before the curfew?"

"Not a lot."

"The house is often dark. Like, pitch dark. No lights anywhere. Almost like the power's been turned off."

"Huh," I said. "What do you make of that?"

"Whoever lives there isn't there very often."

"Wonder how we could find out who owns it now."

"You know who to call? John Shymanski, down the street. He worked for the city. Register of deeds office. Should know how to look that stuff up. And let me know when you find something out, hon, okay?"

✳✳✳

"Don't need to look it up," John said, when I called him seconds later. "House is owned by the Department of Housing and Urban Development."

"How do you know?"

"Tried to buy it. Beryl and I considered turning it into an Airbnb rental."

"Now what kind of tourist wants to stay in a neighborhood full of old people next to a shopping center?" I asked.

"Old people on the road," he said. "Folks with relatives in the hospital. Conventioneers looking to get away from the hustle and bustle uptown. Doesn't matter anyway. I checked the deed, and it's HUD-owned. Bought out maybe two years after Earl died. I made inquiries as to purchasing it. Never heard back."

"They didn't respond at all?"

"Not a peep. Wrote them several times over a year. Might as well have tossed the letters down a well. Then Beryl got sick, and becoming an innkeeper for itinerants kind of lost its allure. After she died, I lost interest in the idea altogether. Far as I know, Uncle Sugar still owns it."

"What does the government need with a house? I could understand if Crosland bought it on a HUD loan and they foreclosed after he died, but why hang onto it? For eight years? With offers on the table?"

"Beats me," John said. "So, Jean told you to call me?"

"Yeah."

"Really. That's interesting. I've been thinking...you know, it's been three years since Beryl died."

"Long time to be alone," I said.

"I was thinking the same thing. Might give Jean a call, once this lockdown is lifted."

"Give her a call now. Can't spread the virus by talking on the phone."

"I'll do that," John said. "We're both eighty. Not a lot of time to waste, eh?"

* * *

Cath and I sat on the screened porch overlooking our postage stamp backyard. I sipped a Corona, because I have a weird sense of humor. Being a recluse does that to you. Cath had a glass of sauvignon blanc. Music from Pandora wafted through the half-open screen door. We'd finished dinner an hour earlier. The sun had already disappeared behind the three-story stand of cypress that separates us from our back-fence neighbors. In the distant west, clouds fluoresced with internal heat lightning. Every several minutes, I thought I detected a faraway faint rumble of thunder. A slight breeze kept the air moving pleasantly, but I knew it would grow into a gale once the predicted storms arrived later that night. Cath surfed on her smartphone, checking up on the grandkids.

"So, what did you learn today?" Cath asked, absently.

"Jean bopped the guy who owned 7848 sixteen years ago."

That got her attention. "Did she?"

"He's dead now," I said.

"Are the two things related?"

"Potentially. Oh, and John has the hots for Jean now."

"John's eighty!"

"So's Jean. Taking her to bed only two decades ago was apparently fatal. Perhaps she's survivable now. You know what they say about snow on the roof and fire in the furnace. Hell, they're only a dozen years older than us."

"With experience comes expertise," she observed. "What about the house?"

"Government-owned. HUD."

"Is that unusual?"

"Damned if I know. They've had it for eight years, though, and didn't respond when John approached them about buying it."

"Oh, hell," Cath said, staring at her phone. "You should see this."

The page for a neighborhood chat board was on the screen. The top message read, *"Anyone know what's going on at 7848?"* It was posted by the woman who lives across Jean's back fence, so I had a good idea where she heard about it. The message was a little garbled, as if the woman had been drinking, a popular hobby among retirees. She mentioned the apparently strange comings and goings at the house down the street, and how the government had not responded to offers to buy it. I smiled. John had called Jean after all.

"So?" I asked. "What about it?"

"Look at the replies," Cath said.

There were twenty-seven replies so far, from up and down the street. Many simply said they had never noticed anything unusual in the cul-de-sac, but a few, especially people who lived close to the house, suggested they had privately questioned why the windows were so often pitch black.

I had awakened a sleeping monster. Nothing is more relentlessly dangerous than a bunch of bored, self-quarantined retirees with too much time on their hands. Now, titillated by the prospect of a mystery in the neighborhood, their imaginations stoked by the unknown, they intended to get to the bottom of things—whatever those things were.

A new elaborate conspiracy theory popped up every fifteen minutes or so, throughout the evening. Well, at least, until about nine-thirty, when some of the neighbors began going to bed. It petered out entirely by the time the late news came on. I was dozing in my recliner. Cath lounged on the sofa, knitting. Outside, the wind picked up, and I could see the flash of chain lightning to the west over the cypresses as the main brunt of the storm bore down on us.

Both our phones vibrated and dinged at the same time. The doorbell security cam had picked up movement near our front porch. I pulled up the app and saw the man in the dark pants and white shirt and suspenders, standing just outside our front stoop. He didn't ring the bell. Instead, he stood there, staring at the seasonal wreath on our front storm door.

"Bud?" Cath asked. I could hear the tremor in her voice.

"It's the guy from 7848," I said. "I'll handle it."

I opened the door and stared at him. I didn't unlock the storm door, because I had no intention of inviting him in, given the viral nature of the time. He pulled a small wallet from his jacket pocket, which he flipped open and pressed against the glass of the storm door, displaying his FBI identification. Lawrence Santangelo, Special Agent. He stowed the wallet and stepped back ten feet. The invitation was apparent. I poked my head just outside the front door. Lawrence Santangelo stayed ten feet away and held up his cellphone, with the neighbor chat app on the screen.

"Did you do this?" he asked.

"Not the post. I might have started the ball rolling with a couple of curious questions. Old people are gabby. Just what in hell is going on, anyway?"

"What do you think is going on?"

"The FBI identification brings up a number of questions. For instance, why isn't the government interested in selling that house?"

Santangelo gave me a dead-eyed stare.

"Wait," I said. "I've read about this sort of thing before. The house is empty most of the time. Nobody knows the people who occasionally show up. It's owned by a branch of the government, and you're with the FBI." I snapped my fingers. "It's a safe house, isn't it?"

"I have no idea what you're talking about," Santangelo said.

"Sure you do. A safe house is the place you take people for protection. Gangsters. Spies. Witnesses to major crimes. Every spy show on TV has at least one."

"What interest the FBI has in that house is our business. Generally, we conduct our business best without a lot of people gawking at us. Your *curiosity* has rendered that impossible. Just wanted you to know. Whatever we're doing here, we now have to start over somewhere else. And, no. I'm not telling you where. Your tax dollars at work. Tell your friend John, if he's still interested, HUD will talk to him about buying the house now."

The storm blew in as he walked down the driveway to the sidewalk. Lightning sizzled overhead, struck a high-tension tower several hundred yards away, and strobed the night into day. A roar like cannons rolled over the neighborhood. Santangelo never flinched and never changed his pace as he marched in the rain toward the cul-de-sac.

The next day, the house was empty. Two days later, a For Sale sign cropped up on the front lawn. In time, the enforced seclusion passed, the virus went dormant, and life returned to normal. A very pleasant couple in their fifties moved into the formerly dark house down the street.

It's nice to have young people in the neighborhood again.

THE END

Retired forensic psychologist and college professor Richard Helms is the author of twenty novels, including BRITTLE KARMA, the third title in his Eamon Gold PI series, set to be released in October 2020. Helms has seventeen major mystery award nominations, including eight Derringer, six Shamus, two Thriller and one Macavity nomination. He is one of only two authors ever to win the Derringer Award in two different categories in the same year (2008). In 2011, his story "The Gods for Vengeance Cry" (EQMM) received the ITW Thriller Award for Best Short Story. His story "See Humble and Die" (THE EYES OF TEXAS, edited by Michael Bracken, Down & Out Books) was selected for Houghton Mifflin Harcourt's BEST AMERICAN MYSTERY STORIES 2020. Helms served as president of the Southeast Regional Chapter of Mystery Writers of America (SEMWA) and the national board of MWA from 2010 until 2012. In 2017, he was honored with the SEMWA Magnolia Award for service to the chapter.

When not writing, Richard Helms enjoys reading, woodworking, simracing, traveling, rooting for his beloved Tar Heels and Carolina Panthers, and just spending time with his grandsons.

Richard Helms and his wife/muse Elaine live in Charlotte, NC.

DEAD IN THE WATER

J.D. Allen

The taste of iron-bitter blood and the reek of rotted fish enveloped Judith Lyons. But her senses quickly abandoned odor and taste to concentrate on the searing pain above her right ear. Her scalp was flayed at best, her skull cracked at worst. Every heartbeat stabbed at the location. Her arms were snugged tight against her body, left to her chest, right hand in the small of her back. The same with her legs. She was swaddled head to toe, wrapped in something massive and damp.

The realization that she been grabbed off the dock sent a pulse of lightning-quick heartbeats pounding in her left ear. *The fuck*? She fought off the adrenaline pushing the throb with a deep yoga breath. *Calm.*

She closed her eyes, even though it brought no further darkness. Judith had been on her evening walk down to the lake—a moment out of the house and away from the confines of the quarantine and the arguing that days home alone in each other's space had exacerbated. Her serenity was cleansing. Meditating to the setting sun, she sat at the end of one of three docks, appreciating the magnificent crimson streaked skies. *Red skies at night, Sailors delight.*

The sound of an engine disrupted the ballad of nature's symphony. The state park being closed for social distancing had made the lake a peaceful wonderland of nature and solace. Living at the entrance to the park had its advantages in normal times. The virus and the quarantine made it even better. Down here at the docks anyway, it was just her and the birds.

A guy in a boat headed to the launch to pull out for the day. He was breaking the rules of the closed park, but it wasn't her job to say anything, Judith returned to contemplative thoughts. Eyes closed, she felt the wake from the boat move the dock under her.

"Hey, ma'am. Ma'am?"

Judith glanced his way. A heavyset man sat at the helm of an old, overly flamboyant bass boat with metal flake paint like you'd see on those 80's road race cars.

"I…I, um got out at the shore on the other side of the lake. Managed to twist my ankle on a rock. You mind holding the boat steady, so I can climb out?"

A big guy like that with a twisted ankle would have trouble. *Dumbass probably got out to crap and couldn't manage the transition from moving boat to moving dock.*

In hindsight, the dumbass finger was pointing right at her because as soon as she'd put her hands on the boat, Fat Boy yanked her by the hair and flipped her weight over the fisherman's chair. She'd landed in a tangle of fishing rods, getting a hell of big trout-shaped lure hooked onto her palm, three barbed metal hooks embedded deep into her flesh, one all the way through and out the base of her thumb.

He slammed the boat into reverse, further assaulting her balance. The boat lurched away from the dock before Judith could manage to get upright. He turned the wheel, and with a switch of gears, they were headed forward. The change in direction sent her back on her ass, with flailing arms, tearing the hooks from her skin.

How many times had Toby lectured her about being in the park off-season? And now, she was even more alone with it closed. Judith had never really been concerned about being down here alone. She was a smart, strong woman. One who never imagined she'd be such an easy mark. She might as well have fallen for the lost puppy ruse.

Getting out of that boat was the only thing she could think to do. Better off in the water. In an instant, she leapt in the direction of the nearest shoreline.

It wasn't so far to shore.

She was a fair swimmer.

But the waters of Lake Jordon were still bone-chilling cold. Her no-wet backpack and boots were no help. She toed off the boots and tried to ignore the mostly empty pack. A bottle of water and a phone didn't weigh much, but the straps kept hanging on her upper arms, limiting her mobility.

She glanced back. Fat Boy in the bass boat made a swamp-turn in her direction. Her life depended on getting the two hundred yards to shore faster than that Evinrude could get the boat to her. The odds were bad. The whine of the massive outboard was a death song. She'd turned and could only side stroke in a vain attempt to avoid the fiberglass hull barreling her way. He wasn't slowing.

Next thing Judith knew she was shivering in a wool banquet. Maybe a rug. The shaking was not so much from cold, but from fear. She wasn't dead, but on the boat. She couldn't see anything. Had no sense of the time she'd been on board or any distance they'd traveled. The lake was a maze of fingers and inlets. She could be anywhere.

The hull moved only with the sway of the water. The lapping would be peaceful in other circumstances. At a dock? Where on the massive lake? She took several deeper, calming, yoga breaths. Apparently, that shit was great for work stress, but no amount of

Namaste was going to fix this.

Voices carried her way. Two males. Judith concentrated. If they were still talking, water lapping on the fiberglass hull drowned them out. Fat boy had only said one sentence to the other. The sound of his voice was not familiar. She didn't recognize him or the boat from other afternoons on the dock. Times when it was busier. She might not even register him among the fishermen and families loading and unloading at the docks.

She struggled with the tight woolen cocoon. Frigid water lapping over the railing wet her blanket and made a tight seal. Fabric stuck to fabric. One foot escaped. Her boots were gone. Lost to the lake as she was run down by a redneck Rivera cruiser.

The head pain was worse. Throbbing, bleeding. She worked the other foot free and tried to separate the blanket from that end.

"Proof of death, man." She made that out. The boat swayed intensely as he climbed into it. Judith felt when he grabbed hold of the blanket and started to pull, unrolling her.

Could she play dead to keep from getting dead? With all the panic and fear, she worried how long she could pull off playing possum. What if they checked her pulse?

She rolled, thankfully landing mostly face down. Fat Boy started the boat. "That work for you?" He paused but added, "Whew. Bitch jumped out the back. Had to run her down. Smacked her with the boat. But now I can drop her back by the docks, and it'll look like an accident. I shoulda planned it that way from the get-go."

Judith held onto that breath because it could very well be the last. Her heart was pounding, her ears ringing, full of the sound of rushing blood. Her stomach threatened to release its contents—pushing bile into her throat. If the veins on her neck were visible, they'd see the thudding blood pressure for sure. Who the fuck would want her dead?

"The money?" Fat Boy again.

A whump on the deck beside her head jolted her into a sharp intake of breath.

"Told you she was a tough nut." It was muddled by the start of the engine. He reversed. "I'll text after she's floating. Don't call it in before that," Fat Boy yelled.

The soggy fabric was dumped back over her head. She tried for small movements of her arms and feet as the boat headed for deeper water, water that was to be her grave. There was something tied around her ankle. The surreal thought of sleeping with the fishes was so absurd it almost made her laugh, but tears came instead.

The slowing of forward motion brought reality clearly into focus. Judith reached for and grasped the rope around her ankle and realized it wasn't tied to an anchor, but a big tire. She had no way to escape that tight knot. She heard her captor singing, confident his job was complete. Judith searched around within her reach, feeling about in the dark for anything.

Her fingers found a metal pole. But it was attached to the boat. Next, she felt the tangle of fishing rods and line and the memory of a lure through her palm shifted pain from her head to her hand. Funny how awareness could amplify pain.

She put her hand on something wooden and smooth. Her fingers scrabbled over it and found a trigger, two triggers, lined up one behind the other. *Shotgun.* The boat lurched. She used the momentum to get to her knees, to grab the gun. She fumbled with the weight for an instant and prayed both barrels were loaded.

Judith trained the business end on Fat Boy's back. He turned. Paper-plate-sized eyes were bright in the one light from the nearing dock.

He stood up out of the captain's chair, stepped toward her. "I'll be..."

Not giving a shit what he'd be, Judith squeezed. At relatively close to point-blank range, the blast sent his oversized torso teetering backward and faltering on the bow. He tremored and twitched, coughed out bright red blood while holding his hand out, and finally gasped a cry for help.

She didn't have it in her to laugh at his plea. Instead, Judith kicked his feet aside and steered the boat toward her park where this hell had begun.

***

Upon inspection, a three-inch slab of skin dangled over the top of her ear. Under the bench seat at the back of the boat, she found a somewhat clean t-shirt to use as a makeshift bandage and tied it around the wound. Of course, her phone had drowned, so up the hill to the house she trudged, shotgun hanging by her side. And she'd have to make it all the way. No one was supposed to be in the park during the shutdown. There had been people protesting downtown just last weekend to reopen everything, if only to boaters and not for campers or hikers that would have more trouble social distancing.

***

The walk to the house was a mile and a quarter uphill. She was barefoot in what had become a pouring rain. The road hurt her water-softened feet with each step.

When she reached the end of her driveway, she stopped for a moment in relief. She could see police lights near the house. They must have been looking for her, but why not down at the lake? Toby had known where she went. He hadn't missed the opportunity to lecture her about not carrying a gun into the park.

She cut through the soft grass and approached the house unseen in the downpour. No one seemed to notice her stop right at the bottom of the stone stairs that led up to the front doors. She was dripping wet with a bloody head and hand.

Judith looked up at the group gathered on her beautifully decorated wrap-around porch. Her husband and two officers huddled near the door, next to the seating area where she and Toby shared wine in the evenings. Laughed. Talked.

"She's a tough nut. I know you'll find her." Toby assured the officer taking notes.

Tough nut.

He'd called Judith that for years. O*ne tough nut.*

And that's what he had said just before tossing a bag of money onto that fishing boat.

"I am." They all turned to look at her standing there. "One tough nut."

The look on her husband's face when he saw Judith, barefoot, bleeding, and bruised but still alive, was one for the scrapbook. She instantly wished she still had her iPhone.

She'd settle for the mug shot in tomorrow's news.

THE END

J.D Allen has been a Killer Nashville Claymore Award-nominee and a Mystery Writers of America Freddie Award-winner. She attended Ohio State University and earned a degree in forensic anthropology with a creative writing minor. In 2018, her SIN CITY INVESTIGATIONS series launched from Midnight Ink. She has short stories several award-winning anthologies. She published nine romance novels before turning to strictly mysteries and thrillers in 2015. She is a former chair of the Bouchercon World Mystery Convention National Board, a MWA member, PAN, FAN, PI Writer's of America member, and previous local Sisters in Crime chapter president.

A CURSED STORY

Karen Fritz

Homicide Detective Jackson Bennett pulled two glasses and a bottle of Scotch from his desk drawer. He poured two fingers of the amber liquid into the glasses and pushed one toward me. Jack said, "I need to tell you a story." He threw the liquid down his gullet, and watched me. "Ryan, mind if I call you by your first name? You should drink up." He motioned toward my glass. "I've read your work. You're a damn good journalist. I need someone with your skill set."

I took a sip of the cheap Scotch and sat the glass on the desk. "So what sort of story is this?"

Jack leaned back in his chair. It groaned under his weight, the sound loud and abrasive in the quiet office. He was middle-aged, a roadmap of tiny veins crisscrossed his nose and cheeks. His complexion was pasty and his countenance fearful. Whatever he wanted to convey was bad.

"Do you believe in curses?" He smiled. "Of course you don't. Until two weeks ago, I didn't either. I do now because I am cursed, and what I'm about to tell you is unusual, some might say unbelievable, strange and scary as hell. "

I took another sip of the Scotch and met his gaze.

He filled his glass again and cupped the tumbler between callused hands and stared at the liquid. "I'm infected with a curse, and all that's required to pass it on to you, is for me to tell you the story.

Once the story has been shared, there's no turning back. The danger is real and the odds of you dying are good. If you want to leave, now is the time."

I'll admit, I was more than a little intrigued. Danger was not new to me. I'd been a war correspondent, hunkered down in the trenches while the enemy barraged us with artillery. I'd jumped out of airplanes into enemy territory, I was used to danger. The little voice in my head told me this was different and to walk away and yet I stayed. I tossed back the last of the Scotch and pushed the glass toward the cop. "Fill it and tell me more." I pulled out a small recorder and held it up to him. "Mind if I record our conversation?"

"Please do. In case I don't make it to the end, you'll need to remember all the details." I studied his face and saw torment and pain. I pushed the start button and nodded for him to begin.

"Four weeks ago Adam Turner came into the station. He told the desk sergeant he wanted to report a murder; his murder. The Sergeant sent him to me. Adam was a young handsome man who was distressed." Jack shook his head. "No, distressed doesn't describe what I saw; panic bordering on hysteria might be a better assessment. When I walked into that interview room, Adam was clutching his head and muttering incoherently."

"Could you make out what he was saying?" I asked.

"At the time, I thought his words were the ramblings of a sick mind. Now I know he was begging the voices to stop their incessant chatter. He wanted silence."

"And that's not a sick mind?"

Jack ignored me and took another long pull from the tumbler. I noticed a trimmer in his hand. His green eyes were bloodshot and watery. He continued, "Adam had large gray, terrified eyes. I'll never forget them." He gave me a sad smile. "In the snippets of sleep I manage to get, I'm tormented by them; always pleading for help." He filled the glass again and tossed it back.

"Jack, maybe you should slow down on the juice."

"Maybe so. But I want to be numb, and I want silence." He held up the glass. "This is the only thing that helps. I've got to finish telling you the story. We don't have much time. During the interview, Adam wouldn't stay seated. He was anxious, afraid and kept moving from the chair to the window. I thought he was on drugs or maybe having some sort of psychotic break. Either way, when he finally settled down he told me the most fantastic disturbing tale I've ever heard."

"Three weeks prior to Adam's appearance in Homicide, he had been a successful local architect. On the day his life changed forever, he'd eaten lunch at a nearby diner and was walking back to his office. He was approached by a disheveled older man. The man was mumbling incoherently and seemed visibly upset. Adam was concerned and called 911. He thought maybe the man suffered from a mental disorder or had a stroke. When the ambulance came, the man fought them, he didn't want to go. Adam said the older man just kept screaming, 'I have to tell you the story.' Finally, they sedated him and took him to the hospital."

"Adam visited the man in the hospital. He was medicated but able to carry on a conversation. He told Adam his name was William. He was a baker by trade, and he was cursed. Of course, Adam didn't believe him, but he felt sorry for him. Adam said William grabbed his arm and told him he had to tell him the story. William looked so desperate that Adam agreed." Jack winced and rubbed the back of his neck. "Anyway, William explained that the man who passed the curse to him said it couldn't be broken unless the originator of the curse removed it." Jack slid a large envelope toward me. "William gave Adam this and now I'm passing it on to you."

I studied Jack for a moment then picked up the envelope and slowly opened it. I dumped out the contents. Scraps of paper fluttered to the desktop. Some of the notes were typed, others handwritten. Jack leaned forward and shuffled through the papers, found a small handwritten note, and handed it to me.

"I've dated them to make it easier for you to construct the timeline." He nodded toward the paper in my hand. "That's the first victim—this is where the curse started."

I read the note twice. Apparently, the author, Ricardo, lived in New Orleans and was a Voodoo practitioner. He became involved with a very powerful Mambos or Voodoo Priestess named Micheline. He betrayed her and ended their affair. In his note, Ricardo wrote that Micheline was furious. A few nights after their breakup, she appeared to him in a dream and cursed him. She told him he would be compelled to pass the story of his betrayal to another male and it would continue with each man burning in Hell's fire to pay for his disloyalty. I laid the note back on the desk. "Wow, this brings new meaning to *a woman scorned.*"

Jack nodded. "I guess Ricardo knew enough about Voodoo to keep a record of when the curse started and he provided the Mambos' name. With each person who is cursed a bit more to the story is added. I'm hoping you'll be able to find the Mambos and break the curse. If not you, then maybe the next."

Believing and yet not believing, I asked. "What happens after the story is shared?"

Jack stared down at his empty glass. "The voices come; horrible, malevolent voices that make you wish for death and there is no reprieve from them."

"And after the voices?"

"Have you ever heard of spontaneous human combustion?"

"Yeah, but that's folklore, isn't it?"

Jack shook his head and poured more Scotch. "No. In the envelope, you'll find my notes. I've provided information regarding this phenomenon. "There have been approximately 200 hundred cases worldwide. Of the four recent burning deaths, three of them have notes included in the envelope." Jack leaned forward sloshing liquor out of the glass. "Ryan, this is real. Don't wait until the voices start calling to you to look for answers because then it'll be too late.

I pulled the bottle of Scotch toward me and filled my glass and took a healthy gulp. "Are you hearing the voices?"

He nodded. "They started a few hours after Adam's death."

"What are they saying?" I asked, uncertain I wanted to know.

Jack squeezed his eyes shut. "Some of it is incoherent. What I can make out is so disturbing I'd prefer not to repeat it. Suffice it to say, the chatter is vile, depraved, and constant."

"In the last stage, is there a warning or do you just burst into flames?"

"Adam, said in the last stage you meet a grotesque version of yourself and then several hours later you'll become a human fireball." Jack tossed back the last of the Scotch.

Jack and his story were giving me the creeps. I got up and walked the perimeter of the small room twice. I stopped pacing and turned toward him. "What happens if the cursed person dies before the third stage? Wouldn't that end it?"

"I thought of that. Seems the Mambos did as well. During this time, no matter how tormented you are, you aren't able to harm yourself. You are bound to pass the curse along to the next person; you can't help yourself."

"How much time do you have?"

"Who knows? A few weeks, days, maybe hours. Either way, the voices are becoming unbearable, and I don't know how long I'll be able to function normally."

I took the envelope. "Are you going to be okay?"

"For now. Go do what you do. Call me in a day or two, but Ryan, don't wait too long. And Ryan, I'm truly sorry I passed this to you."

When I returned home that night, I got in the shower and let the hot water run over my body then I scrubbed my skin raw; maybe hoping to wash away the curse.

Out of the shower and cold beer in hand, I settled onto my sofa and opened the envelope. I laid out the scraps of paper chronologically and read each one twice. They all told the same horrific story with each one providing a few new details. I decided the only way to get the information I needed was to take a road trip to New Orleans. I left my boss a message telling him I needed a few personal days and took a red eye to Louisiana.

I'd been to Mardi Gras several times, enjoyed the garish costumes and parade of revelers but had never given the history or the darker side of New Orleans much thought, until now. Based on the notes left by the first victim, he had met Micheline in the French Quarter in

Congo Square. That would be my first stop.

The French Quarter was alive with tourists, street vendors and a variety of shops; including Voodoo shops. Maybe, I'd find Micheline in one of them. If I did, what would I say? I stopped at several vendors near Congo Square and asked shop owners if they knew Micheline. I quickly realized locals don't give strangers information about Voodoo Priestesses. By the end of the day, I had come up with nothing. However, my palm had been read twice and both times my money was returned. I was told I was cursed and asked to leave—not exactly reassuring. At the end of the day, I found a motel and fell into the bed exhausted. The next day I'd barely gotten started when I received a call from Jack; he was incoherent. I knew the end was near. I made arrangements to get on the next flight out of New Orleans. I hoped I wouldn't be too late.

At the airport, I dialed his number and left a message that I'd be at his home later that night. There was no return call.

Once I landed, I drove straight to Jack's address. Walking up to the front door, I noticed several newspapers strewn across his front yard. There were no lights on in the house. Apprehension crawled up my spine as I rang the doorbell. A minute passed. I rang again. When Jack didn't answer, I hammered the door with my fist. I heard movement and then the door opened just a few inches. A bloodshot eye peered out at me.

"Jack, it's me, Ryan. Let me in."

"Go away. It's too late. There's nothing you can do."

I pushed my way inside. Jack stumbled back barely able to keep his footing. He hadn't had a shower in days and the smell of liquor and body odor made for a noxious combination. He clutched his head and lurched down the hall.

"Make them stop. Please, make them stop." He spun toward me. "I saw it."

"What? What did you see?" I asked.

"Me. I met myself. Ryan, it was . . . all wrong." He reached out his hand as if to touch something. In a whisper, he said, "So real. The face was mine but not. There was such sorrow and despair in his words. "Help me, Ryan. You have to help me."

I maneuvered Jack to the living room and into an armchair. I pulled my cell from my pocket. "I'm calling an ambulance."

He leaned forward and grabbed my arm. "Not the hospital. They can't help me, but you can." He looked up at me, his eyes were so wild with desperation that I stopped dialing.

"What can I do? Name it, you know I'll do anything."

He pulled his service revolver from his trouser pocket and held it out to me. "Please, end this."

I pushed send.

Two days later, I was struggling to meet a deadline. My editor was on my ass, and I was feeling the pressure. My concentration had been off since the night at Jack's house. I was reading the article for the third time when I heard a subtle whisper. Was it my co-worker calling to me, my imagination? The whisper rustled in the back of my brain undefined and vague. But there was no denying what it was, no denying what was going to happen, and no denying what had happened. The voices grew in numbers and volume to the point I could discern the evil depraved things they were saying. Their words slithered and rooted into my mind like a cancer growing and multiplying; destroying all that was good. It was happening just like

Jack said. The curse was real. As for Jack, he was at peace. I didn't need anyone to tell me what happened. I stood, my article forgotten. The compulsion to seek out the uninfected was so strong it forced me forward. I had to pass on the story—the curse.

I walked out of my office and into my coworker's. Sitting at his desk, Carter had no idea what I was about to do. I felt tears slide down my cheeks, and I realized the great effort Jack had exerted in waiting to tell me the story; in giving me a choice. I had failed him. I didn't want to do this to someone else. I tried to fight the compulsion, tried to resist the incredible need to tell the story. At that moment, my beautiful intelligent co-worker, Amanda, walked into the office. I stopped in my tracks and stared at her. Through the vile whispers, a bud of an idea surfaced. Could it really be so simple? Would it work? I recalled Ricardo's recounting of the curse—the story would be passed from one male to another and each would burn in Hell's fire. I smiled at her. "Hey, Amanda, do you have a minute? There's a story I'd like to tell you."

THE END

Karen Fritz **lives in North Carolina with her husband, two daughters, the family pup and one overly curvaceous cat. She is the author of police procedural, *CrossRoads* and the paranormal suspense, *Blind Vision*.**
Please visit her Facebook page at www.facebook.com/ktfritzbook.

PIEDMONT AUTHORS NETWORK, A NEWLY FOUNDED NON-PROFIT ORGANIZATION BASED IN ASHEBORO, NC, FOCUSES ON THE ADVANCEMENT OF LITERACY, WRITING SKILLS, AND LITERATURE OF ALL GENRES WITH AN EMPHASIS ON THE SOUTHEASTERN REGION OF THE UNITED STATES.

9 781951 604097